A SPELL
OF MURDER

A SPELL
OF MURDER

KENNEDY KERR

bookouture

Published by Bookouture in 2019

An imprint of StoryFire Ltd.

Carmelite House
50 Victoria Embankment
London EC4Y 0DZ

www.bookouture.com

ISBN: 978-1-83888-096-5
eBook ISBN: 978-1-83888-095-8

For Jim, Peter and Margaret, whodunit fans extraordinaire

LOCH CLAIMS LOCAL TEENAGER

The identity of the body of a young man, pulled from Lost Maidens Loch at 7.42 a.m. on Sunday, March 23, 2008, has been confirmed as local teenager Patrick Robison. Patrick, who was 17 and had attended Cairnbeath High School until recently, appears to have drowned. Patrick was a well-liked young man in the community, an active member of the boat club and a keen swimmer.

The police are not treating the death as suspicious. Inspector Kim Hyland said that despite being known as a strong swimmer, Patrick's body was found on the north side of the loch, which is notoriously dangerous because of its rocks and the growth of the slender naiad weed, which can restrict the movement of swimmers if they become tangled in it. It has been noted however that no evidence of the weed was found on the body.

Patrick is survived by parents John and Eleanor and brothers Matthew and Duncan, who ask that the community respect their request to be left alone to grieve during these first difficult and sad days.

A funeral will take place at St Peter's Church on Saturday, 29 March at 11 a.m.

Chapter 1

In the sleepy village of Lost Maidens Loch, people sometimes disappeared.

People disappear all over the world, of course: Lost Maidens Loch was not unique in having experienced unusual deaths and unexplained disappearances. But over the years, the small village, huddled at the edge of the loch, had gained something of a reputation. Legend said that the loch was named for a young woman who drowned in it, hundreds of years ago, though nobody could remember exactly when, or who, that young woman was.

In high summer, a mist could hover over the loch at the most unexpected of times, casting the green hills beyond into question. When the fog came in, it could be hard to see your hand in front of your face and all too easy to doubt your senses or forget yourself entirely.

People said the disappearances were something to do with the weather. The more fanciful among them said the loch itself was an ancient portal into a fairy world, but the more pragmatic villagers knew how easy it was to get lost in a heavy fog.

Of course, some also said that people came to Lost Maidens Loch with the *intention* of disappearing. Temerity Love – who had always lived in Lost Maidens Loch and, furthermore, had no intention of leaving it – had enough experience of human nature to know that people's intentions could often be a mystery, especially to themselves. Furthermore, she had a knack for finding the truth about lost things.

*

Love's Curiosities, Inc. sat on a quiet residential street of wide stone houses which in winter seemed to huddle together against the harsh wind and in summer seemed to spread out, as if they breathed in the warm air. The shop's window and door were of the old-fashioned plate glass kind, with tarnished gold lettering that spelled out the shop name in simple capitals, like a private detective's office. A large antique green glass hanging lamp – which signalled whether the shop was open or not – and an oversized yucca plant sat in the window, but if you pressed your face against the glass, a treasure trove of shining oddities revealed themselves.

If a curious browser ventured inside, they would walk into a floor-to-ceiling explosion of antique ephemera. Glass witch balls – hollow spheres of green, blue and clear glass that were once used as fishing floats, then used as lucky charms to protect houses from evil – hung from the ceiling like Christmas baubles alongside various lamps, both glass and copper, some that looked like the type to house a genie inside. The main light in the shop glowed from the vintage crystal of an elaborate golden chandelier, a marvellously gaudy bright-gold, twelve-armed piece, four feet wide, that you would expect to see in the Palace of Versailles.

But not everything in the shop gleamed. There were knotted rope charms, some of which contained swatches of what looked like hair and bone. On a shelf sat a row of thick glass witch bottles – an old British custom, made by witches to repel curses and protect houses; each bottle was obviously very old and sealed with wax. If you asked her, Temerity would tell you that the bottles had never and should never be opened; apart from the likely curse that would befall the opener, the bottle might still contain toxic urine, blood and the rust from the nails that were inside.

In a tall glass cabinet to your left as you walked in, a collection of four genuine shrunken heads – made by the Shuar tribe in the Amazon rainforest in the nineteenth century – followed your steps with their sad eyes. Before Victorian collectors, with their taste for the gruesome, turned the making of shrunken heads into a corrupt economy, these heads had been made by a small number of tribes as magical artefacts to bring revenge upon their enemies.

Rare oil and charcoal portraits of occultists, mesmerists and charlatans, framed advertisements for famous Victorian mediums and huge, grand, silvered mirrors lined the walls. Three antique mahogany and oak tables held collections of crystal skulls, candlesticks, crucifixes and boxes of vintage tarot cards.

The only heat in the building came from either a tempera-mental wood-burning stove or two free-standing electric heaters. Temerity had one positioned near to the shop's desk and her sister Tilda had taken one upstairs with her and refused to give it back. Even with them on, it was always chilly in the house, even in summer.

On that cold February morning, Temerity sat at her laptop, reading an email that had just arrived and listening to the rain beat against the glass. As usual, her long black hair was tied up – today, it was plaited and pinned around her head, tied with a red scarf, a bow at the nape of her neck like a 1950s teenager, though she was nearer thirty. She wore a canary yellow twinset-style cardigan, buttoned up and a black pencil skirt with white polka dots; in contrast, she had thrown a voluminous tartan cape over her shoulders and wore thick navy football socks that were pulled up to her knees. She had a stern face, long and a little horsey with a strong chin, but her smile was warm and quick.

A large blue parrot sat on the top of an upholstered easy chair opposite Temerity: the top of the chair was covered with a thick tartan mat, presumably to protect it from claw marks. The parrot had appeared to be asleep, but now it ruffled its bright blue feathers, disturbed by Temerity's typing and stared at her with a haughty expression.

'Sorry, Hebrides.' Temerity didn't look up from her laptop, but she held out her left wrist for the bird, who hopped onto it and pecked her hand. 'Be gentle.'

'Gen-tle.' Hebrides squawked. The Hyacinth Macaw wasn't supposed to be as much of a talker as some other parrots, but in his forty years, Hebrides had picked up a good vocabulary. Temerity and Tilda had grown up with Hebrides; he had been intensely depressed when their mother passed away, but the sisters had looked after him until he stopped pulling out his feathers and screeching all night. He was slowing down a little in his old age, but not much – he still flew around Lost Maidens Loch and the village every day, incongruously blue against the slate roofs, surprising tourists who came to the loch looking for Scottish wildlife.

'It's not even ten and someone needs me. Can you believe it?' She stroked the bird's head gently, marvelling as ever at its feathery softness. Hebrides ruffled his feathers again, mollified.

'Not even ten!' he replied. 'Time for tea?'

'I know. I know! The world of specialist antiques never sleeps,' Temerity continued, reading the email again. 'I'll make you a cup of tea in a minute. They want me to go to a conference in Alaska, for goodness' sake. Alaska! To give the keynote address.' She sighed. Hebrides closed his coal-black eyes, ringed in a startling yellow, indicating his lack of interest in the matter. He loved tea, usually drinking it from a saucer.

'If they think I'm going all the way to Alaska, they've got another think coming.' She closed the laptop and stood up, depositing Hebrides back on his perch.

'Tea is what's needed here,' she told Hebrides, who screeched in agreement. 'Tilda! Do you want a cup of tea?' she shouted upstairs. There was a muffled yell and the sound of something being dropped. Temerity winced.

'What? What is it?' a disgruntled voice thundered and Tilda, Temerity's older sister by two years, appeared at the top of the stairs. 'You startled me and I dropped *Mrs Grieve's Herbal* on my toe. Hardback. I hope you're happy.' She sniffed, hopping on one leg and rubbing the afflicted foot, whilst still managing to shoot a disapproving look at Temerity.

'I just wanted to know if you'd like a cup of tea.' Temerity grinned.

Tilda, in contrast to her sister, had short, curly brown hair that always looked in need of a comb. She favoured cord slacks, calf-length wool or tweed skirts, tartan pinafore dresses and hand-knitted sweaters and spent most of her time reading.

'Oh. I suppose it's too early for a glass of ginger wine?' Tilda pushed her hair out of her eyes.

'A bit, yes.' Temerity grinned. They had both inherited their parents' taste in drinks: crème de menthe, ginger wine, sherry and, in moments of dire need, brandy with a brown sugar cube.

'Tea, then.' Tilda sighed and walked carefully down the stairs, picking up a fat black cat that was snoozing on the least threadbare tread. 'Scylla! You're too big to sleep there. You'll trip one of us up one day,' she scolded. The cat, apparently not minding being moved, purred and rubbed her cheek on Tilda's wrist. Having two cats (the other, Charybdis, a Russian Blue who was studiously ignoring everything from her bed in the corner) and a parrot could be an interesting experience sometimes; fortunately, after a couple of scuffles, the cats kept themselves to themselves. Hebrides had a very sharp beak and though he was gentle with Tilda and Temerity, he generally disliked strangers and hated other animals.

Love's Curiosities, Inc. was deceptively large, having been extended out into the long back garden. There was still a good-sized garden, but there was also a modern glass extension with a marble and steel kitchen that sat behind the shop.

'I got asked to go to Alaska. Can you believe it?' Temerity flicked the switch on the kettle and got a cream-coloured, cracked-glaze teapot out of the cupboard. She balanced two large mugs on top of a saucer to lift them down from the cupboard, but they overbalanced and fell onto the white marble kitchen top, one of them smashing in three pieces.

'Temerity! Watch what you're doing!' Tilda tutted and pushed her sister out of the way. 'Honestly. That's the third one this month. I'm going to have to get another set.' She picked up the pieces of broken pottery in a tea towel and put them in the bin.

'Sorry.' Temerity sighed. She knew she was clumsy, but she couldn't help it: sometimes it took a long time for her brain to connect with her hands. Maybe it was on account of being so tall. She stood back and let Tilda finish making the tea.

'Alaska! Who has conferences in *Alaska*, I ask you?' Temerity mused, returning to her train of thought.

'Alaskans?'

'Ha ha, very funny.' Temerity rolled her eyes.

She picked Scylla up like a baby, stroking her silky little feet. The notion of witches having animal familiars that they could somehow embody, or converse with, was an old one. You could have a reasonable conversation with Hebrides, as long as you didn't mind his screeches and whistles, but the cats, even if they had been able to speak, probably wouldn't have had anything useful to say. They were incredibly lazy and, Temerity thought, if they could talk, they would probably sound like an elderly romance novelist she had once seen on the news: lying regally on her chaise longue, eating chocolates and drawling out her next story between puffs of a cigarillo.

However, as witches, having animals was a good idea for a number of different reasons. First, cats in particular were excellent at detecting spirits and banishing malignant energies from a house. Sometimes one of the cats would wake up suddenly and stare into a random corner of the house, its hackles raised, and growl for a few minutes. Tilda would comment, *They're ghostbusting again, Tems.* You could tell that was what they were doing, as opposed to listening to a mouse in the wall, because they would just as quickly close their eyes and go back to sleep as soon as whatever it was had gone. If they could hear a mouse scratching, then they'd jump up at the wall and yowl.

The cats also made themselves useful in other ways. Tilda swore by the fact that Scylla, in particular, could always find the right herb in the garden or woods when Tilda needed it for a spell, poultice or other herbal preparation. Quite often, even in the garden, the cat had been able to find a herb that had started to grow wild, not having been planted by Tilda, but whose seed had flown in and sown itself – as if by magic.

Both cats could also pick up changes in the environment – such as a storm coming in, before it had arrived. They were also excellent judges of character. If the cats liked you, you were all right in Temerity's eyes. If not, not so much.

'What's the conference, then?' Tilda asked.

'They have an annual Ancient Chinese Pottery symposium. They want me to do a keynote speech. *Alternative approaches to establishing provenance and authentication*, or something along those lines.' Temerity snorted as her sister poured hot water into the teapot. They'd built this extension some years ago, but all their possessions were either antiques, or not far from being antique, being their parents' things. Therefore, there was a strange contrast between the sleek kitchen and the rather older items it contained.

'Aren't you going to go?' Tilda asked.

Temerity set the cat on the floor. She miaowed in protest and padded off to the large cushion in the corner where Charybdis was curled in a ball. Scylla arranged her hefty frame in the space left and gave a little snore, returning to sleep.

'Goodness. To be a cat, eh? What a life,' Tilda remarked.

'You might as well be a cat. You spend your whole life in a chair, reading or snoozing,' Temerity countered.

'I do not! Managing rare books is a full-time job. I've got to keep up with developments.'

Temerity gave her sister a meaningful look.

'What, like, *Help! This book's still old.*'

'Don't be flippant. Antiques are exactly the same.'

Temerity shrugged, pouring strong brown tea from the old teapot into both mugs.

'Anyway. Don't think I haven't noticed you sidestepping the question. Why aren't you going to the conference?' Tilda took her mug.

'It's too far away,' Temerity said.

'So?' Tilda sipped her tea and watched her sister. 'I'm assuming they've offered to pay your airfare and put you up in a nice hotel.'

'Yes,' Temerity muttered. 'Come on, Tilda. You know I don't like leaving Lost Maidens Loch.' She turned her back on her sister, balancing the tea in Hebrides' favourite saucer – he liked willow ware, maybe because it was blue, like him – and placing it on her desk by his perch.

'Well, I think you should go. I can mind the shop without you. I don't think we should deprive those Alaskans of the best psychic antique verifier in the known world,' Tilda said. 'Quite frankly, I don't know why you hide yourself away out here in the middle of nowhere.'

'You live in the middle of nowhere, too,' Temerity argued, her back still to her sister.

'Yes, but I like it. You yearn for something else. I know you do.' Tilda smiled, but her eyes had a hint of sadness in them. She was naturally quiet and studious, with a caustic sense of humour. Temerity was, of the two of them, the slightly more sociable and *acceptable* one. Her job was, at least, on the face of it, running an antique shop. It was a reasonably normal occupation, whereas Tilda, even though she was a rare book dealer, was known in the village as a herbalist and witch. It made people wary. The fact that Tilda could often be found harvesting mushrooms, tree sap and various unusual plants by the loch or out in the woods made them suspect she was up to no good, and Tilda wasn't someone who felt the need to explain herself. Thus she had few friends and while she pretended that she didn't care, she did.

'Who says I'm not content?' Temerity argued, but she knew her sister was right. A part of her longed to say yes to the invitations that often came her way. Sometimes there were even job offers: universities, auction rooms and museums had all asked Temerity Love to work her magic for them. Yet Temerity refused them all.

'Come on, Tem. This is me. I know everything about you, okay? I know. About Patrick – that you feel responsible. That you can't leave. Somehow, in your mind, losing Patrick is your fault and you think you've got to… I don't know. Stay as a penance. I don't know how many times I have to tell you that it wasn't your fault.'

'Come on, Tils. I don't want to talk about that right now,' Temerity muttered.

'Fine, fine. But you know I'm right.' Tilda raised her eyebrow as she drank her tea.

Tilda was usually right about most things and it pained Temerity to admit that her sister knew the intricacies of her feelings on this matter, too. Still, she'd never say so: it would make Tilda even more pig-headed than she already was. Pig-headedness certainly didn't help Tilda make friends, but Tilda was too obstinate to see it. Temerity had tried to explain that perhaps it wasn't so much Tilda's witchcraft that the villagers had a problem with, but her brusque way of answering when anyone asked her about it.

'You don't know everything, you know,' Temerity often complained. As children, Tilda had always wanted to play schools: take the register, organise games with lots of rules and generally have an excuse to boss her sister around. Later, she had excelled in the hockey team, where her strong thighs and aggressive tendencies made her an intimidating opponent. Temerity, by comparison, hated all sports, daydreamed in most of her lessons and had often bunked off hockey lessons to sit in a hidden spot beside the loch, listening to music and eating chips.

Temerity had only stumbled into her work with antiques because someone had to take over the shop after their parents died and she had a gift for psychometry. She could touch something and know who it had belonged to, or where it had been; she could hold an unusual antique in her hands, or wrap her long, knobbly fingers around a chair leg or a drawer handle and get flashes of information about where it had come from and what it was.

In antique speak, that meant establishing the provenance of an item. That was what she was famous for now, in certain circles. Temerity specialised in magical and occult items because that was what she knew most about, growing up inside Love's Curiosities, Inc. But she was also an expert in bringing clarity and light to the old, odd and lost.

Some might have considered Temerity and Tilda odd, but, unlike many, they weren't lost. Love's Curiosities was their home and always would be.

Chapter 2

As Temerity pushed open the door to The Singing Kettle she heard a girl say fearfully, 'They say it's haunted.' The girl was looking at the sign above Lost Maidens Loch's only tea shop. Inside, the familiar hum of chatter welcomed Temerity in, and she smelt the buttery aroma of fresh scones. The windows were permanently fogged from the steam of Muriel's brass boiler as she made tea all day: in bone china cups for tourists, mugs for the regulars who had come in for their lunch and takeaway paper cups for the boat shed or those who wanted to take a hot drink with them on a tour of the loch.

Muriel was fiftyish, comfortably round in all the right places and always dressed in either a shapeless navy fleece sweatshirt and slacks, or a cream fisherman's sweater, jeans and cracked walking boots, under a spotlessly clean floral-patterned apron. Her sleeves were always rolled up and she usually had a pen pushed through her short grey-blonde hair for taking orders – not that she often used it, as she had an excellent memory. Muriel's family had lived in Lost Maidens Loch for more than ten generations and she thought of herself as its unofficial historian. However, it wasn't just history that Muriel kept for the village: The Singing Kettle was a hub of gossip. If you wanted to know anything that had ever happened in Lost Maidens Loch, then Muriel was who you asked.

'Who says it's haunted?' Temerity held the door open for the girl. *About as haunted as my knicker drawer*, Temerity thought, but she saw the look of disappointment on the poor girl's face and erased the frown from her own. The girl showed her a little guidebook she held in her hand: *The Mysteries of Lost Maidens Loch* by T.L. Hawtry.

'It says 'ere.' The girl was in her late teens and her accent placed her from Yorkshire in northern England, or thereabouts. She pointed at one page, which listed The Singing Kettle as one of the five most haunted locations in the village, with the Post Office, the loch itself, Sutherland's Boat Hire and MacDonald the glass-blower making up the rest of the spooky locales.

'Of course, Dalcairney Manor would also be a fascinating place to visit, but it says here that it's not open to visitors.' The girl turned the page and showed Temerity a grainy photo of the Manor, accompanied by a badly typeset description. Temerity wondered who T.L. Hawtry was; the booklet itself looked very homemade. Probably some local chancer trying to make money from naïve tourists; it wasn't lost on Temerity that all of the locations listed as haunted in the book most definitely *weren't* haunted at all; they were also places that made most of their money from tourists. Temerity felt momentarily piqued that T.L. Hawtry hadn't chosen her shop to be one of the chosen spooky few: there actually would have been a grain of truth in the idea.

She read what the small book had to say about the local Laird:

Dalcairney Manor, the ancestral home of the Dalcairney family, stands on the site of an ancient chieftain's land that the Dalcairneys claim lineage to, though this has never been conclusively proven. The Manor was originally built in the 1500s and rebuilt several times. The family currently comprise the current Laird, David Dalcairney, and his mother, Lady Balfour Dalcairney. The Laird's first wife, Lady Emma Dalcairney, passed away in tragic circumstances. His son, Anthony, from his second marriage to Claire Dalcairney (from whom he is now divorced) lives in London.

'I think the Laird's been ill these past few months.' Temerity handed the book back to the girl; it was their turn at the counter. 'But I've never known the Manor to be open to the public, anyway. They're very private,' she added. *And I don't blame them*, Temerity thought, looking at the book. She'd hate it if her family and life story were being written about in some badly produced book somewhere. It must be terrible to have your privacy invaded like that.

'What can I get ye, dearie?' Muriel asked the girl. 'I recommend the full Scottish breakfast, with tea. My tea's the strongest ye'll find around here. Just what ye need for ghost-hunting!' She nodded at the book in the girl's hand.

Temerity caught Muriel's eye.

'Muriel, I had no idea The Singing Kettle was haunted!' she exclaimed in mock-surprise. Muriel gave her a *shut up* look.

'Ah, of course it is, dearie! I don't know how ye could've missed that. The house's been standing since the 1600s and it used to be a blacksmith's forge, ye know! There're still some nights when I hear the smith's hammer – always three strikes, metal on metal. *Clang, clang, clang!* Temerity raised her eyebrow but said nothing. She knew for a fact that The Singing Kettle had been a fishmonger's before it was a café and that the house was Victorian.

'And d'ye know what? Whenever I've heard that noise, it's like a warning. *Clang, clang, clang!* Somethin' bad happens in the village. An omen!' Muriel continued, warming to her subject. She leaned over the counter for additional dramatic effect and lowered her voice. 'In fact, I don't want to frighten ye, dearie, but I heard the noise just last night. Clear as day.' She stood back on her side of the counter, looking pleased with herself. 'That'll be ten pounds, darlin'. I'll bring it to you.'

The girl followed Muriel's gesturing to an empty table, looking kind of overwhelmed by the unexpected performance.

'Laying it on a bit thick, weren't you?' Temerity murmured as she paid for a cup of the thick, strong tea and a warm cheese scone with butter. 'And since when was breakfast ten pounds?'

'Tourist prices. And I cannae help it if someone's sayin' the tea shop's haunted. Got tae give them some razzle-dazzle, otherwise they won't come, will they? It's good fer business,' Muriel hissed.

Temerity was going to argue back that it wasn't fair to mislead people, when Henry Sutherland barged into the café, banging the door back on its hinges.

'There's been a death! Down at the school!' he cried. He was a big man and he'd obviously run from the boat shed about a hundred metres away, because he was out of breath and red in the face. *Maybe a few more sit-ups, Henry, and fewer evenings in the pub,* Temerity thought to herself.

'Haud yer weesht!' Muriel shouted above the sudden din in the café; it was a Scottish phrase that meant *be quiet*. 'I cannae hear! Henry, did ye just say someone died at the school?'

'Aye, so I hear. Police radio,' Henry panted. Temerity didn't bother asking why Henry had been listening in to what was supposed to be a private wavelength; people in Lost Maidens Loch were notoriously nosy.

'Gods.' Temerity shook her head. 'Looks like your blacksmith was right after all,' she said to Muriel.

Muriel wiped her hands decisively on her apron and pointed at Temerity. 'Okay, lassie. I cannae close the café, but tell the teachers they've got free lunch here, as much as they want.' She looked anxious. 'Oh dear, I hope it wasnae any of the kiddies… or Brenda. I've been warnin' her aboot her heart,' she appealed to Temerity. 'Be a darlin', go and find out for me, aye? I won't rest until I know.'

'I'll go.' Temerity got off her stool and pulled her coat on. 'Don't worry, I'll let you know as much as I can once I've been there. I'm sure it's not Brenda.' Brenda was the school cook and Muriel's best friend. They made a formidable pair of gossips when they got together and Brenda usually stopped off at The Singing Kettle for dinner and a chat on her way home from school. Temerity often saw them together, talking in low voices and watching the customers.

It would be killing Muriel that she had to keep the café open; as chief gossip she needed information as quickly as possible. But Temerity knew that Muriel would give everyone a free lunch that day; it was her way. She mothered them all and today they'd need it, whoever had passed over: a death in a small community was a terrible thing.

Temerity also knew that she was being dispatched as Muriel's eyes and ears and that she'd better get to the school as soon as she could. She knew Muriel well enough to be sure that she'd receive a cool reception at the café forever more if she didn't do as the woman asked, and quickly. Yet there was something else apart from Muriel's request that was drawing her there. It was a strange feeling: a kind of hot compulsion, like being dragged with a rope around her middle in the direction of the school. She might have dismissed it as her own natural curiosity kicking in, but Temerity knew, in her bones, it was more than that.

This wasn't a normal death. As she left the café and started to run to the school, dread started building in her chest like black seawater in a storm. Something was wrong. Something was very wrong indeed.

Chapter 3

The school gates were closed and no one answered from Reception when she buzzed the entry button outside. It made sense that the school would be on lockdown. Temerity caught her breath and nodded to the group of parents gathered at the entrance.

'There's nae point buzzin'. They're gonna send the kids out. No one's allowed in,' one of the mothers said.

'What happened?' Temerity panted. 'We heard at the café someone had died.'

'School sent an email maybe half an hour ago. One of the teachers keeled over in the staff room, not sure who.'

'Thank heavens it wasn't one of the children!' another parent interjected.

The feeling, like choking on seawater, was still in Temerity's chest. She was about to ask if anyone knew anything else about what had happened when Inspector Kim Hyland strode through the crowd, followed by a younger policeman who Temerity didn't recognise.

Temerity couldn't remember a time when Kim Hyland hadn't been the policeman in Lost Maidens Loch: he was an indefinable age, with white hair and deep creases in his forehead – *marks o' the job, aye*, he'd say – but his eyes twinkled when he talked and there were as many laughter lines around his eyes and mouth as there were lines of worry on his forehead. He was stout and of medium height, but Temerity had seen him lift the boats into the shed with Henry Sutherland, the boat master, and race children in the playground after he'd done his regular assembly about stranger danger or fire safety.

Kim worked alone. Usually, village life was unremarkable: the odd burglary, a lost tourist... usually, he could be found at the counter of The Singing Kettle with a cup of tea and a slice of Muriel's fruitcake, reading the newspaper. That was, until the unusual happened – now and again Kim Hyland had to investigate a death.

For Temerity, Patrick's death would always be the worst thing that had ever happened in Lost Maidens Loch. He was her first – her only – true love.

They had met when they were nine years old and Patrick's family had moved in up the street. She and Tilda had stood on the front step of their house and solemnly watched the movers unpacking the van full of boxes and furniture. Patrick, tousle-haired and with kind brown eyes, had come up and introduced himself; Temerity still remembered what he'd said. *I'm Patrick Robison. We're going to be friends.* He was so sure of it and Temerity had wondered for a moment whether she *should* be friends with this oddly self-assured boy with his summer tan and dark blond hair that he pushed impatiently from his face. But Patrick was unusually confident for a child; he had no problem in talking to adults and making them laugh as much as he made Temerity giggle with his constant chatter and his strange exclamations. Within ten minutes of knowing him, Patrick had proclaimed that their house was *extraordinarily bohemian*, which he liked, and the shop was *full of fascinations,* which was true.

Almost from that day on, the three of them had been inseparable: dens in the hills, fishing in the loch, hide and seek in the woods. But one day, when they were fourteen years old, Patrick had kissed Temerity under a coppice of fir trees at the edge of the loch. It hadn't felt odd at all, just the thing that was supposed to happen.

Patrick was Temerity's boyfriend throughout high school. She had watched him win swimming matches, helped him with his English homework: though Patrick could talk the moon from the night sky, he found writing difficult. Temerity, who adored writing and was eloquent on the page, was shy, a better listener than a talker. But they hadn't had a chance to find out who they would be together as adults. Temerity had started her pre-university exams, wanting to study Classics, and Patrick was studying sport at the same college when he'd died and the light had gone out of Temerity's world. No one would make her laugh in the same way again; no one would make her feel as safe and loved as Patrick.

It wasn't just Patrick who had drowned in the loch – the weather could turn fast and a sudden blanket fog sometimes fell over the water, blinding everyone but the most experienced local sailors. There had been other losses; some in the village said that there was a hungry spirit in the loch. Some said there was a beautiful woman that walked over the water and enchanted travellers, leading them to their deaths. And, sometimes, as the great circle of stars traced their dance in the heavens above the misty loch, the old and weak died in Lost Maidens Loch just like they did everywhere else in the world. Still, it had changed her; the ghost of Patrick was everywhere and Temerity didn't want it any other way. If she couldn't have the perfect, sunshiny boy she loved, then she would live in the place that was, at least for her, haunted by him.

'Good morning, Inspector Hyland.' Temerity nodded politely.

'Temerity Love, as I live an' breathe. Shouldae known that yer sixth sense would drag ye up here.' The Inspector nodded politely.

Temerity had helped the Inspector identify a few strange objects of evidence in different investigations in the past. There had been the burglary that had gone wrong at Henry Sutherland's Boat Hire, in which the burglar, a known thief in Glasgow, had been on holiday in Lost Maidens Loch and found it too tempting not to take advantage of the fact that people rarely locked their doors. Temerity had given the Inspector a physical description of the man, which she saw in a vision after handling the lock-picking tools he had mistakenly left at the scene of the crime. Then there had been the case of a tourist who had gone missing for days while walking in the hills around the loch, who Temerity had located using dowsing rods.

As a result of her past successes, the Inspector had contracted Temerity as an official police consultant in the event that he needed her special insights again. She'd felt odd about signing actual paperwork at the station, but the Inspector had insisted.

'I was in The Singing Kettle and Henry Sutherland came running in with the news. I thought I might be able to help.'

'Ye mean, Muriel dispatched ye quick smart tae get the lie o' the land?' Hyland guessed. Temerity rolled her eyes.

'You know Muriel,' she admitted.

The Inspector buzzed the entry button and this time the gate swung open slowly. Standing next to him was the other police officer.

'Aye, I thought as much. Ye may as well stay, though. Ye've a sharp mind an' a good eye.' He motioned Temerity to follow him and the other officer, who walked ahead of Temerity without a word. *Rude*, Temerity thought, but followed them into the school.

*

The woman's body lay on the floor of the staff room and teachers stood around it in a protective circle.

'Ms Hardcastle, is it?' the Inspector asked.

Ms Hardcastle, the school Headmistress, was an occasional customer of Temerity's. Temerity had sourced her a bronze statue of the Greek goddess Hera last year and a Victorian ouija board set the year before. The Headmistress nodded.

'Aye. This goes fer all o' ye: dinnae touch anythin', dinnae move anythin'. My Constable here will be takin' all the evidence from the scene, so if ye could all keep to that end of the room please and let him do his job.'

The teachers shuffled reluctantly away from the body.

'Poor Molly. I don't know what happened. One minute she was making a cup of tea – look, that's her favourite mug. She always drinks out of the same one. We tend to stick to our favourites.' Ms Hardcastle pointed to a red china mug with a tea-stained white glaze interior; there was no pattern or slogan on the mug, Temerity noticed. No *World's Best Teacher* or *Best Friend* or even something like *You Don't Have to Be Crazy to Work Here, but It Helps!* which would probably have prompted an eye roll from Tilda.

Temerity knew the procedure: *don't touch anything, don't move anything*. Even in a misty, tiny Scottish village, the police had their rules. The surprising thing wasn't so much that Lost Maidens Loch had a forensics expert – Alf Hersey, who was also everyone's doctor – but that it had seen as many dead bodies as it had.

'May I?' Temerity looked at the Inspector, who nodded. She knelt down next to the young woman.

'Aye, let's have a look at her,' the Inspector sighed.

Temerity gazed at the young woman's body. There was a slight foam residue at the edge of the woman's mouth; Temerity glanced again at the mug. She bent her head as close as she could to the body without touching it and sniffed, knowing that some poisons could leave a scent after they had been ingested, but she couldn't detect anything.

'What was her name?' Temerity stood up and walked over to where the teachers were gathered. A tallish man, probably in his early thirties, wiped his eyes. He was dark-haired with green eyes that were set rather close together and his face was unshaven.

'Molly Bayliss.' He sniffed. 'I can't believe she's... I mean... this is...' He burst into tears and sat down on one of the mustard-coloured chairs. Temerity watched as Ms Hardcastle rubbed his back like she would a child.

'There, come on, Ben. It's a shock for us all,' she said as he started wailing.

Pull yourself together, man, Temerity thought, looking back at the dead woman. *Everyone else is managing not to fall apart.* She felt, maybe unkindly, that there was something of a performance about his tears, but then chided herself for being unfeeling. Grief struck everyone in different ways. She knew that as well as anyone.

Molly Bayliss was probably in her late twenties and she was – *had been*, Temerity corrected herself – very pretty. Her brown hair was just longer than her shoulders, with subtle golden highlights – today she had worn it loose. Her brown eyes would have been lovely on a normal day, now, they were stretched open with the horror of whatever had been done to her – Temerity speculated a poison that had brought on breathing difficulties or heart arrhythmia intense enough to kill. More than that, her pupils were fully dilated, giving her an even stranger appearance. Molly wore make-up and her fitted cream sweater and navy trousers were smart and well-made.

Temerity remembered seeing Molly around the village, but she hadn't ever spoken to her; on the occasions their paths had crossed, Molly hadn't seemed like anyone that wanted to be sociable. That was fair enough; Temerity liked most people in Lost Maidens Loch, but they were, on the whole, terrible gossips. If you were new to the village and wanted to keep your business to yourself, then good luck to you.

Temerity knew from Kim Hyland's expression that he suspected some kind of foul play.

'Okay. We'll be talking to all ye later today,' Inspector Hyland told the teachers. 'Please stay at school, but ye may want to send the bairns home – where ye can.' He nodded at Ms Hardcastle.

Temerity regarded the younger policeman who stood silently next to Hyland. He was tall and well-built with the kind of dark red hair and blue eyes that showed his Scots heritage. His uniform's epaulette told her that he was a constable. *Is he new to Lost Maiden Loch?* Temerity wondered. *We've never had more than one policeman.*

'He certainly fits that uniform well,' a woman to her left murmured; Temerity didn't feel it would be appropriate to reply, but the teacher wasn't wrong. The scene of a murder maybe wasn't the best place to be appreciating a man in uniform, but Temerity found herself staring for just a moment. The Constable was a very good-looking man. Maybe in his early thirties, he had the kind of face women conjured up in their fantasies: strong jaw, piercing eyes and lips that she briefly imagined kissing. *Get a hold of yourself,* Temerity thought crossly. *This is a crime scene!*

She looked away from the Constable and went back to the body. The Inspector pulled on a pair of latex gloves and squatted down beside the dead woman. He peered at Molly's face and sniffed at her mouth just as Temerity had done.

'No smell of almond,' Temerity agreed. 'Poisoned, though, wouldn't you say? From the foam at the edge of her lips, the speed it happened and the fact that she'd just had a cup of tea?'

Kim nodded.

'Aye, looks like it. The Doc'll confirm.' Hyland sat back on his heels as the Constable knelt down next to them to take evidence bags from their scene of crime kit.

'Ah, sorry, I've nae introduced ye. Temerity Love, local owner of Love's Curiosities Inc., this is Constable Angus Harley.'

Angus nodded curtly and shook Temerity's hand briskly; his grip was firm.

'Welcome to Lost Maidens Loch,' Temerity said. 'Seems like you arrived just at the right time.'

'Seems so,' he replied noncommittally, turned his back on her and started searching the staff room, picking up Molly's red-and-white mug and sealing it in one of the evidence bags. Temerity thought he was rather bad-mannered, but supposed that a crime scene wasn't the best place for social niceties.

'Aye, we'll have our work cut out now.' Kim Hyland sighed. 'Confidentially, I'm being laid out tae pasture and Constable Harley's takin' on the village. We were supposed tae be havin' a month's handover, but I cannae see that happenin' now. Mrs Hyland's gonnae string me up. We've got a cruise booked.' He frowned and reached under one of the chairs. 'What's this now?' he murmured. Temerity looked over his shoulder.

Hyland pulled it out gently and held it up.

The object was maybe five or six inches long, made of metal – *pewter, perhaps*, Temerity thought – with a bevelled handle and a round top with glass on one side, within a frame.

'It's a mirror, aye?' Hyland turned it around in his fingers and laid it down carefully on Molly's chest. 'Lady's hand mirror, I'd say. Though what it's doin' here, I don't know.' He stared into the glass and blinked. 'Hmph. Not a great mirror either, come tae that. Look.' Hyland tilted the mirror in Temerity's direction and she saw that it wasn't the usual silver-backed mirror, but had been painted black behind the glass.

'It's not a hand mirror, though it might have started life as one,' she mused. 'Someone's turned it into a scrying mirror. That's why you can't really see your reflection.'

'Scrying?' Hyland put the mirror into an evidence bag.

'Seeing the future. Like with a crystal ball. The same effect can be achieved with a bowl of water and black ink. The medium, or scryer, stares into something dark and their subconscious allows them to "see" images which they interpret. All manner of cultures have used the method in different ways with different tools,' she explained.

Hyland turned the mirror over. Its reverse side was embellished with a thistle design.

'Well, as long as ye're here, ye may as well do your stuff. What can ye tell me aboot it, darlin'?' He handed the mirror to Temerity, but Constable Harley snatched it away from her hands. She looked up in surprise.

'Sir, with respect – letting a member of the public handle evidence?' He scowled at Temerity. 'Why is she even here? This is a crime scene. Official personnel only.'

The Inspector sighed.

'Angus, I know ye've come from a city police force an' they do things a wee bit differently there. But this is Lost Maidens Loch. You're goin' tae have tae learn that we have our own ways of doin' things. All right, laddie?' Hyland hadn't raised his voice – he never did – but the *laddie* made it plain who was in charge, even if he was due for retirement. He handed Temerity some latex gloves.

'Mind ye, he's right that we can't contaminate the evidence before we've dusted it for prints. Put these on first.'

Temerity dutifully put the gloves on. Hyland removed the mirror from the Constable's hands and passed it back to Temerity. 'Miss Love here has proved tae be a very helpful friend tae me over the years and I'd advise ye tae watch and learn. I'll admit I was sceptical, once upon a time, especially as I've known this one since she was a bairn. But after she helped me find a missing person just with two copper rods, when a whole search team had

failed, I decided tae trust her. And so did the powers that be, aye,'
Hyland added. The Constable nodded.

'As you say, sir,' he replied smoothly, his voice betraying no
emotion, but Temerity met his eyes and thought she detected
something like disdain there.

Ignoring Constable Harley's glare, Temerity took the mirror.
It had the weight of pewter as she'd thought; she knew enough
about antiques to recognise the engraving on the back, which
dated from the turn of the twentieth century. This had belonged
to more than one person, then, though it was hard to tell just
by looking at it when the glass had been taken out and replaced.

'I'd say that this is a scrying mirror used by someone practis-
ing mediumship, fortune-telling or even traditional witchcraft;
depending on when it was adapted for scrying, it might have
been used by more than one person. The mirror itself is over a
hundred years old.'

'Witchcraft, ye say?' The Inspector's eyes widened. 'Ye dinnae
think we have some kinda… occult murder on our hands?'
Temerity's eyes flickered to Constable Harley, who was giving her
a look that, roughly translated, said, *I don't know who you are or
what you think you're doing but that's a big pile of horseshit and I'll
thank you to stay out of police business.*

*I don't care if every teacher in the staff room is swooning over
you,* she thought, as if they were reading each other's minds. *You
might be pretty but I'm guessing you bypassed Charm School on the
way to the Police Academy. And don't swear.*

'I don't know. It's unlikely, but let's see,' Temerity replied and
clasped both hands around the bag, closing her eyes.

Sometimes, when she touched an object, she would see its
whole history: a series of flashback-type visions that showed all
the different places it had been kept, its different owners, rituals

it might have been used in or people that might have read the sacred writing from its thick pages.

Sometimes, there was less: she had no control over what came to her when she touched something. She had been asked to provide provenance for artefacts that, when she touched them, gave her little but the darkness they had been buried in for thousands of years. Sometimes there were unpronounceable names in lost languages or even spirits that had come to inhabit the object and had to be negotiated with, but there was always *something*. Temerity Love had a well-deserved professional reputation for finding – and naming – lost things.

The mirror felt cold in her hands; she shivered, though it was warm in the staff room. It was more than the metal being cold: it was difficult to detect anything from it – no timeline, no flashes of faces and names, just cold, which seemed to radiate from the mirror into her bones. Blackness, like deep water on a moonless night. Temerity frowned and pushed for something more. But pushing against the blackness – like trying to bend the pewter itself – didn't work, so she relaxed instead and turned the mirror over in her hands, so that the glass was facing away from her.

She got a flash of something, then, but just for a moment. *A stag, silhouetted gold against the blackness*; she got a brief sense of something else in the background, but then it was gone. *A stag with its powerful antlers stretching out from its strong head and powerful body, unflinching, somehow... unreal.*

She opened her eyes. Kim Hyland's hopeful gaze and Angus Harley's contemptuous one met hers as she blinked, trying to understand what she had seen. She explained it as best she could.

'A stag?' The Constable shook his head. 'Helpful. Thanks.'

'I've got tae say, ye usually seem tae get more,' the Inspector said, kindly. 'Maybe ye should come back tae the station in a few days an' try again, aye. See what else ye can pick up.'

Constable Harley snorted, but caught Hyland's eye and turned away, busying himself with some paperwork. *Whatever*, Temerity thought, her eyes boring into his back. *I wish you could read my mind because I'd have some choice remarks to give you, you big... wide-shouldered... square-jawed...* she realised she was describing Harley's impressive physique and not actually insulting him, so she just glared at him and hoped he felt it.

'Of course I can, if you want me to.' Temerity was surprised at herself – she had never had quite the same feeling before of somehow being prevented from knowing more about an object. From *seeing* more. It was as if the mirror had been wrapped in some kind of protection, a psychic black cloth. But how could it have been and, more importantly, who would do such a thing? She was puzzled. 'Give me a call at the shop when you need me. I'll be there.'

She thought of the conference. But she could hardly go now, with a murder investigation in the village, could she? It gave Temerity no small amount of satisfaction that she had an excuse to stay home. *It wasn't meant to be*, she thought, as she left the policemen to their work and walked down the quiet school corridor. Alaska was too far away. She was needed here.

She wondered how the other teachers would break the news of Molly Bayliss's death to the children. It was a horrible thing to have to do and nothing that any teacher in Lost Maidens Loch would ever expect to have to say. They would be so upset. In a place like this, people became close. People were good neighbours to each other and many of them were family. Even if you weren't related, people *became* family after a while.

Her thoughts strayed to Patrick's funeral: to the words that his parents had never dreamed they would say, either. To the tears they had cried, that Temerity cried still, when she thought of him. He had been taken from them all just as Molly Bayliss had: young, beautiful, with his life ahead of him.

Temerity hadn't been able to help Patrick. The last time she had seen him, she had experienced the first vision she had ever had, but because it was the first, she hadn't understood what it was.

It was too late when they found him, but if she'd known what she had seen would come true – Patrick, face down in the loch – she would have made him come home with her and not left him. Because it was her first vision, she had dismissed it as morbid thoughts, a waking nightmare. But after Patrick, she had vowed she would always trust what she saw when she touched something or someone. Her vision had never been wrong since.

Therefore, today's insight was even more perplexing. What did a stag have to do with a teacher's poisoning? She had no idea, but it must mean something and she was determined to find out what.

Chapter 4

It was a full moon and Temerity wrapped a long wool cloak around herself before making sure she had the hot water bottle strapped around her waist, on top of her thermal underwear; it was only then that she opened the door and stepped into the night.

Tilda was waiting for her in the garden. It was fully enclosed by tall hedges, which their parents had grown on purpose; they had done much of their conjuring in their magic room, which was now Tilda's library, but sometimes only outside would do.

The cats, Scylla and Charybdis, followed her out at a leisurely pace, their fat bellies brushing the grass. Hebrides was sulking at being kept inside, but if Tilda let him out, he would spend the entire ritual swooping around them, shouting random phrases and generally putting everyone off.

Temerity had placed a flaming torch at each axis of the space of a circle big enough for both of them, marked out in the black pebbles she had gathered at her last trip to the Eastern Scottish coast. The torch at the north of the circle was black, the east yellow, the south red and the west was blue. These were the traditional correlations for the elements: Earth, Air, Fire and Water.

In the centre of the circle, Tilda had set up a small occasional table that they kept in the shed for rituals and covered it with a black velvet cloth. On the table, two storm lamps glimmered against a marble statue of the Egyptian god Thoth, judge of the dead, and a black and gold statuette of Ma'at, Egyptian goddess of justice, balance and harmony. A bronze Middle Eastern-designed censer, smoking with pine resin, sat on an oven glove next to a black glass goblet filled with red wine.

As it was a full moon, the sisters had decided to appeal to the gods for help solving the murder. Temerity had the gift of psychometry, but a little supernatural help never went amiss.

Temerity hugged her cloak around her as she waited for Tilda to finish setting up; it was freezing cold. The moonlight made the bare trees in the garden spectral and otherworldly: rowan, hawthorn and apple – trees associated with witchcraft. The cats padded into the circle and curled up on a blanket that Tilda had placed underneath the altar table; having cat energy present in magic would definitely enhance it. Anyway, unlike Hebrides, they couldn't keep the cats away from a circle, so it was easier to just make them comfortable.

Tilda nodded at her sister and Temerity stepped into the circle so that Tilda – who usually took the lead in these things – could raise the energy circle around them.

'Going Egyptian tonight?' Temerity asked. Western witches often worked with a variety of deities from different cultures, depending on their needs. Egyptian gods were very popular, as were Viking ones, gods and goddesses from Mesopotamia, Greece and of course, Celtic ones, too.

'Thoth and Ma'at.' Tilda pointed to the statues.

'Yes, I know who they are,' Temerity said, testily. Sometimes Tilda seemed to think she didn't know anything at all about ancient cultures, when in fact her whole career was based on them. 'They were husband and wife and both were intimately connected to the land of the dead and the notions of truth and justice. Ma'at was said to weigh the hearts of the dead before their journey to the underworld. Thoth is the god of magic. And books.'

'No need to be like that,' Tilda snapped back. 'I just thought they were appropriate, given the murder. Justice for the dead and all that.'

'Yes. Very appropriate.' Temerity smiled, softening. 'Can we get on? I'm freezing.'

'I don't know why you don't wear more clothes when we do this. I've got five layers on,' Tilda tutted.

'I like to feel diaphanous. Like a witch of old.' Temerity flapped her arms dramatically.

'Hmmph. If you want to feel like a witch of old, you should probably get a few unsightly disfigurements and a disease that's going to kill you by the time you're thirty-five. Times weren't exactly easy for anyone "of old",' Tilda corrected her. 'You'd wash a lot less.'

'Yes, well, you know what I mean. Come on, let's get on with it.' Temerity stamped her feet to spread the warmth up her body.

'Wear your slippers next time.'

'Tilda!'

'Fine, fine. You call the quarters, I always do it.'

'Fine.' Temerity echoed her sister. Going to each flaming torch, she called out to the guardians of each cardinal point: North, east, south and west.

'Great Spirits of the North, of the mountains, of the trees, of the earth, I invite thee to our circle. I command your power and protection on this night. So mote it be!' she called out at the black candle, then turned to the yellow one and repeated the call to the element of air in the east.

When she had finished all four, Tilda outlined the circle by pacing it clockwise, carrying the wine and pouring it carefully around the edge of the circle, intoning, *I consecrate this circle with water*. She repeated the process with the censer for air, with the lamp for fire and finished with sprinkling a handful of earth around the circle's perimeter.

Together, then, they joined hands and closed their eyes. Temerity imagined a golden light emanating up from the edge of the circle and shaping into a dome above their heads.

'It is done,' Tilda said in a low voice and they both knelt before the altar.

'Great Thoth and Ma'at, many blessings upon you. We call you here to our space between the worlds to aid us with your wisdom. One among us has been taken into the land of the dead before her time. We appeal to both of you for help in finding her killer. Can you give us any vision, any clue, as to who this person is? If the dead – Molly Bayliss – has walked in your halls, do you have a message from her for us? Ma'at, if you have weighed her heart, did it contain knowledge of the justice that must befall her murderer? We await your wisdom,' Tilda called out solemnly.

Temerity closed her eyes and made herself as open as she could to any message that might arise. Of the two of them, Temerity was more the mystic, who had intuitions and visions and Tilda was more the occultist, like their parents. To Tilda, wisdom and enlightenment was found in learning, in nature and books. For Temerity, insight came from her visions, her instincts and her heart.

It was silent in the garden, but Temerity could feel the power buzzing inside the circle. Suddenly, both cats, under the table, sat bolt upright and started purring. At the same time, a form started to appear hazily in Temerity's mind's eye. Behind the altar, Temerity saw the figure of the same Egyptian goddess figure as stood on the table. She was much taller than a human, black-skinned and dressed in gold. On top of her head, a black feather sat like a crown; the feather that she used to weigh human hearts. Black and golden wings spread from her arms, surrounding the circle.

Temerity felt a wash of thrilled awe cover her and she bowed her head to the goddess's regal presence.

'Goddess, I am your servant,' she breathed; she could swear she felt the brush of Ma'at's feathery wings on her cheek. For some reason it was the goddess that had answered and not the god, but Temerity had a sudden flash of knowledge that the god, Thoth, would speak to Tilda in his own way.

'Blessed one.' Ma'at's voice sounded in her head, echoey and distant. 'Your lost one has passed through here. She is at rest.'

'Thank you, gracious goddess, for answering our call. Many blessings upon thee.' Temerity heard herself speak, but she didn't open her eyes. 'Is there any clarity you can give me about the one that ended Molly Bayliss's life?'

There was a silence, as if the goddess was on a long-distance line.

'There is nothing. The justice you seek is one that I will pass when the human walks in my hall,' the goddess replied. 'Judgement in life is not my task.'

'But you must know?' Temerity replied. 'You know everything.'

'I know what is in the heart when I weigh it,' she said. 'More than that, I cannot say. Your world is made to be full of challenges. I am here when it is over.'

Temerity sighed.

'Is there anything more that you can tell me?' she asked. Talking to the gods could be maddening. They were so vague.

'Just that I am and will always be,' the goddess intoned. 'Judgement is a heavy responsibility. The one that takes life in your world carries it on his own shoulders as surely as I will weigh his heart, one day.' There was another pause. 'It may be that you see my feather on the shoulder of those whose judgement is coming.'

The image of the winged goddess started to fade. Temerity reached out with her mind, trying to maintain the contact, but it was dwindling. At the last minute, she saw the image of the stag again; a great, antlered stag standing on a Scottish moor. Then it was gone.

Temerity opened her eyes. Her legs were cold and stiff from kneeling.

'How long has it been?' she whispered to Tilda, who was standing up next to her. Speaking with the gods could take you into a strange other time zone where minutes were hours or vice versa.

'Not too long. It's past ten.' Tilda looked at her watch. 'Seems the Egyptians aren't as loquacious as some of the others.' She held out her hand and helped Temerity up. 'Come on, let's close the circle and then we can get inside and swap notes.'

Scylla purred around Temerity's frozen feet, as if she was trying to warm them.

'Good idea.' Temerity's teeth chattered.

*

'So what did you get?' Tilda was busying herself in the kitchen, boiling milk in a saucepan to make hot chocolate, but not before she poured two generous glasses of ginger wine and drained one, setting the other one in front of Temerity on the kitchen table. Both cats had jumped on Temerity in an effort to become a cat blanket; that, with the liquor-like wine, was taking effect. Temerity felt as though she was defrosting a little.

'I had a vision of Ma'at. She didn't tell me much, really. Only that Molly's soul had passed, which we knew.' Temerity gratefully took the hot mug of chocolate from her sister and warmed her hands on it. 'But she did say that I might see her judgement feather on the shoulders of those whose judgement was... imminent, I guess.'

Tilda frowned.

'That doesn't necessarily mean the murderer. More likely it means people close to death,' she commented.

'Hmmm...' Temerity sipped her chocolate. 'I guess so. And does she mean real feathers or, I dunno, I just *see* them on people? Spiritually?'

'Hard to say. In a sense, it could be both. Soothsayers read divine meaning from entrails, feathers... real items imbued with magical power,' Tilda replied, joining Temerity at the table. 'Interesting. Thoth appeared to me.'

'What did he say?' Tilda had also made toast: thick slices of seeded bread from the village bakery, buttered and topped with crumbling white cheese. Temerity took a slice and bit into it gratefully.

'Reminded me to read. Books are important.' Tilda shrugged. 'Also that appearances can be deceptive. He should know, I suppose.'

'God of magic, words, transformation. Similarities to Hermes, the Greek messenger god, and Loki, the Viking trickster deity.' Temerity contemplated her toast. 'What's this cheese? It's different.'

'It's a Wensleydale. Yes, I know. Again, kind of something we already know, but maybe it suggests that whoever the prime suspect is, maybe it's not that straightforward.' Tilda got up, went to the fridge and brought back a jar of plum chutney. 'Here. This'll go well with it.'

'Oh. I forgot. The last thing – I saw that stag again, like I did at the crime scene.' Temerity spooned out some chutney onto her plate. 'Just a stag, with antlers, on the moor. No other details.'

'Maybe it's something to do with the place of death?' Tilda mused.

'But she died in the staff room. It's not a case of a body being moved.' Temerity shook her head. 'I don't think it's that. But it's something. That's the second time I've seen it.'

'Mull it over. Sleep on it. It'll come clear.' Tilda finished her toast and drained her hot chocolate. 'I'm pooped. Connecting with the gods really takes it out of you, eh? I'm going to bed.'

'All right. Thanks for the midnight feast.'

Scylla jumped off Temerity's lap and followed Tilda; she usually slept on Tilda's bed. Charybdis occasionally cuddled up next to

Temerity at night, but she was more likely to choose Tilda, too. Hebrides was forbidden from flying upstairs; if he got up there, he tended to flutter around, confused, looking for a way out. Temerity had once found him, in great distress, halfway up the fireplace chimney in her bedroom.

Temerity pulled her feet up onto the chair, her knees under her chin and pondered. Try as she might, she couldn't work out what the stag represented. What was it?

The cat jumped up onto the windowsill and miaowed loudly. Temerity looked up; Charybdis was staring out at the loch through the window. In the darkness, the lights of the village glimmered like stars.

'What is it?' Temerity frowned. 'You can't go out that way, baby.'

The cat miaowed again and butted her head on the glass.

'Carrie!' Temerity got up, lifted the cat down from the windowsill and stood up again. The view there was a good one; you could see far out over the loch to Dalcairney Manor on the other side. Maybe the cat wanted to go out again; she got up and opened the back door, but Charybdis just purred and looked up at her.

'No? What do you want, then?' she asked. The cat jumped on the windowsill once more and Temerity decided that she'd go to bed. The cat was obviously just playing.

She climbed the stairs to her bedroom, looking forward to the soft warmth of her bed. But all she could think of was Patrick, again, and whether she had seen a feather on his shoulder before he had died. And, for the millionth time, she wondered whether she could have saved him. Her life would have been so different if she had.

Chapter 5

The next morning, Tilda and Temerity were listening to the local radio station, Lost Maidens FM. Inspector Hyland was outlining the details of the case so far and added that Alf Hersey had examined Molly's body and found that she had ingested atropine, a poison.

'In layman's terms, what's atropine?' Temerity asked Tilda across the table. They were eating breakfast: porridge with honey and blueberries and strong black coffee. Tilda always bought the strongest coffee beans she could from a specialist gourmet shop down south; it was delivered in a big wooden crate every month. It reminded Temerity of a little coffin – when it arrived, she'd shout, *Tilda! Mini Dracula's here!* up to Tilda's book-filled garret. Not that Tilda thought it was in the least bit amusing: she threw books down the stairs if her sensibilities were particularly offended, though only the ones that weren't valuable.

'It's used in medicine for a variety of conditions. Myopia, slow heartbeat… soldiers carry it in the event of nerve gas poisoning.' Tilda poured herself some more coffee. The cats were curled up in the corner on a blanket and Hebrides was eating a bowl of chopped-up fruit on the counter, a treat he loved.

'So… it's not a poison?' Temerity frowned.

'Oh, it's poisonous if you take enough of it. A lot of helpful medicines are synthesised from poisonous plants. The wonder of nature.' Tilda stroked Hebrides' bright blue head feathers. 'Two plus two, Hebrides?'

'Four!' the bird squawked.

'Good boy, Hebrides!' Tilda tickled him under his chin. 'Three plus four?'

'Seven!' the bird answered.

'He's getting better at maths every day,' Tilda said, proudly. 'He'll be doing our accounts next year.'

'So you'd have to be a doctor to get hold of it?' Temerity's spoon hovered above her bowl; she hadn't really heard Hebrides' maths accomplishments and was deep in thought about the murder. The doctor in Lost Maidens Loch was Alf Hersey, their neighbour, but Alf had been ill recently and a locum was standing in for him; however, the locum, a Dr Theakstone, was a GP and didn't have experience with forensics, so Alf had helped out in examining the body.

'Maybe the doctor had atropine as a medicine in his clinic and someone stole it and used it to kill.'

'Not necessarily. It originates in plants – you'd just need to know which ones and how much to make someone consume.' Tilda smiled beatifically as she swallowed the thick black brew.

'Four!' Hebrides shouted again; Tilda shushed him.

'Which plants?' Temerity expected Tilda to have to go and get one of her herbals – books detailing the use of plants: as medicine, as poison, for making food and producing oils, essences, draughts and simples. Tilda's collection included some fantastically ancient tomes, handwritten in some cases; even the odd illuminated manuscript, but she seemed to know this without having to consult anything.

'The usual suspects. Henbane, mandrake, belladonna. All poisonous. Fun fact: it's called belladonna, beautiful woman, in Italian, because the atropine in belladonna makes your pupils dilate. Cleopatra used henbane to make her eyes look wide and beautiful – atropine again. So did fashionable French ladies in late nineteenth-century Paris.'

'Hmmm.' Temerity thought of Molly Bayliss's wide, staring eyes. Not so beautiful. But then, Molly hadn't poisoned herself. 'And these plants grow where?'

'Anywhere. Lots out in the wild out here if you know what to look for.' Tilda made a *ta-dah* gesture with her fingers on both sides of the blue ceramic, extra-large coffee cup she was drinking from. 'So that doesn't narrow it down at all. Anyone could find or grow one of those plants. You only need to eat one belladonna leaf and it can kill you. Easier again if you make a tincture. Could easily be deadly, dropped in food or drink.'

'Good Lord.' Temerity twisted her black hair up into a bun under her headscarf, which was black with pink polka dots today. She was still in her bathrobe, which was a powder pink 1950s-style terry towelling robe with a high collar; she also wore oversized black-and-red Minnie Mouse slippers. By contrast, Tilda was already fully dressed in mustard corduroy slacks and a purple sweater with a pin at the neck that had been their grandmother's.

'D'you know, I think I need some of Muriel's famous fruitcake.' Temerity got up, determined to find out what the teachers had said in their interviews. It wasn't something that would be released to the public, but the Inspector might tell her if she caught him at The Singing Kettle, without the new constable.

'You haven't eaten your porridge,' Tilda scolded, so Temerity spooned the rest into her mouth on the walk to the sink and gulped it down uncomfortably.

'I have now,' she mumbled through a mouthful of gloop and left Tilda scowling in the kitchen to run a bath.

*

Sure enough, Temerity found Kim Hyland at the counter in The Singing Kettle. In front of him was a plate of crumbs of what looked suspiciously like fruitcake.

'Ah, you beat me to it.' Temerity perched on one of the high stools next to the Inspector. 'I had a hankering for some of Muriel's cake.'

'Slow day at the shop?' Hyland enquired, smiling back. Today's newspaper was folded in front of him to show the headline: LOCAL TEACHER MURDERED.

'Dead. If you'll pardon the expression.' Temerity waved at Muriel who left the huge, old-fashioned copper boiler behind the counter and came to see what she wanted. 'Muriel, can I have a fruitcake and tea?' She was stuffed from speed-eating the porridge earlier, but she needed an excuse to be at the tea shop. And there was always room for cake.

'Mug?'

'Please.' Temerity looked back at the newspaper, reading the short columns next to a picture of Molly. She had been a beauty, but in the picture her expression was serious and unsmiling.

'Not the most imaginative headline,' she commented, reading. Hyland shrugged. 'And I'm surprised they couldn't find a better photo.'

'Aye, well. That was her official teacher photo, by all accounts.'

'They might have said something like how much everyone loved her or how she'll be missed. There's none of that here.' Temerity turned the page, but the story wasn't continued on the next page. 'Really? Is that it? There's hardly anything here about her.'

'Just the facts.' Hyland sighed. 'Thing is, turns out that she wasnae that well liked. Bairns say she was on the strict side, not that that's anythin' bad in a teacher. Only one of the teachers had anythin' nice tae say aboot her. Some of the others told us that she was a bit too flirtatious with some of the dads, an' the ladies weren't keen on her.'

'Really? How interesting.' Temerity looked at Molly's picture again. 'I guess just because she was beautiful doesn't mean that she was likeable.'

'Aye. Makes nae odds. Someone still slipped poison in her tea.'

'I heard you on the radio. Any idea about where the poison might have come from? Tilda said it could be sourced from a few different plants that would either grow locally, or are easy enough to grow at home.'

'I might've known yer sister would have an opinion.' Hyland grinned. 'Aye. Could be one of the traditional poison plants, could have been that someone got hold of the chemical, maybe someone has access to hospital stores.'

Muriel brought over a huge slab of moist fruitcake, dotted with cherries, sultanas, raisins and apricots with a thick crunchy brown sugar crust on the top and laid it in front of Temerity. She poured tea into both their mugs, topping up Kim Hyland's from a large copper teapot she held with a red tartan oven glove.

'Muriel darlin', yer a bobby dazzler.' Hyland sipped at the hot, dark brown tea gratefully. It was warm in the café, but outside the frost was still on the windows.

'Thanks, Muriel.' Temerity picked up the slice of cake and took a bite: it was rich, boozy and delicious as always. 'I swear, you must put a bottle of whisky in every cake. It's probably not even legal for me to eat it at this time of the morning.'

'Ah, get away with ye! Just a wee dram goes in, that's all!' Muriel tutted. 'It's all fruit. Good for ye.' She went to serve a couple of tourists at a table, topping up their coffee from a steel pot with a black handle. Temerity reflected that if they thought they'd be getting filter coffee or something as grand as Tilda's gourmet beans then they'd be disappointed; Muriel's tea was legendary, but her coffee was instant. She noticed that there was a copy of T.L. Hawtry's *The Mysteries of Lost Maidens Loch* on the table next to them: more audience for Muriel's tall tales.

'So the poison was dropped in her drink? In which case it has to be one of the teachers who were in the staff room at the same time.' Temerity leaned forward. Hyland raised his eyebrow.

'Aye, possibly, but there might be other ways for the poison to hae got intae the cup. It did definitely come from the cup; we found traces of atropine. The inside was old, pretty cracked. Helped to retain the chemical.'

'Interesting. So, who was in the staff room at the time Molly collapsed?' Temerity asked.

Kim Hyland sat back and drank his tea.

'You know I cannae tell you that,' he chided her. 'That's confidential.'

She thought for a minute.

'Okay, you can't tell me who was there. Can you tell me who *wasn't* there?'

Hyland gave her a fond but exasperated look.

'You can work out who wasnae there, if you really must. The kitchen staff, the receptionist, whoever was on playground duty.' He gave her a stare.

'I see.' Temerity looked over at Muriel: Brenda would have filled her friend in on all the details by now. Muriel would know exactly who was in the staff room and who wasn't. Temerity was invested in this murder now, partly because she cared about what happened in the village, but mostly because her vision of the stag was really bothering her. She hadn't had any additional insights about the animal – what it meant, where it was, or what it was doing there. It was driving her mad.

'In fact, if ye want tae help, ye can visit Molly's flatmate with Constable Harley this afternoon.' Hyland interrupted Temerity's thoughts.

'I don't think Constable Harley likes me very much.' Temerity shook her head.

'I dinnae think he likes many people,' Hyland agreed. 'But he's a professional and so are ye. He's goin' tae interview the woman about Molly – if she was seein' anyone, had she had any falling out with anyone, money problems, that kinda thing. Whilst yer there, see if ye can get any impressions from anythin'. Touch her things, see if ye can get any intel.'

Temerity wasn't going to refuse an opportunity to put her mind to rest, even if she did have to endure more of Angus Harley's rudeness.

'Fine. I'll go. Where is it?'

'No need. Harley can walk with ye.' The Inspector nodded to the door of the café which had just opened to reveal Constable Harley, who glowered at them both. If you ignored his expression, he was handsome; for a moment, Temerity indulged herself by imagining his broad shoulders and toned muscles in a traditional kilt and shirt, striding confidently through the mountains.

'Miss Love.' The Constable nodded curtly at Temerity. She held out her hand.

'Please, not so formal. It's Temerity.'

Harley looked at her hand but didn't shake it and turned his attention to the Inspector.

'All statements have been taken at the school, sir.' Temerity half-expected him to salute Kim Hyland, which he didn't, but nonetheless stood expectantly, as if waiting for an order. *Rude, rude, rude*, she thought and ate her cake, irritated by his presence already. *Does he have no actual social skills? Or is it just me that he dislikes for some reason?*

'Thank ye, Angus. We were just talkin'. I'd like Temerity tae visit the flatmate with ye. Ye'll lead the interview, o' course, but I want Temerity tae see if she can get any information aboot Molly from her possessions.' Hyland fixed the Constable with a look that said, *This is happening, so get used to it.* Temerity didn't have to touch Angus's hand to know how he felt about that, but he nodded.

'Fine. Shall we go?'

Temerity wrapped up the remainder of her slice of cake in a napkin and slipped it in her coat pocket. *Fine.*

'Sure, of course, I'm ready.' She put her coat on and followed Harley out of the café.

Chapter 6

The townhouse Molly had shared with Beth Bennett was two streets away from Love's Curiosities, Inc. It reminded Temerity of Patrick's family home, which had seemed so beautifully normal compared to their freezing, damp house full of rotting hunting trophies and bear rugs (Tilda had thrown those all out when their parents died), odd paintings (some of them had turned out to be very valuable) and the books that Tilda now cared for.

Some of Tilda's books had unusual care requirements: a few very old, strange volumes were bound in pigskin, which had to be sponged with a moist cloth every now and again to keep the leather supple. Others had to be regularly re-glued and have their board covers restored or even their gold lettering retooled, all of which Tilda did in a little shed at the bottom of the garden where she could keep all her bookbinding materials.

There had been almost no conversation on the ten-minute walk from the café, which was quite a long time not to talk to someone who was standing right next to you. Temerity tried on a couple of occasions, but got nowhere: *Are you from near here?* Answer: *No*, and *What do you think of Lost Maidens Loch?* Answer: *Interesting*.

Eventually, Temerity gave up and started imagining a more interesting set of questions and answers:

Temerity: *Why are you so rude?*
Harley: *Please excuse my manners. I was raised by wolves.*
Temerity: *Where are you from?*

Harley: *The wolf commune was high up in the Transylvanian mountains. In the winters we ate travelling salesmen.*
Temerity: *What do you think of Lost Maidens Loch?*
Harley: *I'm still getting used to a house that has indoor plumbing.*

She was starting to enjoy entertaining herself in this way when Angus stopped at one of the houses and knocked on the front door.

'Hello?' Beth Bennett looked pleasantly surprised to find a policeman who looked like he'd stepped straight off the Quaker Oats box on her doorstep; she looked at Temerity with rather less interest.

'Miss Bennett, we spoke on the phone. I'm Constable Harley and you might know Miss Love?'

'I've seen her around. Come in,' Beth said dismissively, watching Angus as he walked in front of her into the lounge. Temerity couldn't blame the girl; if she hadn't been the recipient of Angus's appalling rudeness she might have been more enthusiastic about his very fine physique.

'Coffee?' Beth twinkled at Angus; Temerity thought she didn't seem particularly upset that her flatmate had just been murdered, but of course, appearances could be deceptive.

'No, thank you.' He nodded politely and sat down on a leather sofa. Temerity took the matching armchair.

'I'd love a glass of water,' she called out to the girl, who had gone into the adjoining kitchen. Beth returned with a packet of chocolate biscuits, a cup of coffee for herself and a small, grubby glass of water for Temerity.

The compact lounge looked out onto a scrubby garden; Temerity sipped the water, which was warm.

'Not keen gardeners, then, either of you?' she smiled, pointing at the garden.

'I don't exactly have the time to have my knees in the dirt in my line of work,' Beth replied huffily.

Temerity, who actually did frequently have muddy knees and grass stains on her clothes from gardening or doing magic outside, resisted the urge to make a snide comment.

'And what line of work is that, if I may?' Harley had got his notebook out, pen poised.

'I'm a personal assistant. I work in Glasgow,' she replied, crossing her legs. Where Molly had had the type of slim yet curvaceous figure many women coveted, Beth had more in common with Temerity, who was angular and relatively flat-chested, though Beth wasn't as tall as she was. Temerity had always been the tallest girl at school and even when she was a teenager she still towered over some of the boys even in Tilda's year – not that she cared, then or now.

'And how long had you and Molly been living here together?'

'She moved in about six months ago, when she started working at the school.' Beth frowned at Temerity. 'What's she here for? She runs the antiques shop over the road. She's not with the police.'

Talk about me like I'm not here, why don't you, Temerity thought, plastering a fake smile on her face.

'Miss Love is helping us with our enquiries. Do you have an item of Molly's – something she was fond of, maybe, that Miss Love might be able to look at?' Temerity could hear in his voice how much Angus disliked having her along. He plainly thought what she did was theatrical and false – like Muriel's invention of the blacksmith's ghost – but she could also tell that he thought so highly of his own code of conduct that he would never explicitly say this to her. Temerity personally thought it was better manners to be honest about what you thought rather than passive-aggressively implying something but refusing to ever say it, but she supposed not everyone shared that view.

Beth looked suspiciously at Temerity.

'What kind of thing?'

'Anything. A hairbrush, favourite book, teddy bear, ornament.' Temerity shrugged. 'I touch it and I can tell something – usually, more than one thing – about who it belongs to. Inspector Hyland thought it might help the case.' She smiled purposefully brightly at them both. *I don't really care what either of you think*, she thought. *I just want to find out whatever this stag is supposed to mean and what happened to Molly, and then I don't care if I never see either of you again.*

Beth stared at her for a long minute, then got up, went to a bookshelf on the left wall and handed Temerity an egg-shaped amber ornament.

'Here you go. This was hers.'

Beth watched as Temerity held the egg-shaped amber stone in her hands and closed her eyes. Yet the images she got immediately – a young, gawky girl being handed the egg, the same girl holding the egg at a funeral, crying – were all of Beth.

Temerity opened her eyes and handed the egg back to the girl.

'This is yours,' she said. 'Your grandmother gave it to you when you were about seven, maybe eight. It was in your coat pocket, you held it at your grandmother's funeral. You had a black dress on and a brown coat. You were in your teens then. It rained.' She held Beth's gaze and watched her eyes widen in shock. 'I need something of Molly's, please.'

'You… how could you know that?' Beth whispered. 'She couldn't have known that!' she repeated to Angus, who also looked surprised.

'I'm one of the world's most respected psychic provenance experts, specialising in rare and arcane artefacts from ancient cultures,' Temerity snapped. 'It's what I do. Now, can I have something belonging to your roommate or not?'

Beth stared at her.

'Upstairs. Her room is… was… on the right of the stairs. Help yourself,' Beth murmured.

'Thank you.' Temerity stalked out. It annoyed her when normal people didn't believe she could know things, just by touching them – especially when the world's antique experts sought her out for their most difficult cases. She sighed and climbed the narrow stairs, which were covered in a nondescript beige carpet. She remembered chasing upstairs just like this at Patrick's house – *Can't catch me! Can't catch me!* She smiled at the memory, her irritation receding. It wasn't Beth's fault. What Temerity did was strange.

Some people thought that Temerity herself was strange, but as Tilda said, you could never be responsible for other people's opinions of you.

That way madness lies, Temerity thought as she opened the door to Molly's bedroom. *Or if not madness, then severe irritation.*

Chapter 7

Molly's room was sparsely furnished; a double bed without a headboard was topped with a plain blanket and sheets that had once been white, but had gone in with a mixed wash too many times and were now rather grey. The door to the narrow white plywood wardrobe in the corner stood open; Temerity flicked through the clothes, which were generally well made and classic in style; nothing spoke to her as remarkable. It was often knick-knacks or personal possessions that worked for Temerity rather than clothes: she didn't know why. Maybe it was to do with them being washed, or something.

Other than the bed and the wardrobe, the room was almost bare. There was a pile of four well-thumbed paperbacks beside the bed. Temerity flicked through them, but there was nothing of great interest there: they were all of the self-help relationships kind that told single women how to find men.

The only decorative items Molly seemed to possess were some crystals – Temerity recognised black tourmaline, smoky quartz and tiger's eye – and a Russian doll, all of which were arranged on the windowsill. Temerity picked the doll up and closed her eyes.

Instantly, images flooded her mind. First, there was Molly as a child being given the doll from an older woman, a grandmother, maybe. Temerity had the sense that the woman was family, but that Molly didn't know her too well. The woman's face was hazy. Next, there was an argument with another girl: a friend, maybe. Molly snatching the doll from the other girl's hands, who protested, *But I only wanted to look at it.*

Temerity took in another breath and refocused her energies on the doll. She saw Molly, older now, picking up the doll to pack it in a box: she was moving house. Then, unpacking it and placing it on this shelf.

There was something else, but she couldn't put her finger on it. An unpleasant feeling, like being watched. Temerity looked over her shoulder, feeling the sensation intensify. The stairs creaked out in the hallway and she expected Constable Harley to appear in the doorway, but no one came. She walked into the hall holding the Russian doll, and heard Harley and Beth's voices in the lounge downstairs.

Temerity walked back into the room, sat on the bed and looked at the doll. It appeared to be a standard issue medium-sized *matryoshka*, the traditional wooden doll-within-a-doll; this one was hand-painted with a red cloak and a red headscarf over her blonde hair and pink roses on the dress underneath. It was in good condition, but Temerity had noted that they often were: children didn't play with them much, at least, not nowadays. She looked at the base; it was made by a popular and long-standing Russian tourist manufacturer she recognised that had sold nesting dolls all over the world for the last fifty years. It wasn't at all valuable and it could have been bought in London or New York just as likely as in Moscow.

Carefully, she took the dolls apart, revealing the next, smaller one inside. She had opened six when she came to the smallest, an intricately painted identical copy of the rest. Temerity took it out and held it; it was the size of her pinky finger.

The feeling of unease intensified. Temerity had the strong sense that she should put the doll down and leave the house; she laid the dolls on the bed and stood up, ready to go, then caught herself. Where was the sense of foreboding coming from? There was no reason for her to leave: Constable Harley was still

interviewing Beth downstairs and she had only been in Molly's
room for a few minutes.

She made herself sit down and pick up the dolls again, fight-
ing the unpleasant feeling that hit her as soon as she did. It was
something between nausea and anxiety, a feeling that nagged at
her; a sense that she was doing something wrong. Temerity felt
irrationally repulsed; she heard herself doubting why she was
even there. *I should go home, I'm not a policewoman, what right
do I have to be here*, she thought, even though she knew she had
every permission to be here. She dropped the dolls on the bed,
testing herself, and the feelings subsided. She picked them up
again and instantly felt sick and worried.

How strange, she mused, frowning. Temerity looked at each
layer carefully for anything unusual. There was nothing, except in
the last hollow doll, which held the smallest one. Peering into the
light wood interior – the dolls were painted on the outside, but not
within – Temerity could see something written on the base. It was
very tiny and could have been mistaken for a maker's mark or serial
number, except that Temerity knew that these particular mass-market
matryoshkas rarely featured their maker's mark on their bases.

She held it up to the light coming in from the window; it was
still unclear, so she fished her green-rimmed reading glasses out
of her bag – Tilda said they made her look like a 1950s librarian
– and peered at the mark again.

It was a shape, a symbol, four crossed lines inside a circle,
hand-drawn in ink. The ink had bled slightly into the fine grain
of the wood. Temerity stared at it, the nausea threatening her
stomach until she put the dolls back inside each other and replaced
them on the windowsill. Before she forgot it, she drew the symbol
on her notepad, staring at it in the dwindling afternoon light in
Molly's room. It meant something and Temerity was sure it was
what was giving her such a bad feeling.

She looked into Beth's room before she went back downstairs, but didn't go in. Beth's room, by contrast to Molly's, was full of personality: a shelf of framed photos of Beth with friends, pulling funny faces, laughing and hugging. A dressing table groaned with cosmetics arranged messily in various boxes and make-up bags. A row of glass perfume bottles lined the edge of the table.

Clothes hung over a chair, piles of shoes lay strewn in a corner – high heels, sandals, flats, boots. Some of the clothes were still on the shop hangers with the tags on; Beth clearly liked shopping. There was a sound system, framed pictures. Temerity glimpsed a pack of tarot cards bedside Beth's rather more girly white cast-iron bed frame, covered with a turquoise spread patterned with butterflies.

So many people have tarot cards these days, she thought as she walked down the stairs. *Muriel in the café probably has some – anything to busybody into people's lives.* The fact that the mirror found on Molly's body may have been used in witchcraft might be a link to the cards, but it wasn't enough of a connection. Still, it was interesting.

Temerity and Tilda's parents had been occultists and had collected all manner of mystical objects when they had been the original proprietors of Love's Curiosities, Inc. Neither parent had exactly explained what they were doing – the girls would have been too young to understand – but they had talked freely about psychic phenomena, tarot and mysticism.

Their mother had taught Tilda what she knew about herbalism and both parents, when they had realised Temerity's talent for psychometry – knowing by touch – had encouraged it. Their father had always been a mystery – he was distant, affectionate, but always up in the library room, researching or treading around, chanting, doing odd things. Occasionally, an acrid smell would seep down the stairs, followed by billowing smoke if he opened the thick oak door to answer Tilda or Temerity's questions.

After their parents had died, they'd left a record of years spent conjuring spirits, seership, divination and automatic writing in stacks of journals, written and annotated faithfully, intended for the girls. Along with the shop, it was a legacy, including various rare sets of tarot cards, many of them dog-eared from use. Maybe it was because Temerity was familiar with tarot that it didn't strike her as especially odd that Beth had a set – or, maybe, she was right to think that tarot packs were ten a penny nowadays.

Temerity found Beth and Angus where she'd left them.

'So, he was her boyfriend?' the Constable was asking Beth; he looked up from his notepad as Temerity stood in the doorway.

'No way. Wanted to be. He was mad keen on Molly, but she wasn't interested.' Beth shook her head.

'Might they have been seeing each other in secret, maybe?' Harley scribbled in his pad.

'Why would they? Neither of them was seeing anyone else, as far as I know. I can pretty much assure you that Molly wouldn't go within ten feet of that stalker.'

'Stalker?' Harley exchanged a glance with Temerity. 'Why do you say that?'

'Ugh. I told her to report it, but she didn't. He'd turn up uninvited all the time. I mean, she'd see him at work every day, but that wasn't enough for Ben. He sent her flowers, notes, emailed her, texted all hours of the day and night. She'd told someone at school, I think.'

'The Headmistress?' Harley asked.

Beth shrugged. 'Maybe. I don't know.'

'It must have been an uncomfortable working environment for her with that going on,' Temerity said. 'She'd been at the school six months, you said?'

'That's right, it was August. She'd got a job at the school. I was looking for someone to split the rent.' Beth shrugged.

'So this stalking –' Temerity remembered the young teacher in the staff room, wailing over Molly's dead body – 'when did it start?'

'I don't know. I mean, I think they started out being quite friendly. Molly was very flirtatious, so she probably was like that with him at first. But then I know she definitely told him to back off when it all started getting too intense and he didn't.' She sighed. 'She could handle herself. I mean, she was kind of a bitch sometimes, but she didn't deserve it. What happened.'

Harley wrote in his notebook, then flipped it shut.

'Okay, Miss Bennett. I think that's all we need for now. We'll be in touch, but in the meantime, it would be useful if you could avoid disturbing Molly's room. I'm just going to inspect it now, if I may? I won't be a minute.'

Beth shrugged. 'Be my guest.'

Temerity sat down opposite Beth, who gave her a disinterested stare.

'I'm still not sure why you're here. Find anything good up there, did you?' she asked.

'Maybe.' Temerity wasn't going to mention what she had found or how odd the doll had made her feel, but she was curious about Molly still. 'Was Molly Russian? I mean, were her family from Russia originally?'

'Not as far as I know. I think she said she was adopted, though.' Beth picked up a biscuit and dunked it in her tea. 'Oh, the Russian doll. You think she's Russian because of that?' she laughed derisively. 'Not such a great psychic after all.'

Temerity was thoughtful. Even if Molly's adoptive parents had been impeccably loving and kind, maybe she had struggled with the knowledge that she had been given away. Wouldn't such a thing have made her difficult at times, sharp-tongued, even a bit unlikeable?

Temerity's eyes followed Beth drinking her tea, but there was something suddenly on Beth's shoulder. A shadow, something

Temerity couldn't quite make out. What was it? A trick of the light? Temerity didn't think so.

She changed the subject.

'I saw some tarot cards by your bed. You'll have to give me a reading,' she said, casually.

'I said you could look in Molly's room, not mine,' Beth snapped.

'I didn't go in. I just saw when I was walking past,' Temerity said, breezily. 'Have you been reading them long?'

'No. I got them for my birthday. To be honest, they're so complicated, I've hardly used them. Not really my thing.'

The shadow on Beth's shoulder shifted; Temerity frowned at it. It was almost… she shook her head. It came into focus for one brief moment before Beth stood up and it disappeared: a black feather, sitting on her shoulder.

'Oh.' Temerity nodded. 'Never mind.' She heard Angus coming down the stairs and got up. 'Well, thanks for letting us talk to you,' she said, politely. Only a few nights ago she and Tilda had connected to the great goddess of justice, Ma'at. What had she said? That feathers would show Temerity who was guilty – whose judgement was near.

There had definitely been a feather on Beth's shoulder. A spirit feather; something born in the astral realm.

Temerity was taken aback. *Did this mean Beth was their murderer?*

'No bother.' Beth dismissed her, but was all smiles as she followed Temerity out into the hall. 'Constable Harley, are you sure you don't need to ask me anything else?' she beamed, but Harley shook his head.

'Nothing else for now.' He handed her his card. 'If you think of anything else, get in touch. I may come back to follow up this issue about the stalker teacher.'

'Any time.' Beth gave him a bright grin. 'Come and take down my particulars any time you want, Constable.'

They walked up the path and onto the street; it was only after Beth Bennett had closed her front door that Temerity glanced at Harley and noticed he was blushing. Usually she would have to stifle an impulse to laugh, but the feather had got her thinking.

'What?' He caught her eye and she shook her head.

'Oh, nothing,' Temerity replied. She certainly wasn't going to tell this logical oaf about her vision. He'd think she was mad.

'I don't know what you're laughing at,' Harley muttered.

'I'm not laughing,' Temerity protested, wrapping her scarf up around her neck. 'I'm thinking.'

'Fine. Think away. But I did absolutely nothing to encourage that, you know…' Constable Harley pointed back at Beth Bennett's house. 'All the… flirting.'

'I think you'll live,' Temerity replied, lost in her thoughts. She hardly noticed when he strode angrily ahead of her. *Who else was she going to see a feather on – and why?*

Chapter 8

They were walking past Love's Curiosities, Inc. when Temerity's mobile phone rang. Shielding her ear from a vicious wind that had appeared out of nowhere, she tried to hear who was speaking, but it was hard to make it out. Temerity signalled to Angus that she had to take the call; she beckoned him to come into the shop to get out of the cold.

'I was going to call you... yes, no, it's a great honour...' Temerity was struggling to hear the person on the other end of the line; it was the Alaskan university, following up on their invitation to speak at the conference. She motioned for Harley to go through to the kitchen, where there was a sofa along one wall and eight comfortable, cushioned chairs that sat alongside a scrubbed wood dining table. He followed, obediently.

'No, it's just that...' She listened to the enthusiastic conference manager at the other end of the phone, watching Harley move through the house. She felt momentarily bad for not listening to him earlier; he'd looked so discomfited at Beth Bennett's uncomfortable flirting. He sat down at the dining table, upright and started looking through his notepad.

'Yes, I know... yes, it's a very interesting panel... oh, that's very kind of you to say, but—'

She listened further, sighing.

'No, I'm sorry, but I have to decline your kind offer,' Temerity said with more confidence in her voice than she felt.

Leaving Lost Maidens Loch was too much of a wrench for Temerity. She made up excuses to stay in the shop – she was too in-demand, the shop wouldn't cope without her, or the places she was invited to were too remote, too far away. But the simple truth was that she didn't want to leave Patrick. His bones were in Lost Maidens Loch. She had left him once before and she hadn't been able to save him. She wouldn't leave him again.

Anyway, she was involved in the murder now. Murders were important.

Temerity ended the call and walked into the kitchen, deliberately banishing Patrick from her mind.

'Cup of tea? Coffee? Freezing out there.' Temerity flicked on the kettle and opened the cupboard for mugs. She expected him to refuse, but he looked up.

'Tea would be welcome. I didn't have any earlier.'

That's possibly the most polite thing he's ever said to me in the brief time we've known each other. Temerity tried not to show her surprise and spooned loose tea from a canister into one of the old teapots.

'No, well, that was probably wise. I wouldn't have put it past Beth to drug your tea and keep you there as a sex slave,' she joked.

'I don't think that's very funny. Modern slavery is nothing to joke about,' he replied, seriously.

'Sorry,' she muttered. *He really has no sense of humour. I guess the wolves didn't make time for amusing conversation*, she thought. There was an uncomfortable silence.

'Important call?' Harley cleared his throat, changing the subject.

'Oh… not really,' she said evasively, pouring hot water on top of the tea leaves which gave off a pleasantly bitter aroma.

'Really? It sounded like it was.'

Temerity sighed.

'Oh, it's just this university. They want me to come and speak at their conference, but I can't go.'

'Why not?' Harley accepted a mug of steaming tea and poured in a little milk from a small silver jug she placed on the table. It almost tipped over, as Temerity had accidentally rested it half on top of the edge of a magazine, but Harley rescued it in time.

'It's a long way away.' She stood next to the dinner table, resting her hip on it as she blew on her tea to cool it down.

'What do they want you to do?' he asked; she explained about the keynote speech. Harley looked at her with a curious expression. 'So you really… you're psychic? It's real?'

'Psychic provenance. I have the gift of psychometry: knowing something from touching it. It's useful in the antiques and collectables world.'

'How?' His expression was polite, but she knew he still didn't believe her, despite witnessing her tell Beth Bennett where her amber egg came from.

'How is it useful, or how do I do it?' She sipped her own tea. *At least we're having an actual conversation now. Drinking from crockery instead of a free-running stream beneath a full moon has obviously civilised him temporarily*, she thought, smiling to herself.

'Both.'

'It's useful because dealers, auctioneers, owners, potential buyers – they don't always know the whole life story of an object. That's called provenance. If you can provide full provenance for an object, it has a higher value.'

'But… what's the value in you saying something belonged to someone or came from somewhere in particular if it's just your –' he waved his fingers in the air – 'your vision, or whatever? You can't prove it.'

'No, but I can often tell investigators where to look for ownership documents, receipts, that kind of thing. I can tell which country to look in, what family has something important in their vault that will complete the story. If the object's lost, I can tell them where it is.'

Harley held her gaze steadily; she didn't drop it.

'So if I gave you something of mine, you'd be able to tell me things about myself you couldn't know.'

'That's right. Well, I can tell you what comes to me. Whether I conceivably could know it or not is irrelevant. I could go through your bins for a year and possibly find out the same thing, but it doesn't really appeal.'

'Convenient.'

'Not really, no.' Temerity was beginning to get irritated. 'For instance – Molly Bayliss owned a matryoshka doll.' Harley looked blankly at her. 'A set of Russian dolls? You know, one inside another one?' she clarified.

'Was that what you touched when you went up to her room?'

'Yes. And when I touched it, I felt physically ill. Anxious. I wanted nothing other than to get out of there. I saw someone – a woman, a relative, I think – giving it to Molly. I saw her, when she was younger – Molly had a temper and she didn't like people touching that doll. And I found this symbol drawn inside it.'

Temerity went over to where she had slung her handbag over an antique dinner chair as she'd come in and retrieved her notebook, bringing it back open to the page with her drawing of the four crossed lines inside a circle.

'Are you sure you didn't just feel ill because you... might be ill?' Harley asked, then took the notebook and frowned. 'This could be anything.'

'Yes, it could. And no, I feel fine now. It could be a clue, though.'

'What is it?' He looked at Temerity's drawing distrustfully.

'I have no idea. The only thing it reminds me of it is a magical glyph, or sigil. Something used in different occult traditions.'

'Occult? Meaning…? Molly Bayliss was a witch?'

'No. Meaning that's what it might be, that's all.' She sat down at the kitchen table.

'What does a glyph… or sigil… do?' He handed it back to her.

'It's a kind of compressed symbol containing the power of a magical working,' she said. *I shouldn't have to explain this to you, Wolfman. Transylvania's full of this kind of weird cultural history.* Temerity realised that she was actually starting to make herself believe that Angus Harley *had* been raised by Transylvanian wolves, which was funny, but she thought she should probably concentrate on reality for the moment.

'A spell?'

'I suppose you could see it like that, yes.'

Harley rolled his eyes.

'It might be a manufacturing brand,' he said. 'Occam's razor: whatever the most likely reason is, it's probably that.'

'Well, I'd agree, apart from the fact that I know that manufacturer – I did a valuation job for someone a while back. They sent me a whole box of dolls and the brand that Molly had, I can tell you, only have a maker's mark on the base of the biggest outer doll. And they're as common as the cold. This mark was hand-drawn inside the last doll. Not printed.'

'So you really think this is… witchcraft?' Harley looked doubtfully at the doll.

'Maybe. It's a possible link to the mirror found with the body.'

'But isn't witchcraft… all a bit… made-up?' Harley sipped his tea.

Temerity was about to disagree vociferously when there was a flurry of feathers and Hebrides flew into the kitchen, screeching, with his claws out, straight at Angus Harley.

The Constable stood up in a panic and dropped his mug; it shattered on the stone flagged floor. *At least it wasn't me this time*, Temerity thought briefly.

Hebrides landed on Harley's shoulder and dug his claws in hard, screeching loudly. His considerably large bright blue wings – when both wings were outstretched, as they were now, they were about four feet wide – smacked Harley's face a number of times. Parrots loved their owners but disliked strangers; Temerity also wondered whether Hebrides was taking umbrage at Harley's dismissal of witchcraft. She kind of hoped he was.

'Hebrides! No!' Temerity scolded him. The parrot's beak was very sharp and could easily draw blood. 'Naughty! Hebrides, gentle!'

She held out her hand and Hebrides, submissive now, hopped gently on to the back of her wrist with a guttural growl, as if to say, *Sorry, but I don't like him*. Temerity suppressed a smile and stroked Hebrides' downy head.

'Hebrides! Come back!' Tilda trotted into the kitchen, with a cross expression on her face. 'Oh! Sorry. I didn't know you'd come home. He just came back in from being out and I forgot to close the door. Hello, I'm Tilda.'

Tilda proffered her hand, but the Constable just stared at it, obviously shaken.

'Angus, I'm so sorry! I forgot to warn you about Hebrides. He's very protective of us, but he's a softie really. Sit down, you're okay. I don't think he hurt you.' Temerity took a quick look at Angus's neck and cheek but Hebrides hadn't broken the skin.

Tilda clicked her tongue and the bird flew to her instead.

'So sorry,' she repeated. 'I should have closed the door.'

'That's… all right. Angus Harley.' The Constable held out his hand shakily.

'Oh! The new constable.' Hebrides sat on Tilda's shoulder now, making a purring noise and looking for all the world like nothing had happened. 'I heard.'

'Is that... are you allowed to have a pet that... big?' Harley asked.

'Oh, yes. He's a Hyacinth Macaw. Definitely one of the biggest ones, but actually one of the gentlest. Macaws actually make good pets as long as you have the right environment and give them lots of playtime; they have the flock mentality, so they like being part of a family. Hebrides loves puzzles, he talks and sings. He does make a racket first thing in the morning and last thing at night, but we're used to it.'

'Oh... right. I suppose I didn't... really expect to be attacked by a massive bright blue bird, that's all. My mistake,' Harley said, rubbing his shoulder. 'He really dug his claws in. Ow.'

Temerity peered at Harley's uniform jacket; there were puncture marks where Hebrides had clung on.

'Oh no. You're right, I'm so sorry.' She shook her head. 'You're going to need to disinfect those. We keep him as clean as we can but it's best to be on the safe side. Let's have a look.' She went to peel back Harley's jacket but he pulled away.

He looked uncomfortable. 'That's fine, I'll sort it out later.'

'It's no trouble at all. We've got Tilda's antiseptic ointment in the bathroom. It's tea tree, garlic and ginger. Come on, I'll show you.' Temerity pointed to the bathroom door. 'I don't want to be responsible for killing our new police constable by giving him septicaemia. I'm not taking no for an answer.'

'I'm sure it'll be all right,' he grumbled, but followed Temerity to the bathroom that led off the kitchen. There was another bathroom with a vintage claw-footed bath upstairs, in which Tilda took long baths and read romance novels. It was an unexpected character trait for someone so caustic in her manner, but deep down, Tilda was an unabashed romantic. Sadly, real life just never measured up to the heroes and heroines she read with such devotion.

Temerity and Tilda actually tended to use the downstairs bathroom to bathe Hebrides, but Temerity didn't feel like it was a good time to mention that and anyway, it was clean and tidy. They'd kept the original avocado suite that their parents had installed in the 1970s: it was still in good condition and neither of them had the time or energy to want to change it.

'Wow. This is something else.' Harley blinked at the vivid purple tiling that covered the entire wall space.

'I know. Our parents had great taste.' Temerity opened the medicine cabinet on the wall and took out a brown glass jar of Tilda's anti-microbial salve. 'You'll need to take your jacket and shirt off and I'll put it on for you.'

'I'd rather put it on myself.' Harley held out his hand for the jar. 'I'm fine, really.'

'Don't be silly. You can't reach it as easily as I can,' Temerity replied.

'Really, Miss Love. I must insist.' He held out his hand for the salve. 'Please.'

There was a slight, uncomfortable pause. *Have it your way, Wolfman. I was just trying to help. Don't eat the salve when I'm gone.* Temerity was irritated that he wouldn't let her help. It was as if he just didn't want to admit that he needed her for something.

'Fine. Wash your shoulder area first with the soap there, that's also antiseptic, then put the cream on. You can use the small towel on the top there, it's clean.' She pointed to a small pile of handtowels in a basket by the sink and handed him the glass jar. Harley nodded.

'Will do.' He nodded.

Temerity pulled the door closed after her and returned to the kitchen, then remembered that she hadn't explained how much of the salve to use. If you used too much it tended to get into your clothes and was hard to wash out.

'Sorry, I forgot –' she pushed the door slightly ajar, catching Harley bare-chested at the sink – 'Oh…'

He was as muscular as she had expected, with broad shoulders and large, tight biceps; as he leaned forward over the sink, the muscles in his back flexed. But it was his shoulder, the one that Hebrides had sat on, that Temerity couldn't help staring at. Down one whole side of his torso, burn marks twisted and scarred his flesh into red-and-white patterns. Some of the burns trailed onto his back.

He turned around in surprise.

'Oh. Sorry.' Temerity blushed. 'I, errr… I forgot to say – only use about a pea-sized amount.'

'Right.' He stared at her, waiting for her to leave. Temerity realised she was staring. 'I'll manage.' Harley repeated, his cheeks colouring. He was embarrassed; she could tell he hadn't wanted her to see his scars.

'Right. Yes, of course. Sorry.' Temerity blushed and shut the door, mortified.

A few moments later he came out of the bathroom, fully dressed. Temerity had gone to sit at her desk in the shop.

'I put the jar back in the cupboard,' he said stiffly.

'Thanks.' Temerity looked at her laptop. 'I'm so sorry about just now, I didn't mean to—'

'It's fine,' he interrupted. 'I really should be off, anyway.'

'Right.' There was another awkward pause. 'How did you… they're burns, aren't they?' Temerity asked shyly.

'Yes. I got them in a fire,' he said and gave her that polite but dismissive nod she'd seen so many times already. 'Thanks for the tea. Be seeing you.'

The door had closed before Temerity had time to say anything else. Temerity sighed. Scylla, the fat black cat, jumped into her lap.

'Yes, darling. He's a tough customer, that one.' Temerity stroked Scylla's velvety ears thoughtfully. She wondered what had happened to Angus Harley in that fire; it would have to have been a bad one to come away with scars like those.

'I suppose I'll never know,' she told the cat, who chirruped at her. She clicked on the icon for the internet. Angus Harley might want to remain a mystery, but the sigil inside the Russian doll might give up its secrets with a little more research.

Chapter 9

'Temerity, I just can't believe that a teacher from my school was murdered. Murder! And in school hours, too. It's not even like Molly had some sort of double life in the evenings, as far as I'm aware, anyway. She didn't get mugged, she didn't get accidentally involved in... I don't know, a bank robbery that went wrong. Murdered. In my staff room! I just don't think I'll ever get over it.'

Laura Hardcastle shook her head and wiped a tear from her eye. Temerity handed her a tissue from the box on her desk that she used mainly for picking up fragile items in the shop, or wiping down the furniture on the rare occasions that one of the cats brought in a mouse and laid it out as an offering for her.

'It must have been such a shock,' Temerity agreed. It was three-thirty in the afternoon and Laura had come by after the school day for a chat. Sometimes, people liked to unburden themselves to her.

Laura had, in fact, come in on the pretext of wanting to buy something, but Temerity could tell that really, she just needed to talk. Not that Temerity wouldn't sell her something if she was interested; takings were almost non-existent for this time of year. At least she had her consultancy work, otherwise she and Tilda would be living on bread and water.

'I can't tell you how much.' Laura sighed. 'She wasn't the best teacher we've ever had and she wasn't overly popular. But she was one of mine, nonetheless. I interviewed her. I gave her the job. I feel somehow responsible.'

'You're not responsible.' Temerity reached out and squeezed Laura's hand. 'Come on. These things happen.'

'I know. But you always imagine this kind of thing happens in a city somewhere. Not in Lost Maidens Loch.' Laura sipped the mug of coffee Temerity had made her and sat back in her chair. 'What a week.'

'You say that, but the village has had its share of unusual goings-on,' Temerity said.

'Hmmm. I suppose so.' Laura leaned forward. 'Last week, Mr McKinley. This week, Miss Bayliss. This year is doomed.'

'Ben McKinley?' Temerity remembered the teacher who had cried in the staff room.

'Yes. Well, I shouldn't really say…' Laura looked evasive.

'All right.' Temerity sat back, knowing that the teacher wanted to tell her something.

'Well. The thing is, we had to give Ben a formal warning. For harassment of his fellow teachers. One in particular.' Laura shot Temerity a meaningful look.

'Molly?'

'Yes. She complained he'd been following her home, texting her late at night about non work-related things. Personal things, if you get my meaning.' Laura raised her eyebrows. 'Clearly, whatever my teachers do in their own time is up to them. We don't specifically say that they aren't allowed to have relationships with each other, but it's not ideal.'

'Were they in a relationship, then?' Temerity asked.

'He says yes, she says – *said* – no. She complained he was harassing her at work, demanding that she go out with him, interrupting her classes, even, to call her out into the corridor so he could talk to her. It was affecting her work and she said she didn't feel safe.'

'Have you told the Inspector all this?' Temerity asked. 'Someone else said much the same thing about him. It sounds like this gives McKinley a major motive for killing her.'

'I told him. I don't know that it makes him a murderer, though,' Laura said. 'I've put him on suspension while the Inspector looks into it.'

'What did McKinley think about that?' Temerity picked up her coffee and drank it. As usual, it was the bitter, thick variety Tilda liked. She made a face and put the mug down.

'Not much, as you can imagine. He couldn't believe I was going to heap misery on him by suspending him after the love of his life had just died. I didn't remind him that "love of *her* life" wasn't exactly how she thought of him.'

'Hmmm,' Temerity mused. 'So, who do you think did it, if not Ben McKinley?'

'I have absolutely no idea. But I hope this all gets sorted soon. I've got nigh on a hundred worried children thinking that there's a murderer on the loose. They're terrified, the poor things. I'll certainly rest easier once the culprit's been caught.' Laura shrugged.

'Of course,' Temerity agreed. 'I think we all will. But why don't we take our minds off it for now and look at some of the new stock? I've just had some lovely new candlesticks in.'

'Yes. You're right. I need to distract myself with some retail therapy.' Laura smiled ruefully. She held out a hand for Temerity's as they stood up; startled, Temerity froze. She could feel the worry and concern flowing from the teacher; it was as if it swam under Laura's skin and into hers. Despite her professional façade, Temerity could feel just how anxious the head teacher was. 'It's just that... I haven't been sleeping. It's horrible, Temerity. I keep reliving it in my dreams... walking in to the staff room and seeing her there, sprawled out on the carpet.'

Temerity gave Laura an awkward hug. Other people's emotions could be overwhelming sometimes and she didn't like to pull away when people needed a hug or their hand held. But having the gift of knowing through touch could often be difficult. You got more than you might expect.

'It'll be okay. I have faith in the Inspector,' Temerity reassured her.

'But what if Ben *did* murder her?' Laura appealed to Temerity, gripping both her hands tightly. Temerity subtly tried to pull them free, but she couldn't break her friend's hold. 'What if I've had a murderer under my nose all this time? With the children? I'd never forgive myself.'

A wave of confusion and grief swept over Temerity. She managed to extricate her wrists from Laura's grip.

'We never really know who the people are that we live with, day to day,' Temerity said, quietly. 'All we can do is live in good faith that they are who they say they are.' People in Lost Maidens Loch had secrets. It was that kind of place. Who knew what shadowy truths lay behind their smiles?

'And if they're not?' Laura demanded.

'Then it's still not your fault. The only person responsible for Molly's murder is the murderer, whoever that may be.' Temerity tried to smile reassuringly. *When did I become the village therapist? I'm not that good at it,* she thought.

Laura blew her nose and wiped her eyes. 'I'm sorry I got so emotional.'

'Don't be sorry.' Temerity felt awkward. She never really had got the hang of the sage village witch thing, dispensing wise advice by a crackling hearth. That kind of thing was more Tilda's style: despite her occasionally brusque manner, Tilda was great with people who came to her for genuine help. It was just the non-believers she had little time for. 'Let's have some sherry, shall we? Or a crème de menthe. That usually cheers me up.'

She went over to an antique drinks cabinet in the shape of a globe – they'd been quite popular in her parents' day – and opened the top of the sphere to reveal a number of bottles and glasses. Laura chuckled wryly and came to stand next to Temerity.

'My goodness. It's like the 1970s never left,' she said and took out a bottle of brandy. 'Go on, then. For the shock.'

'Of course. It's purely medicinal,' Temerity answered seriously and handed Laura a vintage green brandy glass. 'I think I'll join you.'

As she handed the glass to Laura Hardcastle, Temerity glanced at the unusual clip in the Headmistress's black hair. It was in the shape of a stag.

Chapter 10

There was no one else in The Singing Kettle when Temerity got there the next morning. She'd been hoping to run into Inspector Hyland to find out more about what the other teachers had said about Molly, but he wasn't in his usual place at the counter. She wondered if she should mention the stag on Laura's hair slide. Was it coincidence, or something more? She didn't know, but it would be interesting to find out what Laura had said in her police interview, and whether the Inspector was suspicious of her in any way.

'Morning, darlin',' Muriel greeted her. Today she was wearing a tartan apron which read *Dinnae teach yer granny tae suck eggs* over her standard jeans and fleece. 'What's it tae be today?'

'Breakfast, please. Cooked.' Tilda, a principled vegetarian, refused to have meat in the house, so Temerity often had a full Scottish at the café: sausage, egg, bacon, baked beans, black pudding, warm potato scone, fried mushrooms, toast and tea. If you had one of Muriel's breakfasts, you didn't need another meal until dinner that night.

'Right ye are.' Muriel turned away and laid three strips of thick bacon into a waiting frying pan, already bubbling with oil. 'Mind ye, I should scold ye, Temerity Love. Ye never came back from the school tae have a blether like I asked ye.'

Temerity had completely forgotten.

'Oh, Muriel. I'm so sorry!' She felt terrible.

'Ah, don't worry. I've got ma sources.' Muriel added a large slice of black pudding into the pan and cracked two orange-yolked eggs into the pan. The sizzling made Temerity's stomach rumble.

'So what did they say?'

Muriel looked around her as if checking no one was listening, even though the café was empty. She leaned confidentially towards Temerity.

'Seems that the teacher, Molly, wasn't that popular with the parents, for one thing. School received complaints that she'd been rude, shouted at the kids too much.' Muriel raised her eyebrow. 'And apparently she didnae get on with her flatmate either. Inspector Hyland says ye went up there with the new Constable.'

'He asked me to,' Temerity said, defensively. So far, none of this was news. Laura and Beth had said as much.

'Aye. Well, seems that poor Beth Bennett picked the wrong one tae move in. Molly had an affair with Beth's fiancé. Beth had already asked her to leave, given her notice, like, when she died.'

'Molly Bayliss had an affair with Beth Bennett's fiancé?' That threw things into a different light and gave Beth a very good reason for wanting Molly dead. Crimes of passion could be deadly. Temerity resolved to ask Angus if Beth had let that particular fact slip while she was making cow eyes at him. She suspected not.

'Aye. How're you getting on with the new policeman, then? Takin' a shine tae him? Yer not the only one, I can tell ye.' Muriel turned the bacon and buttered some toast, shaking her head. 'Place like Lost Maidens Loch, if a good-lookin' single man turns up, lassies lose their heads.'

'I have not taken a *shine* to him, Muriel. In fact, he's quite rude and standoffish,' Temerity remarked. She considered telling Muriel about her raised by wolves theory, but she didn't think Muriel would get it.

'Aye, well. What's fer ye will no go by ye.' It was a phrase that meant if something was meant to be, then it would come to pass, whatever happened. Muriel placed the large plate of breakfast in front of her. 'That's five pounds, darlin'.'

'Hmmm. What else did you find out? Don't hold out on me, Muriel, I know you know more.'

Muriel sucked in her cheeks.

'I don't know what ye mean!' she protested.

'Muriel. Come on.'

Muriel sighed.

'All's I know is that the other teachers didnae like her much. The kids said she was too strict, she wasnae a team player, didnae play nice in the staff room, lots of arguments. The only one she was popular with was that Ben McKinley. I never liked him. He comes in from time to time but he's always a difficult bugger, wants to know what I cook the sausages in, where do I get the eggs from. Eat the food or don't eat it, don't quiz me on where I get it,' she grumbled.

'They were seeing each other, then?' Temerity asked, innocently, as if she didn't know.

'According to him they were. In secret, because of workin' together.' Muriel scoffed. 'I think it's a lovers' quarrel. Him or that boyfriend of the flatmate that she stole, they'll have done it.' She nodded confidently. 'Inspector says Ben has an alibi because he was on playground duty when she drank the poison, mind ye.'

'Was he?' Temerity frowned. Presumably the poisoner would have to have been present to drop the poison into Molly's mug after she had made the tea, which meant it had to be one of the other teachers. It could have been Laura Hardcastle – a headmistress could be anywhere in the school at any time if she wanted. But what would her motive be?

'Aye, lots of kids and teachers say he was, the whole break, didnae come inside. So maybe it's the other one. Beth Bennett's fiancé.'

'But she was poisoned at school. How could the other guy have been there to do it? Who is he, anyway?' Temerity cut an egg in half and mopped up the bright yolk with the thick bread Muriel had cut from a large loaf behind the counter.

'Dunno, darlin'. She never brought him in here that I know of.' Muriel shrugged. The door opened; Temerity looked round to see Inspector Hyland, bundled up in his coat, hat and scarf. 'Ah, good mornin', Kim. The usual?'

'Bless ye, Muriel, aye.' Kim Hyland took off his coat and hung it up on the pine coat stand in the corner of the café. 'Mornin', Temerity! Just the lassie I'm looking for. I hear yer parrot tried tae kill ma new constable.' The familiar twinkle in his eye showed he was joking.

'Hebrides is the best burglar alarm a girl could ever have.' Temerity shrugged.

'Aye, well, I take it Angus wasnae tryin' tae burgle ye?' Hyland enquired.

'No. He came in on the way home from Beth Bennett's house and Hebrides got a little… territorial.'

'Hm. So, Angus tells me ye found somethin' there. A Russian doll?'

Temerity nodded and recounted what she had seen, but also the strange sensations she'd experienced touching the doll and the hand-drawn sigil inside it.

'Odd. Ye felt funny when ye touched that mirror as well, aye.' Hyland regarded her completely seriously; unlike Angus Harley, Kim Hyland knew that there was more in heaven and earth than could be dreamed of.

'Yes,' she agreed.

'Apparently, Beth and Molly didn't get along. Maybe she got her revenge with witchcraft somehow.' Hyland accepted a mug of coffee from Muriel. 'What d'ye think? More popular nowadays, I understand.'

Temerity made a face.

'I did see some tarot cards next to her bed. But if I'm being totally honest, I don't think Beth Bennett's a witchy type. She just doesn't have it about her. And I asked her about the cards and she said they were a gift. She's hardly used them.'

'She might be lyin'.' Hyland sipped his coffee.

'She might, but I don't think she is. Not about that, anyway. What do you know about Beth's fiancé? The one that Molly's supposed to have gone off with?'

'News travels fast.' The Inspector raised a salt-and-pepper eyebrow at Muriel, who avoided his look. He sighed. 'Guy called Andrew May. Works at the same company in Glasgow, firm of accountants. She's a PA there. Beth told Angus she'd been seeing him a few months and then after Molly moved in, she came downstairs one morning tae find them canoodlin' on the sofa. She told Molly tae pack her bags. This was aboot a week before Molly died. We havenae been able to speak to him to substantiate her claims, though.'

'What was Beth doing on the day of the murder?' Temerity loaded sausage and baked beans on her fork, savouring the breakfast. She recalled the feather she'd seen on Beth's shoulder. It was supposed to be a sign of guilt, but what was Beth Bennett guilty of? Even though she didn't really like Beth, Temerity didn't feel in her heart that she was the murderer. Her instincts tended to be right, but instincts wouldn't stand up in a court of law.

'She said she was at work, but Harley checked yesterday and they said she was off ill that day. Stomach bug.'

Temerity chewed her food thoughtfully.

'You'd remember if you were off sick just the week before, wouldn't you?'

'I would have thought so, aye.' Muriel deposited another full Scottish in front of Hyland. 'Thanks, darlin'.'

'So Beth doesn't have an alibi?' Temerity frowned. 'Would she have done it?'

'Murders have been done for less.' Hyland shrugged. 'Affairs of the heart are always the most savage. But no one saw her at the school that day; the school has high fences and every visitor has tae sign in at reception.'

'So it couldn't be her…'

'Hm. Maybe, maybe not. People are ingenious when they want to be.'

'What about Laura? Ms Hardcastle?'

The Inspector frowned at Temerity and stopped chewing his food.

'The Headmistress? What aboot her?'

'Does she have an alibi?'

'Aye, she does, as a matter of fact. Why ask aboot Hardcastle, though? Ye suspect her?'

'It's nothing. Just… the stag. I saw the stag in the vision when I touched the mirror. I saw Laura yesterday, and she… she had a stag design on her hair clip.'

Kim Hyland smiled and returned to his breakfast.

'No offence, Tem, but I dinnae think our police work should be based on ladies' fashions. As I say, Laura Hardcastle has an alibi for the mornin' of the murder. She was in her office doin' paperwork; the receptionist swears she never left till mid lunchtime, and that was when she heard a commotion from the staff room.'

'She still could have left without her receptionist noticing,' Temerity argued. Hyland snorted and almost choked on a bite of sausage.

'I assume ye've not met Brenda,' he said when he'd recovered. 'Brenda could tell ye what time a magpie flew past and how many feathers it had.'

Temerity sighed.

'Fair enough. I didn't exactly want it to be Laura, but… I don't know. The stag thing is driving me crazy,' she explained. 'What about this Ben guy? Beth said he was stalking Molly. Stalkers often turn into murderers.'

'Aye. He says they were seein' each other.' Hyland speared a hash brown and poked it in a glob of ketchup.

'He can say what he likes now. Laura Hardcastle told me that she's put him on suspension for workplace harassment, though.' Temerity thought of Ben in the staff room: how he'd wailed. He'd been inconsolable. Was it all a pretence?

'Hm. I know. He was out in the playground when it happened. We're goin' tae go and talk tae him again about the stalkin'. We can check emails and texts so it should be pretty easy tae see if he's lyin' aboot that, anyway.'

'Good.' Temerity finished the last of her tea. 'So, what else can I do?'

'Research that mirror. I want tae know who it belonged tae. Can ye do that?'

'Of course. Can I see it again?' she asked.

'I'll send Harley around with it later. You'll be in?'

Temerity balked at the idea of seeing Angus Harley again so soon after walking in on him with his shirt off, but she nodded.

'I'll be home. I've got work to do.'

'For what it's worth, I think ye should go to that conference in Alaska.' Hyland burped and covered his mouth with a paper serviette. 'Excuse me.'

'Who told you about that?' Temerity demanded.

'Constable Harley mentioned it. He said you weren't going.'

'Well, not that it's any of your business, but I don't want to go,' she snapped.

'Hey! Dinnae have a go at me! I'd rather you stayed here and helped me oot. God knows I'm not gonna get to go on that cruise with Kathleen otherwise,' the Inspector muttered. 'But I know how talented ye are, darlin'. Don't hide yer light under a bushel, is all I'm sayin'.'

'Noted.' Temerity shrugged on her coat and hat for the walk back to the shop.

'I'll send him over at the end of the day!' Hyland called out as she left. Temerity waved, shouted a goodbye at Muriel and stepped out into a storm.

Chapter 11

Temerity opened the shop door and looked down the dark cobblestone street. The wind was vicious and rain sliced down from heavy black clouds, edged in a murky yellow from the full moon behind them. She had run home from the storm, returning home from The Singing Kettle at about ten; all day after that, the storm had lashed the village.

It was past six o'clock and Angus Harley hadn't turned up with the pewter mirror. Irritated once again, Temerity closed the door, flipped the *Open* sign to *Closed* and slid the old lead bolts into place. If he wasn't going to come, then he should have called to let her know. It was plain disrespectful, and that was all there was to it. She entertained herself by imagining herself berating him:

> Temerity: *Why are you so rude?*
> Harley: *Please excuse me. I was raised by wolves.*
> Temerity: *I feel like we've had this conversation already.*
> Harley: *[howls sadly]*
> Temerity: *Why didn't you turn up? I waited in for you. I could have done something else. There were a variety of sparkling social events I could have attended.*
> Harley: *Please accept these animal entrails as an apology.*

Still, she had managed to do some research while she was waiting. Mirrors like the one found by Molly's body were common enough and often part of a dressing-table set with a hair brush and comb. The thistle detail indicated that it was Scottish, but that didn't help Temerity much; she knew it was more than a hundred years old because of its similarity to others from that time she'd seen at antique auctions. She sighed and adjusted her green-rimmed glasses. Sometimes they pinched; she rubbed the bridge of her nose thoughtfully.

The fact that the mirror had been customised in the way it had, with the glass painted black, was more interesting. Witches usually made their own magical tools, believing that they could be imbued with the witch's power in the creation process. There was also a value in recycling items and not buying them mass-produced, supporting capitalist manufacturers. Temerity knew that the Inspector would be dusting the mirror for fingerprints, but when she got hold of it again she felt sure she could find out much more if she could handle it without the latex gloves this time. If she could only dispel the strange confusion she had when she held it. It was much the same kind of fog as when she had touched the Russian doll, only she had got more information from the doll. Both items had clearly been bewitched.

Charybdis the Russian Blue, who Tilda and Temerity sometimes called Carrie, snaked around her ankles as she stood by the door. She was, as a rule, haughty and standoffish, but today she seemed to want Temerity's attention.

'What's up, sweetie?' Temerity crouched down and stroked the dense fur around Charybdis's ears. 'What's wrong with my Carrie-Cat?'

The cat miaowed and went to the door, scratching at it.

'You want to go out? But it's blowing a hoolie out there.' Temerity frowned. Charybdis rarely ever went out; she deigned to do her business in the garden, but she would waddle back afterwards and curl up on a blanket.

Carrie scratched at the wooden door again.

'Hey! Naughty.' Temerity sighed and opened the door again to let the cat out; sometimes, in a storm, the cats dashed wildly around the house, up and down the stairs, completely contrary to their usual sedate habits. You could tell if a storm was coming if they did that, but the storm was already here.

But Charybdis didn't run out into the street; she sat primly bedside Temerity's feet, as if waiting for something to happen.

'Carrie, I'm not going to stand next to an open door all night. I'll catch my death,' Temerity tutted and was closing the door when she saw a door open a way up the street and her two neighbours, Alf Hersey and Harry Donaldson, emerge, wrapping themselves up in scarves and coats. Alf and Harry were both in their sixties, though they kept pretty fit. Harry still rowed and both of them were into hill walking and yoga. That was, until recently: Alf, the village doctor, had been at home recovering from a heart bypass. Harry waved at her.

'Alf, what on earth are you doing, going out in this?' Temerity called out as she buttoned up her baby-blue twinset cardigan against the cold. She had an old Godzilla-print T-shirt underneath it which really wasn't protection enough against the weather. She was also wearing red Capri pants and her Minnie Mouse slippers.

'Haven't you heard? There's a boat lost on the loch. Three tourists on board. Been on the radio, they need rowers. Going to see if we can help!' Harry called out.

'Oh, Lord. Wait, I'll come with you.' Temerity grabbed her coat, a long grey-and-black winter houndstooth and buttoned it up. There was no point taking an umbrella: the wind was too fierce, so she picked up her rainproof gloves and a fleece-lined brown leather deerstalker Tilda had bought her as a joke a few Christmases ago. Temerity actually quite liked it.

Tilda appeared at the top of the stairs.

'Tem, I just heard on the radio… oh. Hi, Harry. Are you going to help?' she called down. 'Hang on. Two minutes, I'll come with you.'

Tilda emerged a few minutes later, bundled in a purple wool coat that had been their mother's, with green wellingtons underneath and a mustard wool scarf wrapped around her head.

They ventured into the storm.

*

By the time they got to The Singing Kettle, it had become the centre of a rescue operation.

'I told them not tae stay out long. And not to go over by the Manor.' Henry Sutherland, who owned and ran the boat shed, was telling the Inspector as they walked in. 'It's my fault. I should hae known a storm was comin' in. But they were so insistent.'

'Ah, now.' Muriel appeared with a tray of mugs of hot chocolate and coffee. 'Ye cannae have known. It's just unlucky, aye.'

Depending on what you wanted to believe, Lost Maidens Loch was named after an ancient legend that a mythical lady had drowned in the loch – or you could believe the more likely explanation that its name was inspired by its shape, which was, if you looked at it from above, the shape of a girl's head with long hair.

The rounded part of the 'head' was to the west of the village, which sat on the south side of the loch. The ends of the Maiden's 'hair' stretched out to the east, alongside the main road that ran in and out of the village, in three twisting, narrow straits that were shallower than the main part of the Loch. However, they were thick with an unusual river weed that could stop boats. Sometimes, people and swimming dogs got tangled in it, too.

Dalcairney Manor sat on the north side of the loch, across from the village. If you didn't want a meandering drive along tiny roads (that often flooded) to get from one to the other, you took a boat across. Yet boats making the full journey across the loch were rare, because the Laird didn't often leave his home and the Manor accepted few visitors.

Tourists could take Henry Sutherland's twice-weekly loch boat tour, which skimmed the edge of the black water, taking in the breath-taking views and local wildlife. Near to the Manor, there were rocks under the water that Henry could navigate in daylight, but they were dangerous to those who didn't know the loch – and even more dangerous in a storm.

'Thanks for coming.' Hyland took a mug of coffee and drained it; Temerity accepted a hot chocolate and coughed at the first sip, not expecting the whisky Muriel had added with a liberal hand.

'Of course. I'm sorry we didn't get here before.'

'I can row, if you need anyone. Or handle a motorboat.' Harry, a retired PE teacher, took off his hat and stuffed it in his pocket: his hair was shaved to his scalp, disguising his receding hairline. He and Alf had lived down the street from Love's Curiosities for as long as Temerity could remember.

'Great. Talk to Henry, he's going to take a boat out and see if we can find them on the water. We've called the coastguard, they should be here soon. You all right with a boat in this weather?'

Harry nodded.

'Reckon so. I was in the Navy. You don't forget this kind of stuff.'

'Right ye are.' The Inspector nodded.

'What about us?' Tilda asked. 'What can we do?'

'Angus – Constable Harley – is organising search groups on foot. Walk around the loch, see if you can spot the boat.' Hyland pointed at Harley, who was standing a few feet away. Temerity felt guilty for thinking he had been rude not to turn up to the shop with the mirror. But how was she to know he was coordinating a rescue mission? *Raised by wolves. A human would have called*, she thought crossly.

'All right. Tils, you're coming?'

'Sure. But Alf, I think you should stay in the warm.' Tilda looked concernedly at Alf, who coughed. Alf and Tilda had become close friends since he'd had his heart problems; Tilda would go round with various herbal concoctions aimed at improving his general health. Alf, the village doctor, had known the girls since they were children and Temerity suspected that he understood Tilda better than most, especially now that they had become friends as adults. Good doctors like Alf understood people's characters as well as their bodies: Temerity suspected that Alf knew that Tilda was lonely and that her spiky manner shielded a sensitive soul. Tilda's herbal medicine had helped, in fact, Tilda had said, glowing with pride one night a few weeks ago. Temerity was happy: it was a good thing for Alf to have someone keeping an eye on him. It took the burden off Harry a little bit and it gave Tilda someone else to talk to beside her sister and the cats.

'I'm fine, it's just coming in to warm air after cold air. It'll go in a minute.' He coughed again, harder.

'You will not. You'll just make it worse.' Harry frowned, putting his hand on Alf's forehead. 'Stay here and let Muriel fuss over you.'

'What? While you're off being an action hero? I don't think so.' Alf sniffed. 'If people need medical attention, they'll need me.'

'The coastguard's been called and the ambulance is on standby!' Muriel interjected; she'd obviously made herself the unofficial head of the rescue operation. 'It's okay, Alf darlin'. We know yer a hero, but Harry's right, aye. Stay in the warm. We dinnae want tae lose ye for another few months.'

'Come on, Alf. Harry's the James Bond of Lost Maidens Loch,' Tilda teased. 'Let him go and be a hero. I'll stay with you if you want. I need to pick your brains about a herbal tincture, anyway.' She winked at Temerity. 'Go on, Tem. We'll catch up with you later.'

Alf sighed.

'Fine, fine. I'll stay here. But if you need me, call the café.'

'No problem.' Harry gave Alf a kiss on the cheek. 'You shouldn't have even come out. I told you.'

'As if I'd be able to stay at home while all this was going on.' Alf rolled his eyes.

Temerity tapped Angus on the shoulder.

'Temerity Love, reporting for search duty.' She purred in an exaggerated sexy secretary voice. Angus turned round, a confused expression on his face.

'Oh. Hello.' He didn't smile and Temerity felt her little joke – not even a joke, really, just a slightly amusing voice – deflate, leaving an uncomfortable silence between them. *Oh, for... just, why do I bother?* she thought. Patrick would have laughed uproariously.

'I've come to help with the search?' Temerity repeated, straight-faced, feeling mortified. It had just been a joke, but she'd temporarily forgotten that Angus Harley didn't understand jokes, probably on account of his wolf heritage.

'Right. Thanks. Well, you might as well walk around the loch to the Manor with me, if you're up for it?'

Temerity shrugged. 'Fine.'

'It's a rough walk in parts, but we might be able to see something—' he continued.

'I'll be fine. It's not like I haven't walked by the loch before,' she snapped.

Great. Another wordless walk with Humourless Harley, Temerity thought. She looked around for anyone else to invite along with them so that she would have someone to talk to, but most people had left already; Tilda and Alf sat at the counter, laughing about something with Muriel. Temerity had noted that when she and Tilda had walked in, a few eyes had turned their way, assessing her sister warily. Temerity wondered what they thought Tilda would do – summon a calm to the storm, or, perhaps more likely, they thought she had something to do with it in the first place. Though many villagers had nodded to Temerity – she made a point of being out and about in the village most days, chiefly because it drove her mad being cooped up in the shop – they had ignored Tilda. Some of them even made the old sign against the evil eye.

I need to get Tilda out in society more, otherwise she's going to moulder away with those old books, she thought. If Temerity was like Hebrides, who needed to fly in the wild, then Tilda was like the cats: content to stay in one place, asleep, until dinner time.

Still, she was glad to see a pot of tea and some cake between Tilda, Muriel and Alf. *Ah, come on. That's just not fair,* she thought, though she was happy that Tilda was socialising. Temerity would have vastly preferred a gossipy night in the café than tramping out in the rain with the monosyllabic Constable Harley. *Typical that it takes three missing people on a stormy night to get Tilda out of the house.*

She considered making an excuse, but Angus Harley was holding the door to the café open, waiting for her.

'Coming, coming,' she muttered, following him out into the storm.

Chapter 12

Temerity was irritated to admit that Angus was right. Walking the perimeter of the loch in a storm was not pleasant.

The weather was still raging around them and Temerity realised that it didn't matter that the Constable maintained his usual silence; she could hardly hear herself think in the din of the thunder, wind and rain, never mind follow a conversation with someone who probably just wanted to howl at the moon. She was glad that she'd pulled on her wellingtons at the last minute, because the ground around the loch had turned to deep, sticky mud that squelched when she walked and threatened to pull her boots off more than once.

Angus had handed her a powerful police torch as they walked out of the village and the streetlights faded into blackness.

'Keep it focused on the ground in front of you. You don't want to fall over. Keep an eye on the loch, though. We might see the boat, or if it's capsized, we've got to look for swimmers. Or bodies.'

'Right.' Temerity trod behind Angus, shining her light over the black loch water, looking for anything that seemed unusual. Every now and again, lightning lit up the whole loch. In those moments, the brightness gave the loch an unnerving silver clarity, like a black-and-white photo, stark and somehow unreal.

They had been walking about half an hour when they came to a group of willows that formed a protective semicircle.

'Stop here for a minute!' Harley shouted above the wind. He beckoned her into the little natural shelter and took a silver flask out of the pocket of his overcoat. 'Medicinal!' he shouted, uncapping it and handing it to her. *Gods. The Wolfman knows how to loosen up*, she thought, reasonably taken aback. *Maybe I've totally underestimated him. This whole time, he was desperate to get me alone under a tree and ply me with hard liquor.*

Temerity took a gulp and felt the whisky warm her stomach immediately.

'Can't get too cold,' Harley commented; either the wind had died down a little, or the trees really were protecting them a little from the storm, because suddenly Temerity could hear him better.

'It is chilly.' She handed the flask back to him. 'Thanks.'

He took a gulp and shivered.

'Horrible night to be lost on the water. I hope we find them.' For once, Temerity appreciated his sincerity. It *was* a horrible night to be lost: the loch was unforgiving at the best of times. Its purple mists may have inspired thousands of tourists' holiday pictures, but she knew the real dangers that lay in the water.

Temerity stared out onto the water; above them, the searchlight of the coastguard helicopter beamed across the water, the choppy noise of the helicopter blades intensifying then falling away as it flew over the loch, searching.

'There's something about the loch. It... I don't know. Every so often, it takes someone. A sacrifice, in a way,' she said, remembering. She didn't often allow herself to think too deeply about Patrick, the boy she had loved; the boy who she hadn't been able to save. But here, in the storm, the loch beside her, it was impossible not to.

Angus followed her gaze.

'You lost someone?' he asked softly.

Temerity blinked back sudden tears.

'How did you know?' She wiped her eyes on her sleeve, trying to control herself. 'Did the Inspector tell you?'

'No. Just… it's in your voice.' He stood next to her, very still, and there was something in his steadfast presence that was comforting. *This isn't how this is supposed to go*, she thought. *It isn't as funny if the Wolfman turns… nice, all of a sudden.*

'It was ten years ago. My… my boyfriend at the time. His name was Patrick Robison. Everyone loved him. He was on all the sports teams. Kind. Funny. He drowned. He'd been swimming, they said.'

'Wasn't he a good swimmer?' Angus asked, handing her the silver flask again.

'He was on the college swimming team. That's what I never understood.' Temerity didn't want to remember it all again, but she couldn't help it; something made her want to confide in him. 'But it was my fault. I could have saved him.'

'How? Were you there?' he frowned, taking the flask after her.

'I saw him on the Saturday afternoon; we went for a walk, it was sunny.' Temerity remembered every single detail of that day. The sun on Patrick's hair, making it blonder than ever. The smell of sunscreen, the tang of the lemon in the crab sandwiches she'd made for them to eat. 'I had to go home. I had this history project to finish. I left him there, he was reading. I even remember the title of the book.'

'So, he decided to go swimming after you left?' Angus concluded. 'He probably got a cramp or something. It wasn't your fault. I know you must have felt terrible, losing him. But victims of trauma, people experiencing grief, they often think that whatever happened was their fault. But it's not.' He put a hand on her arm.

'You don't understand. I *saw* it. I saw what was going to happen and I didn't stop it.' Temerity looked away; lightning lit the loch again, transforming it into that same strange between–place, like an illustration in an eerie fairy-tale storybook.

'What do you mean, you saw? You saw him drown?'

'No. I… had a vision when we were together that afternoon. It was the first time it had ever happened, so I didn't know what it was. But I saw his body, dead in the water. I was kissing him, I closed my eyes and I had this sudden, vivid picture in front of my eyes. I opened my eyes and he was there. I thought it was a weird kind of daydream. And then, the next day, when I heard, I knew I'd seen it before it happened.'

There was a silence.

'Are you being serious?' he asked, finally.

Temerity sighed heavily.

'Yes,' she said, her eyes meeting his. 'I wish I wasn't, but I am. I can touch people and know things about them. I can touch objects and know where they've come from, where they've been. I couldn't do it before that day and I don't know why it started then and I don't know how I do it, just that I can. And it kills me. Because every single time that I help someone, it reminds me that I didn't help the person I loved. I know you find it difficult to believe, but you'll excuse me if I don't really care what you think.'

The tears came again and Temerity closed her eyes, feeling them run warm down her cold cheeks. If he'd lived, she and Patrick might have built a life together. They might have moved away from Lost Maidens Loch; had a family, walked distant mountains, swum in jewel-like seas. They might have had a life of laughter. But she had lost him. So she stayed in Lost Maidens Loch, because that was where his bones were and would always be.

She needed to walk. If she stood there any longer, looking out onto the loch, thinking about Patrick, she felt like she would break down altogether. Temerity strode off, out of the protection of the trees, shining her torch ahead of her on the boggy path. Angus ran after her.

'Temerity, wait!' He ran a few paces to catch her up. 'Temerity. I'm sorry, I didn't want to upset you.'

She shone her light onto the water, looking for shapes in the gloom. She didn't want to see anything; the memory of her vision of Patrick played at the edge of her mind. Face down in the water, cold, his skin greyish after a night in the water. He was still beautiful, but the thing that had made him Patrick was gone.

'People in the village call me *witch* behind my back. They don't believe until they need me,' she said a little hysterically. Temerity breathed in the night air; the wind was dropping now. She wished she had never come out.

'*Are* you a witch?' he asked.

'In a way. Tilda more than me. I just have vision, a type of clairvoyance. Psychometry. Our parents were occultists. Tilda's taught herself more of what they knew than I have. She's got their old books.'

'Occultists, like… crystal balls?' He looked genuinely ignorant of what she was talking about. 'I'm sorry. This is all completely new to me. I was brought up to be rational about things. My mum was a geneticist. I didn't know… people actually were… witches.'

'I'm as rational as you are. It's not an either/or situation,' Temerity snapped, irritated again. She was still upset. *Shut up about things you don't understand, Wolfman.* Angus couldn't be more different to Patrick: humourless, plodding, serious, no social skills.

'Right. Okay.' His tone was neutral; she couldn't tell if he was angry or not. They walked on in silence; Temerity saw they were approaching Dalcairney Manor and stopped, shining her torch ahead, onto the edge of the loch in front of the Laird's home. It was a tall, imposing, grey stone Manor house with manicured gardens at the front, leading down to the loch side; Temerity remembered them being better tended than they were now.

Angus stopped beside her and touched her arm.

'I don't really understand your visions, or witches... But I can see how painful it was, losing Patrick. I'm sorry,' he said solemnly.

'Thanks.' She met his eyes and saw that he was genuine. Her heart softened a little.

'I'm sorry if I'm a bit... standoffish, sometimes,' he said. Temerity was aware that his hand was still on her arm. She felt warmth coming from him and it surprised her. The warmth of friendliness and caring. 'I find it hard to get to know people.'

'Okay, well, thank you. I appreciate that,' she repeated, not knowing what else to say. His touch was strangely healing, pushing the painful memories away. 'But you don't have to be standoffish with me.'

He removed his hand from her arm.

'I'll try.' He smiled. Temerity thought it was the first time she had seen his smile and it lit up his eyes very nicely. *Now, come on*, she castigated herself. *Don't get carried away, Temerity Love.*

Something moved on the water. She shone her torch onto it. A dark shape lay at the edge of the water.

'I think we've found the boat,' she said, pointing.

Chapter 13

They ran alongside the loch as best they could for the few hundred metres there were left, but the mud pulled at their feet, slowing them down. Finally, they found their way onto the small private beach at the edge of the Manor's gardens; Temerity thought that *beach* was an exaggeration, really, especially in the rain; it was a strip of sandy earth maybe twenty metres wide. The storm had made it as boggy as the pathway, but Angus held her arm as they negotiated their way to the edge of the water. Temerity shone her torch onto the side of the upturned boat; the Sutherland Boat Yard logo was bold against the stark white of the motor boat: a black stag's head against a white background.

The thing was, Temerity realised with a sense of defeat, as far as stags went, they were everywhere in Scotland. The proud stag on the moor was a pretty common image on everything from whisky bottles to the Headmistress's hair clip to a local taxi firm and even this, Sutherland's Boat Hire. It made her vision feel all the more useless.

'Damn,' Angus muttered and took his police radio from his belt. The crackle of interference rang out across the quiet loch, then after Angus made his short report, the Inspector's metallic, amplified voice told them to stay put. In the distance, Temerity heard the returning helicopter.

'What's happening here?' A man's voice rang out in the darkness. 'I saw your torches. You do know that this is private property?'

Angus shone his torch towards the house and they watched a portly, balding man halfway down the long, gentle incline of stone steps that led from the house to the end of the garden.

Temerity had met the Laird before, but only once, a long time ago. She had been a child then and the Laird had come to the shop to see her parents. Maybe they'd found him some rare decorative piece for the Manor: a Faberge egg, an original Lalique lamp. All adults had looked the same age to Temerity, then, but as he grew closer now, she estimated that he was perhaps in his late fifties or early sixties.

Angus waved and held up his police badge.

'Good evening, sir. I'm so sorry to trespass on private land, but we're engaged in a search and rescue operation. I'm Constable Angus Harley. This is Temerity Love.'

The Laird, quite out of breath even though he had only been walking, stopped for a moment.

'Search and rescue? Ah. I heard the helicopter. Who is it?' He came to stand by them on the muddy sand.

'Small motor boat there, sir.' Angus shone his torch out to the boat. 'And three tourists. The storm must have overwhelmed them.'

The helicopter grew closer and lower over the water; the vibration from its blades created a choppy tide on the loch. Temerity put her hands over her ears. Down the road that led into the village, visible through the trees at the edge of the Laird's estate, she saw blue lights flashing. An ambulance was on its way and what looked like the Inspector's patrol car.

'Right, let's see what we can do!' the Laird shouted over the noise. Angus's radio crackled again and he brought it right against his ear to hear it properly.

'It's the Inspector. Says the helicopter has sighted the three guys. They're down the loch from here, but they've managed to get out of the water. We need to take a boat down and get them, though, because the helicopter hasn't got its rescue cage operational.'

The Laird nodded.

'Right you are, Constable. I've got a boat moored up just here. I'll go with you.'

'Errr… Right you are, sir. Temerity, can you stay and talk to the Inspector when he gets here?'

Temerity didn't think the Laird looked at all strong enough to be pulling half-soaked accident survivors into his dinghy or whatever it was, but Angus was in charge here.

'No problem.' She nodded and watched the Laird lead Angus down the small beach, uncovering a motor boat from under a tarpaulin and pulling it into the water. Almost as soon as they made it onto the loch, Angus's torch showing the way, Kim Hyland's car screeched to a halt on the gravelled drive to the right of the house. Temerity ran up to meet him.

'The Laird's taken Angus in his boat to get them,' she explained.

'Ah. Okay, great. I'll radio the coastguard, tell them tae shine a light on the guys.' He made a quick call on the radio and then shook his head. 'I tell ye, Temerity. I'm definitely too old for this.' He laughed, sounding relieved. Temerity thought everyone would probably go to bed feeling relieved tonight. 'I forgot David had a wee craft. Not that he's used it for a while.'

The ambulance had also arrived; Temerity looked up to the house, seeing a light come on in an upper window. A face looked out briefly at the commotion and then disappeared again; Temerity couldn't tell if it was man or woman, young or old.

They walked down to the beach with the medics, waiting for Angus and the Laird to reappear. The helicopter was a way down the loch, shining its light down onto the edge of the water. The rain had stopped, at least.

'So you know the Laird? I suppose you'd have to…' Temerity asked Hyland as they stood there, hugging themselves to keep warm.

'Aye. Good man. He's been ill these past years, so ye won't have seen him in the village much. Looks old. Younger than me, though.' Hyland sighed and shook his head. 'Terrible shame, aye. What with him losin' both wives, too.'

'Oh, right.' Temerity remembered that the awful leaflet purporting to list all the haunted locations in Lost Maidens Loch had said something of the sort in it about the Manor; she'd forgotten, but she thought she'd known the story once. 'He was married twice?'

'Aye. Second wife divorced him. I hear she's livin' in Italy now, doin' pottery or somethin'. Their son's the heir to the lands. Anthony. Lives in London. He doesnae visit very often. First one, now, that was terrible.'

The cold had settled in Temerity's bones now and she was freezing; she wondered if it would be bad form to ask to go inside the Manor.

'What happened to the first wife?' Her teeth were chattering; she tried to stop them, but her body had taken over. The Inspector gave her a concerned look.

'Look, Temerity, you dinnae need to wait with me. Go up tae the hoose an' say I sent ye in for a dram.' Ever since he had interviewed her after Patrick's death, the Inspector had looked out for her. She knew he respected her and that she was a grown woman now, not a teenager grieving for her lost love. But it was always there between them: the memory of that day. He had always been kind.

'A drop of whisky would be welcome,' Temerity admitted. 'I'll go up in a minute. What happened to the first wife, though?' She flexed her hands: even inside her gloves, the cold had made them feel like blocks of ice.

'I'm surprised ye dinnae remember. She was supposed to have drowned in the loch. Terrible accident, her bein' pregnant an' all.'

Hyland exhaled into the cold air; his breath was a white cloud of steam. 'You wouldae been young then. Maybe five or six.'

'Maybe. I remember him coming to the shop once.'

'Hmmm. Well, maybe. Thing was, she was never found. He was out on his boat – that same one, maybe – searchin' for days after the coastguard had given up. He was a right state, I can tell ye. No wonder. Not the same since.'

'That's awful.' Temerity could imagine some of the grief the Laird must have felt – but losing a baby, too – that was beyond imagining.

'Aye.' The Inspector pulled a pipe out of his pocket, fumbled with a packet of tobacco and started to pack the bulb of the pipe with it. 'A bad business.'

Temerity shivered.

'Now get up to the hoose. Someone will help ye warm up. I'll come up with the rest o' them in a wee while and we'll give ye a lift back,' Hyland added.

'I will. Thanks.' Temerity was too cold to argue, so she followed the long stone pathway up to the manor and then walked around to the front of the house. She rang the bell on the imposing medieval-style front door and listened to it reverberate through the house.

Chapter 14

It wasn't until Temerity was sitting on one of the three large, comfortable tweed sofas, in front of a roaring fire in a large stone fireplace and with a mug of tea clasped between her hands that she started to cry.

It was as if the warmth dissolved her icy limbs and her tears were the melted water. Her freezing body had been holding her sad memories of Patrick stiff and immoveable; in front of the Laird's hearth, she let them go. There were some that she only let herself remember now and again, as if they were special jewels that would tarnish in the air if kept out too long. There was the first day they met, as children; there was their first kiss under the fir trees. But there were other moments that, in the moment, she sank into. She remembered Patrick when they had gone into Edinburgh one day to watch a show at the festival; before they went into the theatre, he had taken a rose from a nearby flower stall and bowed theatrically, deep from the waist, offering it to her. *My lady*, he had proclaimed loudly, embarrassing her. She had blushed; she remembered wishing Patrick wasn't always so theatrical in public. But now, Temerity wished more than anything she could have one more day with Patrick; one more moment where he tried his hardest to make her laugh.

It was a beautiful room. A silent, unsmiling housemaid had admitted her after she'd explained she was with the rescue operation, then disappeared without a word. She had returned in a few minutes accompanied by the housekeeper, a kindly, middle-aged woman who introduced herself as Liz.

Temerity supposed that there had been a time when the Laird's Manor had had an army of maids dressed in mobcaps and starched white pinnies. The maid, who stood stonily at the edge of the room, was dressed in a black shirt and black trousers, with her light brown hair pulled back into a severe bun. Temerity felt oddly discomfited by her presence; there was no reason for her not to at least look vaguely approachable.

'Oh, now! Don't cry, dear! Did you know the people they're looking for? Friends of yours?'

Liz, by contrast, sat down next to Temerity and put her arm around her shoulders. She wore a plain, olive-green cardigan with a sensible wool skirt, thick tights and brogues, like many sensible Scottish ladies of a certain age – and not unlike Tilda.

Liz disengaged her arm and tucked a tartan blanket around Temerity. She'd arrived with a tray of tea, a thick slice of a delicious coffee and walnut cake and a large glass of whisky, as the Inspector had predicted. He had obviously taken the hospitality at the Manor many times.

'Now, you just warm up as much as you can,' Liz fussed. 'Goodness! It was just as well I was still here; I was about to head off for the night.'

Temerity wiped her eyes and took a sip of whisky.

'It's just been an emotional night,' she said, taking a deep breath. She was feeling a little better. Patrick's loss was always with her, but most of the time she kept it locked away. Still, a warm fire, a drink and something to eat were helping.

'Aye, I don't doubt it! I suppose it must have been years since the coastguard came out. Of course, every time it happens, I expect that David thinks of the first Lady Dalcairney. God rest her soul.' Liz shook her head. 'This is going to bring it all back.' She sat on the end of the sofa and looked sympathetically at Temerity. 'Of course, that was before my time. But it's such a shame not to have more children in a house like this. Do you have little ones, dear?'

Temerity shook her head.

'No.'

'Ah, well. Still time.' Liz patted her leg. 'I was never blessed.' She sighed. 'No, it's just me, Sally here –' she gestured to the silent maid glowering at them from the corner – 'Mind ye, Sally's only been here a short time, she's only a young lassie as ye can see. Then there's the Laird, the chef and Lady Dalcairney – oh and if Anthony comes home, of course, not that he's here more than once a year. He's a darling.' Liz smiled mistily for a moment. 'Nowadays they get a local firm of cleaners to come in twice a week, that's more than I could do on my own, of course. In the old days they'd have live-in maids and a cook with her own scullery and kitchen maids. Very different now. There's a private chef makes all their lunches and dinners and if they have a dinner party, that kind of thing. I make the breakfast. Other than that, I'm more of a carer. Sally does the nights, generally,'

Temerity put down her glass.

'Did you say Lady Dalcairney? But I thought she died. In the loch.'

'Ah, bless ye. No, Lady Dalcairney, the Laird's mother. She's quite old now.'

Temerity remembered the face at the window.

'Oh. I didn't know.'

'Oh, aye. Quite a character.' Liz's expression inferred this was kind of an understatement. 'Speaking of the Lady, I'll have to go up and check on her, if you don't mind?' Liz got up and straightened her skirt with both hands. 'You'll be all right? If you need the bathroom, there's one along the corridor there. Second door on the right.' She pointed out to the door they'd come in.

'Yes. Of course. Thank you for all this, Liz. I'm so grateful.'
Temerity really was; she thought how nice it must be to have a
Liz around all the time to provide tea and reassurance.

'Ah, you're welcome. I'll pop back in when the rest come up,
wanting the same!' The housekeeper walked out and Temerity
heard her making her way up the stairs. Temerity realised that
she was starving and demolished the delicious cake in no time
at all. It was obviously homemade, rich and moist and studded
with large walnuts. Temerity washed it down with the golden tea
and felt refreshed. Sally remained in the room; Temerity could
feel her staring at the back of her head. She turned around and
smiled encouragingly.

'Have you worked here long, Sally?' she asked, but Sally
regarded her mutely, an odd expression on her face.

All right then, Temerity thought.

Now that she was warm, Temerity got up to have a look
around. The room was very grand; hand-painted wallpaper
featuring Scottish birds covered the walls: Grouse, Ptarmigan,
Fulmar. The grey stone fireplace was almost as tall as her and
wider than her arms stretched out. The stone mantel was engraved
beautifully with leaves and twisted stems, with a deer running in
a wood, surrounded by pheasants.

Temerity luxuriated in front of the hearth a little longer before
moving on. Above it was a portrait of a man with a white beard –
she assumed it was the Laird's father, perhaps, or another ancestor
– in full Scots dress, depicted against the Scottish countryside.

She was drawn to the long windows to her left, which were
curtained with thick, luxurious garnet-coloured curtains that
swept the floor. The curtains were not fully closed and through
them, Temerity could see a different angle down to the edge of
the loch. The helicopter had landed on the Manor house grounds,

its lights on: Temerity watched as the two medics hoisted one man onto a stretcher and into the helicopter.

Thank the gods they were found alive, Temerity thought.

Her gaze strayed to the gardens at this side of the house. Unlike the manicured lawn with its intermittent bushes that might have at one time been trimmed into precise shapes, these gardens were wilder, lit by occasional lights winding around tree trunks and garden uplights that cast strange shadows here and there. There was a glass door which led onto a terrace and she opened it curiously, stepping back out into the cold.

Without the indoors light reflecting on the windows it was hard to see, but Temerity could make out that this was a mix of overrun kitchen garden, orchard and herb garden. There were maybe thirty or more apple trees at the end of the garden which looked like they had been left untrimmed for a few years, the branches growing into each other to make gnarled canopies. Away from the searchlight at the edge of the loch, the weak beam from a crescent moon shadowed the trees, the black clouds casting them into darkness, moment to moment. Closer to the house, there were cabbages, broccoli and chard growing in raised beds and a greenhouse that needed a good clean, but it was clear that this part of the garden hadn't been attended to that carefully for a while.

The herb garden sat separate to the vegetables, with plants that had spread haphazardly along the spiral design that was marked out with heavy stones. Temerity recognised mint, parsley, rosemary and lemon balm, but the rest were unfamiliar to her. Tilda would have known. Temerity wondered if this part of the garden was the private chef's responsibility: she doubted it. A live-in cook and probably a team of gardeners would have once made sure that all of this was kept up to date, but the Laird had let it all go. Temerity wondered if the Laird had money problems.

'I sent ye up here to warm up, Temerity Love, not freeze yerself into an ice cube again.' Inspector Hyland's voice boomed from behind her, making her jump. 'Come inside. Yer letting all the heat out.' He waved her back indoors, where Angus Harley was standing with his back to the fireplace and the Laird, David Dalcairney, was pouring whisky from a crystal decanter into four glasses, one of which was hers.

Chapter 15

'Well, that was dramatic.' David Dalcairney sighed and handed a glass to Temerity. 'Miss Love, I refilled your glass – I hope that's all right.'

'I'm sure I'll manage it. We weren't properly introduced – I'm Temerity Love, of Love's Curiosities,' she added the shop name to see if he remembered that visit.

'Ah, of course. The antique shop.' He shook her hand; his hands were still cold from being outside. 'Sally, Liz – thank you, we'll let you know if we need you.' With that, he dismissed his staff.

'I think you visited once?' Temerity prompted him: she was curious to see what he would say. The Laird's brow furrowed as if it was hard to remember.

'I'm sorry, my memory isn't what it was,' he said, politely, but Temerity sensed he was lying. 'So you're an antiques expert? I'll have to remember you if I need something valued for insurance. Most of this has been in the family so long that it's been catalogued already, though.' He gestured to the paintings and some vases and glassware in a display cabinet.

'You have some lovely pieces there,' Temerity nodded.

'Thanks so much for your help, sir,' Angus interjected. 'We're indebted to you. Much longer out there and those men might have been far worse off.'

'How are they?' Temerity tried not to think of Patrick, face down in the loch. They were luckier than him, anyway. She felt a stab of envy for whoever was waiting for them to return; they'd come home. Patrick never would.

'They'll be all right. Exposure. They were very cold and wet, but hopefully no lasting damage. They managed to swim to the rocks and get out of the water, which was what saved them,' Angus explained. 'They lost control of the boat in the storm and probably hit a rock this side of the loch; there's a hole in the boat the size of my head.'

Temerity exhaled.

'They were lucky,' she said. The Laird nodded, looking into the hearth.

'Luckier than some,' he said, quietly. There was a respectful silence; everyone knew what he was referring to. Dalcairney looked up from the fireplace. 'Still. Ancient history, eh?' He drained his glass and poured himself another; it was obvious from his complexion that he was a heavy drinker. 'I hear you've got a murder case in the village. It's all happening in Lost Maidens Loch at the moment, it would seem.' He straightened up suddenly, holding his stomach, a look of agony impacting his face. 'Sorry.'

Temerity thought that the Laird would be better spending his time going to see the doctor about whatever it was that was paining him so badly rather than apologising for it, but she kept quiet.

The Inspector nodded.

'Aye. Local teacher. Young lassie, too. Terrible shame,' he said. 'Ye should probably sit down. Ye don't want to overdo it.'

'And what do you know so far?' Dalcairney enquired, but nonetheless sat down on one of the sofas. 'Probably just indigestion. Please excuse me.' The Inspector looked slightly uncomfortable.

'Well, of course, there's details we can't discuss, David.' The fact that the Inspector was on first name terms with the Laird showed the status he held in the village; Temerity supposed they had known each other a long time. 'But it's a poisoning case. One main suspect.'

'Oh, really?' the Laird held his side again: something was clearly giving him discomfort. 'I shouldn't drink. Too acid on the stomach. But on days like this…' He grimaced.

'Aye, me, too. Supposed to be off the demon drink,' Hyland agreed, grinning. 'Easier said than done, though.'

'So the suspect… can you say who it is?'

Temerity thought that Dalcairney was pushing a little too hard for details, but on the other hand, as Laird, the village was his concern.

'Not at this stage,' Hyland said apologetically. 'I'll let ye know when we make a charge, though. Shouldnae be long.'

Temerity gave Angus a look, but he was impassive. Who was this number one suspect they thought they had? Beth Bennett? The boyfriend, Ben McKinley? She hadn't known that they were so far along with the case. But, she had to remind herself, she was just a civilian. Neither the Inspector nor Angus Harley had to tell her anything.

'Ah, of course. Well, it's good to know that you've got it all under control. Not that I'd expect anything else, Kim.' Dalcairney got up from the sofa. 'I'm afraid you'll have to excuse me. My stomach's really flaring up; I think I need to lie down. Well done all, for tonight. Your commitment to Lost Maidens Loch is truly commendable.' He nodded to them all and left.

'Poor guy.' The Inspector sighed. 'Hard night for him, aye.'

'He helped me pull those guys into the boat. That was not easy.' Angus nodded.

'Aye, well, I was talkin' about his memories, more, but you're right. He's not well, either, by the looks of things.' Hyland put his whisky glass back on the table and stood up. 'Come on. Let's get home.'

Liz appeared in the hallway, carrying an empty silver tray.

'Ah, take care now.' She handed Temerity her coat.

'Thanks for taking care of me, Liz.' Temerity smiled. 'Come and visit my shop next time you're in the village and I'll repay the tea and cake. It was delicious.'

'Ah, it was nae bother.' Liz held up a finger. 'Wait, I'll give ye the recipe.'

'Oh, there's no need—' Temerity protested, seeing that Harley and the Inspector were waiting for her, but the housekeeper was already writing it down. She folded the paper into a square and pushed it into Temerity's pocket.

'There ye go, lassie. Make yer own.' She smiled.

'Thanks again.'

Temerity followed the two policemen out into the large hallway; the staircase led up in a graceful sweep behind them. She looked up as she walked out: for a moment, she thought she glimpsed a woman at the top of the stairs, watching her.

*

Inspector Hyland drove down Dalcairney Manor's long gravelled drive and out onto the main road into the village.

'Quite a night,' he said. 'Those guys'll think again before they take a boat out in a storm.' He sighed. 'Tourists. They'll be the death of me.'

'I'm still surprised that Henry Sutherland let them take the boat out,' Temerity said, watching the empty road unfurl in front of the car. It was almost ten o'clock and she was exhausted.

'Aye. Nae doubt he'd had a dram or two this afternoon. I'll be havin' a word with him about it, don't ye worry,' Hyland said, grimly. 'Old Henry's not as on the ball as he once was. He shouldae known that storm was on its way.'

'That guidebook for tourists – *The Mysteries of Lost Maidens Loch*. Full of incorrect information, including the idea that the whole village is apparently haunted, including the loch.' Angus's expression was stony. 'I appreciate that it seems to be bringing in more business to the village, but if it means that we end up with tourists constantly having to be rescued by the coastguard, I don't think it's a good thing.'

For once, I agree with you, Temerity thought, tiredly. *We must stop agreeing like this, Wolfman.*

'I know. I've seen it,' Temerity said. 'Muriel seemed to be very happy about it.'

'*Muriel* is charging tourists twice the goin' rate for breakfast, pretendin' that the café's haunted by some blacksmith.' Hyland snorted.

'Aye, well. I'm going to be looking into who wrote it,' Angus replied. 'And believe me when I say, when I find out who it is, they're going to get a talking to.' His tone softened. 'Anyway. Thanks for your help earlier, Temerity.' He turned around his seat. Temerity blinked, then opened her eyes wide; the movement of the car had started to lull her to sleep.

'Oh. That's all right. I didn't really do anything.' She felt uncomfortable; they'd been in the middle of what was heading towards an argument when she'd seen the upturned boat in the water. 'I hope I didn't... I mean, I... earlier, I got a bit emotional. What we were talking about.'

'Don't apologise. I could have been kinder.' He turned away and looked out of the window. There was a silence in the car that continued until the Inspector pulled up outside Temerity's shop.

'Here ye go, lassie.' He nodded at her. 'Sleep well, now. No bad dreams, aye?'

Temerity got out of the car; the streets were still slick with rain, but the storm had passed.

'All right.' She waved the car off and went inside.

But there were dreams. In them, she ran after Patrick, shouting his name, but he showed no sign of being able to hear her. She woke with her cheeks wet with tears.

Chapter 16

'Rise and shine, sleepyhead.' Tilda put a mug of steaming hot chocolate on Temerity's bedside table and opened the curtains.

Temerity's walls were painted a blue so dark it was almost black and her wide cast-iron bedstead was white, though the paint was slightly chipped. The sheets were plain yellow, which contrasted beautifully against the deep blue. Against one wall, there was a Chinese cabinet featuring a tarnished, mottled mirror on one panel and a painting of a peacock in a courtyard on the other. Bronze and silver statuettes of Hindu and Greek gods and goddesses crowded the room's deep windowsill. An almost life-size bronze statue of a Thai prince, sitting cross-legged and playing a flute, sat in the opposite corner to the wooden cabinet. An oil painting of the loch hung above her bed, showing it covered with mist.

'Mmmmph.' Temerity grumbled at the early Spring sunlight that stung her eyes and pulled the duvet over her head. 'Go away.'

'It's past ten and I made you hot chocolate, so I won't go away, if it's all the same to you.' Tilda got under the covers at the other end of Temerity's bed and rested her feet on the pillow next to her sister's head. As usual, she wore thick socks to protect her toes from the cold. If you didn't, the draughty old house would give you chilblains. 'Tell me all about it.'

Scylla, the fat black cat, had followed Tilda up the stairs and jumped heavily onto the bed, instantly turning herself around in a ball and snuggling next to Tilda's legs, between them on the bed.

'Scylla! Not when I'm holding a hot drink,' Tilda scolded the cat, who purred. 'You don't think the rules apply to you, do you, kitty?' Tilda sighed. 'And I suppose you're right. You're earning your keep, keeping the bad spirits away.'

Tilda and Temerity believed, like their parents had, that cats provided a kind of spiritual protection for the house. Either way, the cats hunted mice and voles out in the wild land behind the house and brought them in regularly as gifts. The catty sentiment was nice, but it was still disgusting, especially if you stepped in half a dead mouse in your slippers when you were still half asleep in the morning.

Reluctantly, Temerity sat up. The room was cold, so she reached for a black knitted bedjacket she'd embroidered with red woollen cherries and put it on.

She sipped the chocolate. It was thick and sweet; Tilda made it with a French powdered chocolate that came from the same gourmet shop as her coffee. 'What do you want to know? We walked around the loch; it was freezing. Harley and the Inspector and the Laird helped with the rescue. I went up to the Manor. A nice woman called Liz gave me whisky and cake. They were tourists. Henry Sutherland rented them the boat when he shouldn't have.'

'The storm was absolutely lashing,' Tilda agreed. 'We were stuck in the café for ages. Just as well Muriel had provisions.'

'I saw.' Temerity grinned. 'How's Alf?'

'Not so bad. He's started a phased return to work. Tell you what he did tell me, mind you,' Tilda said conspiratorially, stroking the cat next to her. 'The locum, Theakstone?'

'Yes?' Temerity warmed her hands on the mug.

'Alf thinks he's been stealing drugs from the surgery. Maybe selling them.'

'What? Surely not.' Temerity was shocked. She was about to say, *Things like that don't happen in Lost Maidens Loch*, when she realised it wasn't true. Odd things happened in the village all the time.

'Well, Alf said he looked at the stock and they seemed low on some things that weren't accounted for. He checked and they hadn't been prescribed. You know Alf, he's a control freak. He's hated not being able to work.'

Being the doctor in a place like Lost Maidens Loch was a big deal and Alf took his responsibilities very seriously. He'd delivered babies, visited the elderly members of the village who found it hard to get out of the house, sometimes just for a cup of tea and a catch-up, knowing what an awful effect loneliness could have on health. He treated childhood viruses, ran an addiction clinic in his own time and had even been known to drive villagers to their hospital appointments in Edinburgh.

'I know.' Temerity and Tilda knew Alf and Harry pretty well now; as neighbours, they often popped in for coffee, or, sometimes dinner. Harry had helped the sisters when bad weather had blown a tree over in the garden. 'I wouldn't be surprised if he taped his own hair to the filing cabinets. So, what was missing?'

'Painkillers, mostly. The kind of thing that people want to buy illegally.' Tilda sat up and leaned towards Temerity. 'And, guess what else? They had a small store of atropine. Not much, because Alf said it's not something you'd anticipate needing much in a place like Lost Maidens Loch. But they did have some and it's gone.'

'Goodness. So… someone could have bought atropine? From Theakstone?'

'That's what Alf thinks. He's going to talk to the Inspector about it, but it's hard to prove. They don't have any CCTV at the surgery, so either Theakstone confesses to having sold drugs, or we find someone that's bought some. That's the only way we'd be able to get him.'

'Hmmm.' Temerity drained the last of her hot chocolate. 'If Alf's right, that is. He might not be, you know. He's been off the job a while. He's getting older, he had a major operation. He might just be… I don't know. Paranoid.'

'I know. But I don't think he's wrong. He hasn't forgotten how their drugs inventory works.'

'Well, if he's right about the medicine disappearing, he might still be wrong that it's Theakstone selling it. It could be someone else.'

'He does seem the obvious choice, but yes, you're right. I don't know who, though. No one else has keys to the surgery apart from the locum and Alf. Anyway, surely the real question is not so much who's sold the drugs, but who bought them. The murderer.' Tilda's eyes glowed. 'It's a definite lead.'

'It certainly is,' Temerity mused. 'And he's going to talk to Kim about it?'

Tilda nodded.

'Yep. You're going to ask him about it, aren't you?'

Temerity tried to look unconcerned.

'I might. It's our village, after all. We should all care about this murder.'

'You're not actually the police, though. You do know that?' Tilda nudged her sister's shoulder with one foot. 'There's a difference between psychic investigation and police work.'

'I know! I'm just helping out.' Temerity pushed Tilda's foot away.

'You seem to be spending quite a lot of time helping Constable Harley in particular.' Tilda reached down beside the bed and placed her mug on the bare floorboards, avoiding her sister's gaze.

'What's that supposed to mean?' Temerity snapped, blushing.

'I mean, you went out onto the loch with him last night. You went to talk to that girl together. You hang out in the café with him all the time. Oh, and you made him take his top off while he was here, let's not forget.' Tilda sat up and rested her head against the tall iron bedstead, one eyebrow raised.

'I do not hang out with him *all the time*,' Temerity protested. 'Anyway, he's awkward. He hardly talks. When he does, he's usually spouting some narrow-minded rubbish about the world always being logical. And he's got no sense of humour. At all.'

'Just saying. People are starting to notice.' Tilda wagged her finger at her sister. 'You know what they're like here. Gossips.'

'There's nothing to gossip about,' Temerity snapped again. 'Honestly. All I'm doing is trying to help out; at the detriment of my work, by the way. I've got an inbox full of provenance requests I haven't been able to get to for days.'

'Hmm... any other conference offers?' Tilda needled.

'I don't know. Maybe.'

'The next one that comes up, you should go.'

Temerity bridled. 'I might not want to.'

'No. But you should.' Her sister gave her a look. 'All this stuff at the loch. I know it's upsetting for you. All the more reason to get away. I don't understand why you refuse to. It's like you... you anchor yourself here out of a sense of obligation or something. He's gone, Tem. You can't bring him back.'

Tilda wasn't being unkind, but her version of kindness was often of the tough love variety.

'I know, Tils.' Temerity's voice was quiet. Outside, a crow cawed. 'Let me be.'

'I don't want to let you be. I want you to be happy,' Tilda insisted.

Chapter 17

This time, Temerity saw the shadowy feather on Ben McKinley's shoulder immediately.

She sat at a bare white melamine table in a bare beige-painted room next door to the main interrogation room. No one knew she was there except the Inspector, who had asked her to observe him interviewing McKinley.

Her room had a window, but it wasn't a real window. It was a two-way glass partition between the room she was in and the one in which Kim Hyland was making McKinley and his lawyer comfortable next door. She could see them, but they couldn't see her.

The interrogation room next door was exactly like she'd seen on TV shows: sparse with one table in the middle which held a recording machine; two chairs on each side of the table. There were no windows and the walls were painted a depressing beige.

Temerity watched as Hyland placed two plain white mugs on the table in front of McKinley and the woman next to him, who must be his lawyer, then sat down, saying something with a smile. Temerity reached over to switch on the intercom between the rooms, a silver toggle switch underneath the window.

'—only instant coffee, I'm afraid,' the Inspector was saying. Temerity knew that he used being jovial to put suspects at their ease. She remembered him saying to her once, *I've been at this game far tae long, lassie; an' if it's taught me anythin', it's that ye catch more flies with honey than with vinegar.*

McKinley didn't look reassured by Kim Hyland's friendliness. His face was a white mask of tension; his jaw was set, as if he was gritting his teeth. He made no move to pick up the mug.

The feather on his shoulder was clearer than the one Temerity had seen on Beth Bennett: McKinley's had a clear shape and, even from where Temerity sat in the next room, she could see its fibres. It was a deep blue this time.

Temerity stared in disbelief at the feather. Not because she thought Ben McKinley was innocent, but because this was the second feather she had seen in only a few days. She hadn't felt, in her heart of hearts that Beth Bennett was a murderer, which was why she hadn't done anything to try to persuade Harley or the Inspector to probe further. But now, here was a feather on McKinley's shoulder too, so what did that mean about Beth? She didn't know what to make of it.

Hyland leaned forward in his chair and switched on the machine. He spoke his name, McKinley's name and the time and date into it and nodded to the lawyer – a smartly dressed woman with short grey hair – indicating that she should add her name and presence. Having done that, he sat back and looked pleasantly at the teacher.

'So…' His voice was relaxed, as if the three of them were out fishing or sitting around a table at The Singing Kettle. 'Tell me about Molly.'

McKinley looked at his hands.

'What do you want to know?' he asked, quietly. Temerity remembered his uncontrollable cries that day in the staff room; this felt very different. He was controlled now, reserved and secret like a locked case.

'When did you meet?'

'Her first day. At school.'

'You liked her from the start?' Hyland still reclined in his chair, but his eyes were bright.

'Course. Nothing not to like,' McKinley replied in the same voice.

'Pretty girl,' Hyland observed neutrally.

'Obviously.' McKinley sounded almost dismissive. 'She was...' He took a deep breath. 'She was... lovely. As a person. Not everyone got that – I mean, she had a sharp tongue when she wanted to, she kind of put people off before they could get to know her. But she was a good person. I saw that.'

What a hero, Temerity thought, drily. She wondered again at the significance of the feather. Did that mean Beth and Ben were both guilty of Molly's murder, or were they both guilty of something else, possibly unrelated? If that was it, then surely everyone in Lost Maidens Loch should be sporting a spirit feather on their shoulder?

'The others...?' Hyland enquired. Temerity wondered whether she should mention the feather visions to him, but she decided against it for now. Kim Hyland was very understanding of her witchy ways as a rule, but until she really understood what the feathers meant, she thought she should probably keep the information to herself.

'The other teachers. I'm one of the only male teachers – not that unusual with young children. Working with women is great but they do get catty from time to time. They turned on her.'

Temerity reflected that it was hard to know the truth now that Molly was dead: all there was to listen to was hearsay. Ben certainly had a rose-tinted memory of Molly Bayliss, but as the saying went, love was blind. In this case, love might also be cause for murder.

'I see. But as I understand it, she spurned your advances.' Temerity smiled at the Inspector's old-fashioned phrase, but McKinley didn't seem amused.

'Not exactly. It was my fault; I asked her out too soon, before we'd had time to become friends. *Of course* she said no at first.' McKinley appealed to Hyland. 'Come on. You're a guy. You understand. They always say no at first – that just means they're a decent girl. Not a tease. She was playing the game. She said no, but she wanted me to keep trying.'

The Inspector blinked. In her room outside the interrogation, Temerity was startled by the use of the word *tease* as much as the sentiment. She hadn't known that there were young men in this day and age who had such backward views about women.

'In my experience, laddie, if a woman says she doesnae want to go out with ye – or if she doesnae want tae cuddle up tae ye at the flicks, or she's sick tae death of goin' on holiday tae St Andrews fer that matter… that's Mrs Hyland I'm talking aboot there, a cruise it is this year, aye…' Hyland shook his head, reached into his pocket and pulled out his pipe and a packet of tobacco. 'Then I've found they tend tae mean it.' He stuffed the bowl of the pipe with the brown strands and nodded. 'I dinnae think calling lassies *teases* comes into it, either, but maybe that's ma old fashioned opinion,' he added.

Good for you, Inspector Kim Hyland, Temerity cheered silently.

McKinley looked away sulkily.

'Well, whatever. We were friends. I wanted to be more.'

'Aye. Tell me aboot her housemate, Beth.' Temerity knew that Hyland was only changing the subject temporarily; he hadn't finished asking Ben about his feelings for Molly, but he was going to let him think he had. Ben relaxed visibly. He sat back in his chair.

'What about her? She was jealous of Molly.'

'Seems a lot of people were. What's this aboot Molly stealin' Beth's fiancé?' Hyland asked.

'I don't know about that. She didn't mention it to me.' But Temerity couldn't help noticing that Ben's cheeks were flushed and his eyes had widened. Temerity realised that the brief minutes when McKinley had managed to project a disinterested, unemotional image must have been an effort for him: he was far too emotional a person to manage to appear cool for long.

'Miss Bennett walked in and found them at it on the sofa, I'm told,' Hyland continued. Temerity shook her head. There was no knowing whether it was true or not. However, she knew that Hyland wanted to push this man's buttons and see what he did.

'I don't believe it,' Ben hissed.

'Miss Bennett says it happened. Would you say she – Miss Bennett – was a liar?' Hyland enquired gently.

'She must be! People lie all the time,' McKinley spat. 'Molly wouldn't do that. She wouldn't do it to—' He broke off. 'She wouldn't have done that to me. She knew I loved her. She loved me, too, I know she did.' His voice broke and he leaned forward onto the table. 'Oh God, I miss her! I loved her! Molly, please come back, please…' He sobbed and pummelled his fists on the table like a child. Hyland exchanged a glance with the lawyer, who as yet had said nothing.

'Ben, would ye like a minute to calm down?' the Inspector asked with great civility, but McKinley sat up suddenly. 'I didn't kill her!' he shouted.

'All right, Ben. We're just talking.' Hyland placed both hands flat on the table.

'Well, why else am I here? If that's what you think, why don't you just come out and say it?' he shouted again. The lawyer murmured something to him, but he ignored her. 'No! Come on! I've got an alibi, you know! I wasn't even there. I was in the playground, all the kids saw me and the whole of the staff room know I wasn't there. Why aren't you asking them all these questions? They could have actually done it.'

'We're talking to lots of people.' Hyland's voice remained calm. 'You were… close. It's obvious we'd want to talk to you.'

McKinley looked away, but said nothing. Hyland studied him for a moment.

'Do you know how Molly died?' he asked, his voice still gentle.

'Course. Everyone knows,' McKinley retorted.

'Ben, I have to ask you. Have you ever bought or sourced the poison atropine?' Hyland leaned back in his chair again, watching the teacher's face.

'What? No, of course not!' McKinley looked appalled at the thought; she was viewing this all from behind the glass, but Temerity thought he was being genuine. 'Why would I ever do that? I loved Molly. I… wanted her to love me.'

'We'll have to search your home, as a standard procedure. We've already searched the school; I hope you understand.' Hyland made it sound as though it was just a formality, but she knew it definitely wasn't.

'Do I have a choice?' McKinley looked sulky again. Hyland gave his hail-fellow-well-met grin, as if this was just between friends.

'Well, ye could say no, of course, Ben. Absolutely. But then, the thing is…' the Inspector puffed on his pipe, which Temerity was pretty sure he wasn't allowed to smoke inside the police station 'If ye refuse, it creates a ton of paperwork for me, aye and then we'd still have tae do it, just with more papers. I know ye don't have anythin' incriminatin' at yer hoose, why would ye? But it's just one of those things, aye.' He blew out a plume of pipe smoke. 'See what I'm sayin'?'

'You're saying I don't have a choice,' McKinley repeated dully.

'I suppose I am, yes. Ye got anythin' else ye want tae tell me, Ben?' Hyland steepled his fingers together and watched as Ben picked up the mug, drank from it and put it back on the table.

'No.' McKinley thought he'd done the interview, that it was over, Temerity could tell from his expression. But she knew he remained the Inspector's number one suspect. Hyland nodded and spoke the time into the recorder, then stood up to usher Ben McKinley and his lawyer out of the interview room.

After five minutes or so, the door to the room Temerity was in opened and Hyland came in, carrying the white mug McKinley had drunk out of in one plastic-gloved hand. He placed it on the table in front of her.

'See what you can do with it,' he said, sighing as he sat down opposite. 'Did ye see him lose his temper? Changeable fella. What Mrs Hyland calls "mercurial", aye.'

'The god Mercury, or Hermes, is the messenger. He's quick-minded, persuasive and changeable. He's also a great magician. The master of magic, in fact,' Temerity mused as she picked up the mug. 'I don't think Ben McKinley's a master of magic.'

'Reckon I agree with ye there, lassie. He's got some strange ideas about women.'

Temerity raised an eyebrow.

'He sounded like someone who watches those videos on the internet about how to pick up women in bars. You know, those guys –' Temerity clicked her fingers – 'what do they call themselves? Pick-up artists. It's all based on these misogynist ideas about women being some kind of brainless prey motivated by displays of wealth that they can manipulate with neurolinguistic programming.'

Hyland looked blank.

'Neuro-what-now?'

Temerity grinned.

'Don't worry about it. I just mean, he seems like a bit of an idiot. Insecure, definitely.'

'Agreed. Mrs Hyland would have his guts for garters if she heard what he said then.' Hyland shook his head. 'Doesnae necessarily make him a murderer, though.'

'Hmmm. I might not get that much from the mug, you know, he only touched it briefly. It's not something that's really his,' she warned. Hyland shrugged.

'Just good tae get yer feeling on him,' he admitted.

Temerity took the plain white mug in her hands and closed her eyes. An object like this, which had been used by so many people (and went through the dishwasher every day) was a very different proposition to get information from than something which had been treated as sacred its entire life. But nonetheless, it had its own energy.

What came to her first was a kind of greyish mesh of faces: it was the entirety of everyone who had used the mug; a quiet fog of remembrance. She took in a breath and named who she was looking for: Ben McKinley. She concentrated on her breathing, remaining centred. She saw his face in her mind and then Molly. She felt his emotion for Molly, suddenly: a craven, lustful wanting that obsessed him. The wanting Molly was so intense that Temerity had to draw in a deep breath. It was unsettling.

Temerity tried to search Ben's feelings for Molly through this small link with him, but all she could sense was that intense desire for Molly – a belief that she was his true love and that their futures were fated to be together. And then, in a flash of vision, Temerity saw Molly's body on the floor of the staff room, the foam at the edges of her mouth, her stare rigid. She was seeing Molly through Ben's eyes for an instant, but there was only horror in Ben's heart; Temerity felt his shock and disbelief. She could hear him muttering, *Oh no, no, no, Molly, no.*

She opened her eyes and let go of the mug.

'It was a surprise to him that she died. He was horrified when it happened,' she said, slowly. 'I don't know. It's strange. All I'm getting from him is how much he wanted her. Like, insanely. He was obsessed with her. He believed very strongly they were going to spend the rest of their lives together.'

'Odd. I got the sense he was hidin' somethin'.' The Inspector frowned.

'I did, too. But all I can pick up from this are his recent feelings, I suppose.' She picked up the mug again and closed her eyes. She imagined the scene in the staff room as vividly as she could: Molly's body on the floor, her poisoned mug that had rolled away, Ben crying, his shock, the teachers standing around. She tried to sense anything else, anything new that she hadn't picked up already. There was something, but it was faint. It was a sensation against her fingers; it wasn't the ceramic cup. It reminded her of when she put her hands in her coat pockets and found an old receipt in there. She frowned.

'Paper. He had paper in his pocket when she died. I don't know what that means. No idea what type of paper. Just… he could feel it against the tips of his fingers when he stood there, looking at her body. Sorry, that's all I have.'

'No, lassie, that's helpful. Ye never know when this will all come in useful,' Hyland mused.

'Nothing I say is legally binding,' Temerity reminded him. 'You can't prove any of this. It's just impressions. But they're always right.'

'I know. It helps me, aye. In the same way as yer antiques. Ye find a way in with yer gift, then ye find the facts easier when ye know where tae look. Thank ye, as always.'

'Did you mention to Constable Harley I was coming in today?' Temerity enquired innocently, since Harley hadn't appeared at all.

'Ach, no. He's away busy. Tracin' Molly's real parents, her bein' adopted. Ye never know, some kinda clue there.' Hyland got up and waited for Temerity to follow him out of the room into the corridor. The little station comprised Hyland's office, overflowing with papers, files and which smelled permanently of pipe smoke; one holding cell, hardly used, and the two interrogation rooms. Harley used a desk in the small reception area.

There was a part-time receptionist, Dora, a local mother who did a couple of hours a day. Dora didn't bother to hide the fact that she spent most of her time gossiping, knitting or organising her children's doctor, dentist and haircut appointments as well as their many after-school club activities.

'Okay. Well, stay in touch.' Temerity waved as she got to the door and pulled on her coat; Dora eyed her with a certain amount of suspicion. No doubt by the end of the day, everyone in Lost Maidens Loch would know she'd visited the station. Temerity didn't really care. *Do your worst, Dora*, she thought. *While you're at it, book me in at the hairdresser's. I'm overdue for a cut and blow-dry.*

She walked out into the crisp, frosty morning and plunged her hands into her coat pockets. Just like in her vision, crumpled paper brushed against her fingertips: she pulled the paper out, smoothing it. It was a sheet with a letterhead at the top: an ink drawing of Dalcairney Manor. Temerity's first thought was that this illustration was the one that had been shoddily reproduced in *The Mysteries of Lost Maidens Loch*, by T.L. Hawtry: no doubt cut out and photocopied, which would account for its blurriness.

The paper had been folded into a neat square, but Temerity's fingers had fiddled with it without thinking. *Oh, the cake recipe.* Temerity remembered the housekeeper at Dalcairney Manor writing it out for her. She hadn't had the heart to tell Liz that she'd never baked a cake in her life. Still, it had been delicious – she'd give the recipe to Tilda.

Only, it wasn't a recipe at all. It was a scrawled note which said:

There are things you should know. Come to the house when you have time.

– Liz.

Chapter 18

'Pretty nice.' Tilda parked the car and leaned forward, gazing up the long drive to Dalcairney Manor. 'I've never been in.'

'Well, nor had I until the other night,' Temerity agreed as they drove up it slowly and parked at the wide front of the house. Spring was coming and today there was no mist over the loch; the sky was a bright blue and, as Temerity opened the car door, a fresh breeze blew pleasantly on her skin. She rang the doorbell and heard the sound echo inside the house. 'Oh. There's a really weird maid. The night of the rescue, she never said a word the whole time. Dressed all in black and glowering at me from the corner like the Bride of Dracula.'

'Consider me warned,' Tilda replied, getting out of the car and slamming the driver's side door shut.

Liz opened the door. She was once more dressed in a calf-length wool skirt and a buttoned-up cardigan over a fine knit sweater. Despite the coming of Spring, Lost Maidens Loch was still pretty chilly.

'Ah. I thought you'd have called first.' She looked temporarily discomfited, as if deciding what to do.

'Sorry, I just thought… from your note… that you might not want to talk on the phone,' Temerity whispered. She'd shown the note to Tilda when she'd got home yesterday, who had suggested they visit the house. Her actual words were, *let's beard the lion in his den*. Tilda was prone to using archaic phrases because of all the old books she read.

'No, no, it's all right. Come in.' Liz stood to one side to let them in.

'This is my sister, Tilda,' Temerity said.

'Hello, dear.' Liz smiled tightly; clearly, she was uncomfortable with them being here. 'Do come in. The Laird is in his study just now; Lady Dalcairney is in her garden, but she'll be having her weekly hydrotherapy bath in a short while, so we can talk then. Let me show you to the kitchen.' She hurried them down the hall and into a large, traditional kitchen and pulled out two chairs from the kitchen table for them to sit at. 'I'm sorry, maybe I should have visited you. Will you bear with me for a short while? I need to accompany Lady Dalcairney when she's up and about. She's not too steady on her feet and she needs help going up and down steps, things like that.'

'Of course, don't mind us.' Temerity nodded. 'We'll make ourselves at home.'

'Right, okay then. Sally will be back in a minute; if you want anything, ask her, but she's almost at the end of her shift,' Liz mumbled and went to the door at the far end of the kitchen, pulling it closed behind her.

'Something's definitely up,' Tilda said in a low voice after Liz had gone. 'She's as skittery as a mouse.'

'Hmmm.' Temerity frowned.

Tilda got up and started looking through the cupboards.

'Tils! Stop it,' Temerity hissed.

'She said make ourselves at home. I'm looking for coffee. I bet they've got some good stuff,' Tilda protested. 'There. See? Coffee.' She waved a bag of ground coffee at her sister. 'Now, I need a cafétière or something.' Tilda pottered around the kitchen until she found an Italian-style stove top coffee jug and started spooning the ground coffee into it.

'What do you think she wants to tell us?' Temerity picked a tangerine from a fruit bowl in the middle of the kitchen table and rolled it between her hands.

'How should I know?' Tilda was frowning at the coffee pot. 'But the Dalcairneys must have secrets. A family this old, there's bound to have been lots of strange stuff over the years. Maybe something connected to the search the other day. That's when she met you, so it makes sense.'

'What would that be, though? We found the men; they were all right. What else is there to know?' Temerity started peeling the orange without thinking; something wasn't right here.

Suddenly, the door from the hall opened and the Laird appeared. He looked startled to find Tilda and Temerity in the kitchen.

'Oh! I'm sorry, I heard voices and I thought it was Liz with my mother. I needed to remind her about something.' He frowned. 'You're friends of hers?'

Temerity stood up and held out her hand.

'Temerity Love. We met a couple of nights ago. I was here with the rescue operation? I own the antique shop in the village.'

'Ah, of course, Miss Love. I'm so sorry, it was all rather dramatic that night, wasn't it? And this is…?' He looked enquiringly at Tilda.

'This is my sister, Tilda. She lives with me and specialises in the rare books part of the business,' Temerity explained. Tilda set the coffee pot down and came to shake the Laird's hand.

'Sorry. Liz said to make ourselves at home. I was putting some coffee on. D'you want one?'

The Laird looked slightly thrown off balance but smiled.

'Actually, I would. Thank you.' He sat down at the table and Tilda returned to the stove.

The door opened again and Sally appeared in the kitchen, then stopped as if startled when she saw the Laird and the two sisters. She was dressed exactly as before, all in black. Temerity wondered if it was a uniform or if she just chose to appear that way. Her complexion was pale and spotty; she was quite young, Temerity reckoned, probably only twenty or twenty-one.

'We're fine, thank you, Sally,' the Laird snapped; Sally retreated back through the kitchen door without a word. Temerity exchanged a glance with Tilda as if to say, *See what I mean?*

'So… of course, I visited your shop once or twice. I was quite friendly with your parents for a time. A long time ago now.' The Laird continued as if Sally had never entered; he faced Temerity and took an orange from the bowl. He looked tired and pale.

'You bought antiques from them?' Temerity finished peeling her orange and broke it into its segments, deliberately appearing casual about it.

'One or two. But it was rather more of a…. personal reason for visiting. I take it that you both know what your parents' interests were?' he replied. Temerity wondered why, if the Laird had known her parents, he hadn't mentioned it on the night of the accident.

'They were occultists.' Temerity ate her tangerine and Tilda brought three cups of steaming black coffee to the table, taking a seat opposite the Laird.

'Temerity's psychic, did you know that? She specialises in psychometry. I'm a herbalist,' Tilda said, sipping the coffee. 'We inherited more from them than a shop full of Louis Quinze furniture.'

'I see.' The Laird raised his eyebrow.

'May I ask what you saw them about?' Temerity knew it was rude to enquire, but her instinct was shouting at her that this was somehow important. The Laird sighed.

'It sounds silly. But it felt very real to me at the time…' He played with the handle on his mug. 'I was married twice. I don't know if you knew that?'

Tilda nodded.

'We're sorry for your loss.' Her voice was clipped and formal, but nonetheless kind.

'Thank you. My first wife, Emma, drowned in the loch. She was carrying our child. Her body was never found. Two years later, I married Claire, the mother of my son, Anthony, but sadly the marriage didn't last.' He sighed; Temerity wanted to reach out, touch his hand, hug him, something that would take away the grief she could see was ageing him.

'That's terrible,' Temerity said. 'I'm sorry.'

'If I'm honest, the marriage to Claire didn't last because I was still mourning for Emma. Terrible thing. Just terrible. At the time, I needed some kind of support and I heard that your mother was a psychic medium. I wanted to speak to Emma. I needed… something.'

Temerity nodded.

'She took pity on me and we sat down in a séance, the three of us: your mother, father, and me. It was upstairs, above the shop. Your mother had made it very esoteric in that room. There were statues of Egyptian gods that stood floor to ceiling. Shelves and shelves of books and the floorboards were painted black. They'd painted a huge pentagram at the centre of it, a magic circle. I didn't understand all the symbols. We sat down on it. She'd lit a very smoky incense; I do remember that smell. Like a church.'

Temerity nodded again, not wanting to break the Laird's stream of memory. The room that their parents had used for magic – which was now Tilda and the rare books' domain – still held the woody aroma of frankincense.

'Nothing came through, but your mother said she had picked up something else. A curse which had been put on Emma and the baby.'

'A curse?' Tilda looked interested.

'I'm sure you think that's ridiculous. I've never mentioned it to anyone apart from you, actually. I don't know why I'm telling you all this now, apart from that your parents tried to help once.' Tears had appeared in the Laird's eyes. Temerity obeyed her instincts now and put her hand gently on his arm. 'I'm sorry, Miss Love. What must you think of me?'

'It's not at all ridiculous,' she said softly. 'Remember that we're the children of two occultists. We know what they were doing up in that room. This is the least of it.'

'What else did Mother say about the curse? Did she know who had cast it?' Tilda questioned.

'She tried, but it had been concealed too well. Whoever cast it was very thorough, she said.'

'Interesting. And you had no inkling of anyone that might want to harm Emma and the baby?'

'None. Emma was loved by all who knew her,' the Laird replied. 'After that, I didn't go back. Maria, your mother, wanted me to – she was intrigued by the curse, but I couldn't… it was too upsetting.'

'Of course.' Temerity had a thought. 'Do you have any items that belonged to your first wife? I might be able to tune in with her spirit that way. Give you some clarification. Peace, maybe, after all this time.'

The Laird shook his head.

'Honestly, I'd rather just let it lie, now. It's been too long. But thank you.'

Temerity looked at his grey pallor; at the shadows under his eyes. *You've carried the worry of this curse too long,* she thought, but she didn't say it. He had come to terms with it in his own way, even if it was making him ill. You had to let people walk their own paths.

'Well, if you—' She broke off as the back door opened and Liz walked in with an elderly woman on her arm. Temerity felt a sudden chill go up her spine: a sharp breeze had blown in behind Liz as she entered.

'Ah, Mother.' The Laird sprung up from his seat and went to go and take her arm. 'Ladies, this is my mother, Lady Balfour Dalcairney. Mother, this is Tilda and Temerity Love, from the village.'

'I know who they are,' Lady Dalcairney rasped; her voice had been ruined, either from years of smoking or shouting; Temerity suspected both. 'And I won't have them in my house!'

Chapter 19

'Mother!' The Laird looked shocked. 'Please don't be rude to our visitors!' but Lady Dalcairney wouldn't be silenced. She hissed and spat at Temerity and Tilda and made the old gesture of protection from the evil eye. Temerity exchanged a look of amazement with Tilda and stepped back.

'Witches! You're the curse on this house! I repel thee in the name of God!' She wrangled her arm free from Liz, reached into her blouse and pulled out a gold crucifix on a long chain and waved it at them.

'I'm so sorry, I don't know what's got into her.' David Dalcairney blushed as he and Liz caught Lady Dalcairney's flailing arms and guided her firmly into the hallway. 'I'll help Liz make her comfortable and I'll be back.'

'We should go.' Temerity stood up. 'We're obviously upsetting her by being here.' *Gods, this got weird quickly*, she thought. *It's like someone just turned on the horror B-movie filter.*

Tilda glared at her and cleared her throat.

'No, stay!' Liz called over her shoulder. 'Don't worry. This isn't your fault.'

'We'll be here!' Tilda called after them; the sisters listened as Liz and David guided Lady Dalcairney up the stairs.

'Well, that was… unexpected,' Tilda said.

'For want of a better word. That woman's got bats in the belfry.' Temerity rolled her eyes.

'She must be going senile. Poor thing.'

'Not so senile that she didn't know who we were,' Temerity mused. 'But what was all that about a curse on the house?'

'The same curse as the Laird was talking about, I guess. They've both come to think of it in the same way. The loss of the two wives like that.' Tilda drained her coffee.

'No one's ever hissed at me before. Like a cat.' Temerity still felt quite affected by what had happened: it was shocking, really, for anyone to think that they needed to protect themselves from her. And yet Lady Dalcairney had, because she was terrified. Temerity had seen it in her eyes.

'She was scared of us. Confused,' she said.

'That's how it is with dementia. You can't keep a grip on what's real. I think paranoia is common with it. You think people are trying to kill you, that kind of thing. It's so sad.' Tilda nodded.

Liz reappeared in the kitchen.

'The Laird's just quieting her down now. I'm so sorry about that.' She straightened her navy blue cardigan, under which she wore a plain cream blouse with an enamelled pin featuring a blue and purple thistle at the neck. 'She gets muddled. I don't know why she responded to you in that way.'

'She called us witches. So, she knows something about us. It wasn't random,' Temerity said.

'Yes. I think she remembers your mother and father from when they were alive. You do have a resemblance to your mother. And the night of the rescue, she asked who was here. I would have told her you were here then. She's got it all confused in her head, though. Ah, I see you've made some coffee.' Liz busied herself cutting some cake and laying it out on a plate with some biscuits, which she set down on the table. 'Here, help yourselves.'

'You knew our mother?' Temerity was surprised. 'I didn't think you'd worked here that long.'

'Oh, I haven't, but I had a friend who used to live in the village and I used to come and visit her. I remember my friend pointing out your mother in the village, once or twice. She was a very striking woman,' Liz responded breezily.

'So, what was it you wanted to tell us?' Tilda said, taking a china plate with painted roses and two shortcake biscuits. 'Your note wasn't exactly clear.'

'Well, it's delicate. I wanted to speak to you first, because you seem to have a relationship with the Inspector, Temerity… and I didn't want to go straight to him. I wasn't sure, you see.'

'Sure of what?'

Liz sighed.

'I wasn't sure if it was him I saw. But I think it was.'

'Who? The Inspector? Where?'

'No, dear. The man he's been questioning. My friend Dora told me – you might know her; she works at the police station?'

Temerity rolled her eyes, not surprised in the least that Dora had told all her friends about Ben's interrogation. Suspect confidentiality clearly wasn't a top priority in Lost Maidens Loch.

'Ben McKinley.'

'Yes. Well, he was here, you see. One Sunday. I wouldn't normally be here on a Sunday, but I'd popped in because I'd left my cardigan, you know how it is. When you get older, you can be a little bit absent-minded. Anyway, I was in the kitchen and I looked out and I saw him. He was in the garden, talking to Lady Dalcairney.'

'Ben McKinley, the teacher? How can you be sure?'

'Well, I didn't know who he was then, dear. At the time I thought there was a new gardener, or maybe a friend of the Laird had popped in. It wasn't my business.'

'When was this?' Tilda asked.

'A month or so ago. It was mid-morning and she was taking her daily constitutional. That means, generally, she sits outside for a short while if it's sunny and it was bright that day. She likes to potter around the garden, but she needs help for that now. It was mid-January, I think. Unseasonably warm.'

'And did you hear what they were talking about?' Temerity asked.

Liz looked offended. 'I don't eavesdrop, dear. It wouldn't be fitting.'

'Right. Do you have any idea what it might have been about, then?'

'None at all,' Liz said. 'But the thing is, dearie, I was just on my way out and I noticed that something was missing. Now, as you can imagine, a house like this is absolutely full to the brim with knickknacks. Cigar boxes, perfume bottles, vases, candlesticks, that kind of thing. And it all needs polishing and caring for, which is my responsibility, though Sally often helps.'

Temerity nodded.

'Of course.'

'Well, the thing is, there was a hand mirror of Lady Dalcairney's that I'd put out downstairs for polishing. There were a few things; a matching hairbrush, a couple of brass vases, some ornaments. I'd put them on the hall table to do on Monday when I came back in. And the mirror was gone.'

Temerity exchanged a glance with Tilda.

'Can you describe the mirror?'

'Yes, of course, dear. It's made of pewter and it has a thistle design on the back. It's been in her family for many years. At the time, I just assumed that the Laird or Lady must have moved it and not told me, though they wouldn't usually do something like that. But then, when Dora told me that a mirror just like it was found next to that poor girl's body… and then, with him being the prime suspect in the case…'

'There are other leads that the Inspector is following up,' Temerity interjected. 'We don't know that it was him.'

'Oh, of course, dear. But I wanted to tell you. About the mirror. It must be the same one.'

'It might not be. But even if it is, it doesn't prove anything except Ben McKinley being a thief,' Tilda added. 'Though it's odd that he was here in the first place. Surely, if we ask Lady Dalcairney…?'

'I doubt she remembers, but you can ask her. I would have suggested asking her just now if she hadn't got so upset. You can see how she is.'

'I think the mirror was placed purposefully at the crime scene,' Temerity said, thoughtfully. 'It's quite a large thing. It's not exactly something that Molly would have just carried around, tucked into her pocket. I got the impression it was there for a reason.'

Temerity didn't add the fact that the mirror's glass had also been painted black, making it into a scrying or magic mirror. If it had been stolen, then that was something that could have been done to it afterwards.

'Was there anything strange about the mirror?' Temerity wasn't going to mention it to Liz, but wanted to see if she knew about the black glass. If she did, then it had already been customised before it was stolen, which threw up a whole other set of questions.

But Liz shook her head.

'No. It's a hand mirror, you know, part of an old-fashioned set. It belonged to Lady Dalcairney's grandmother and she inherited it. She's always been very sentimental about family heirlooms.'

Temerity nodded. If Ben had stolen the mirror, that would imply that he had made it into a witch's magic mirror before giving it to Molly. As a gift, maybe? But why? Neither of them had showed any sign of being involved in witchcraft. Temerity didn't count someone's flatmate owning a pack of tarot cards as being involved in any way.

'Would Sally have taken it?' Tilda asked. Liz looked surprised at the suggestion.

'Oh! I don't think so,' she replied, but she sounded uncertain.

'How long has Sally worked here?' Temerity asked. 'Do you trust her?'

'Of course I trust her! I don't know how long… a year, no more than that.' Liz frowned. 'I can't think she'd be involved with all this.'

Temerity wanted to ask more about the silent maid, but she couldn't think of a way to phrase it without sounding unkind about Sally's silent manner, so she decided to leave it for now.

'Is Lady Dalcairney a very religious woman?' Temerity asked, remembering the gold crucifix.

Liz sighed.

'Oh, yes. Very much so. I understand that the Dalcairneys have always been good churchgoers. As they should be, of course.' Liz sighed. 'Though I do think it's slightly encouraged her… imagination, let's say. It's not her fault, of course, it's the dementia. But she does have an obsession about the family being cursed. It's quite the task to talk her down from a full-blown panic sometimes. Once she knocked over a candle and set her quilt on fire. It was a wonder she didn't burn to death.'

'What does she think, at those times?'

'Oh, that someone wants to kill her. She's still grieving for her two daughters-in-law. She thinks the second one's dead, too, though I do keep telling her she's living in Italy. I'm sure that's it.'

'Is there anything else you want to tell us?' Tilda asked.

'Well, I don't know if this mirror business is relevant. But do tell the Inspector if you think it is,' Liz said.

'I will,' Temerity said. 'You could have told him yourself, though. They interrogated McKinley this week. This would have been key information.'

'Ah, well, I didn't want to disturb him with something that might have been silly,' Liz confessed. 'He must be so busy. But I thought you'd want to know, either way.'

'Of course,' Temerity agreed.

'Well, ladies. I'll have to see you out because the hydrotherapist will be here any minute for Lady Dalcairney.' Liz stood up and dusted crumbs off her skirt.

It was only then that Temerity noticed that Liz's wool skirt was embroidered at the hem with a pattern of golden feathers.

'Will she be all right?' Tilda was asking as she followed Liz out into the long corridor. Temerity, frowning, walked behind. Was this just a coincidence, or was there another suspect in Lost Maidens Loch?

'Oh yes, don't worry. She's fine,' the housekeeper said. 'I take good care of her.'

They said their goodbyes and the sisters got into Tilda's car. Sally was nowhere to be seen, but as Temerity raised her gaze to one of the upper windows, she saw a figure in black watching them. She felt a shiver go down her spine.

'Well, that wasn't what I was expecting,' Tilda said as she started the motor.

'Me neither.'

'That maid is kind of spooky,' Tilda added.

'I know,' Temerity agreed, thoughtful.

The embroidery on Liz's skirt was just as much of a sign as the spirit feathers on Beth and Ben's shoulders. Was Liz involved in all this somehow, or did she have some kind of other secret? What was Liz guilty of?

'The Inspector's going to want to hear about it. I better give him a call. Can you drop me off at the station?' Temerity added.

'He's more likely to be at Muriel's, but sure.' Tilda headed down the drive. 'I think there's something more going on there. That maid Sally is suspicious. And I don't feel like Liz told us everything.'

'No.' Temerity looked out of the window; mist had lowered onto the loch and the bright morning was gone. 'I don't think she did.'

Chapter 20

Temerity stood on the top rung of her rickety stepladder, carefully cleaning the huge gold-leaf chandelier with a soft rag. The radio was playing an all-1950s internet station and Temerity was singing along when the door opened and Angus Harley stepped into the shop. She wasn't expecting him, or anyone, really – she'd started to consider being closed for a couple of days a week at least in the tourist off-season. The regulars of Lost Maidens Loch didn't tend to find themselves in need of esoteric artefacts that often.

'Oh!' Caught off guard, Temerity nearly toppled over, and fought the impulse to hang onto the chandelier. Instead she crouched down, grabbing on to the ladder which swayed precariously. Harley strode over and steadied it, holding out a hand for her to step down safely.

'You should be careful on that thing,' he warned, unsmiling. 'Looks like it's going to fall apart any minute.'

'It's fine.' Temerity, annoyed that she'd only just avoided swinging from the chandelier like a monkey in front of a man she still regarded as having the social skills of a wild animal. *Touché, Wolfman: touché*, she thought. 'It's lasted this long.'

'All the more reason to get a new one?' he commented as she climbed down.

'We'll see,' she replied tersely, thinking, *my stepladder is none of your business*. 'Can I help you?'

'Ah. Yes. The Inspector sent me. You said the housekeeper at Dalcairney Manor gave you some information.'

'Yes, she did.'

'So… can I have it?' Harley looked uncomfortable.

'Oh. Right. Sure, sit down.' Temerity dusted off a leather sofa and pushed a box of books that had been delivered yesterday for Tilda to one side. 'How's the case, anyway?'

Hebrides flew in, swooping gently and landing on Temerity's desk. She'd given up trying to stop him doing it and had to accept his claw marks on the walnut wood. Angus gave the bird a cautious look.

'Progressing. I went up to talk to Beth Bennett again earlier today,' he said, getting his notebook and pen out of his pocket.

I bet she enjoyed that, Temerity thought.

'Oh. And?'

'Her alibi checks out. I had to push her on it, but she was playing hooky from work that day and shoplifting, would you believe it? The stores she went to in Glasgow have confirmed they've got her on CCTV at the time Molly died.'

'Shoplifting?' Human nature never failed to amaze Temerity. 'But… doesn't she have a pretty well-paid job? Surely she doesn't need to—'

'Naughty girl.' Hebrides squawked and Temerity had to hide her grin behind a cough.

'It's not always about needing to,' Harley said, frowning at Hebrides. 'A lot of people do it for the excitement. The challenge, I suppose. Who knows? Anyway, Beth Bennett was stuffing lingerie in her handbag in a department store at the time, so I think we can count her out of our considerations.'

'Wow. Okay.' Temerity sighed. 'And what about Dr Theakstone?'

'We're not sure about that yet. He says he was in Edinburgh on the afternoon of the murder so we have to see if we can find anyone to corroborate that, but we never thought he actually had a reason for killing Molly, more that he might have supplied the atropine. The Inspector has investigated Alf Hersey's accusation that Theakstone could have sold or stolen drugs, but it's impossible to prove without the testimony of someone he sold them to.'

'I suppose so. Tilda said Alf did seem very certain about it.' Angus shrugged.

'We need evidence. I mean, Theakstone is new to the village, so there's that. We don't know much about him other than his professional record, which is clean.'

'And McKinley?'

'We'll be searching McKinley's house shortly. We're waiting for the warrant to come through to do it.'

'Do you think you'll find something incriminating?' Temerity asked.

'Don't know, yet. But he did it, don't you think?'

'I don't know,' Temerity said truthfully and told him everything that Liz had told them.

'Interesting.' Harley scribbled everything down in his book; Hebrides watched him through one open eye, occasionally ruffling his azure feathers.

Tilda wandered into the shop, reading a large leather-bound book as she walked. It was right in front of her face, so she didn't see either Temerity or Angus until she had almost fallen over them. Temerity made out the title in German – *Buch Aller Verbotenen Kumst*. Her German wasn't that great, but she mentally translated it as something like *Book of All Forbidden Arts*.

'Oh, hi. I didn't see you there,' Tilda remarked, unnecessarily. 'Constable. Not planning to take your clothes off in our bathroom today, are you? Just so I can be prepared.' She smiled beatifically at Angus, who raised an eyebrow.

'I'll let you know,' he replied; he seemed to be getting used to Tilda.

'I'll be over here on the edge of my seat.' She rolled her eyes. 'Oh. I know what you'll find interesting. I heard a rumour about Dr Theakstone.'

'What rumour? From who?'

'I heard Muriel talking to her friend, that one from the school…'

'Brenda.'

'Right, Brenda.'

Angus frowned and raised an eyebrow.

'I wouldn't exactly consider either of them to be a reliable source of information,' he muttered. 'Go on.'

Tilda stroked Hebrides' head softly. 'Well, Brenda says she thinks Theakstone's an addict.'

'An addict?! Of what?' Temerity interjected.

'Maybe a drinker, maybe painkillers. Brenda said the guy had definitely had a hangover every time she'd gone in and her appointments are early, between eight and nine. She's had some kind of ongoing problem with her bowel,' Tilda explained, raising her eyebrows. 'Anyway, she said he was behaving oddly.'

'Right. Well, I'll have to follow this up. But, maybe next time, could you tell Brenda and Muriel – and anyone else – if it affects a murder case, could they maybe tell the police? Or could *you* tell us?' Angus got up. Temerity could see he was annoyed.

'Tilda's telling you now,' Temerity pointed out.

'Whatever. It's been a long day.' Angus sighed.

'Don't be like that, Hunky Policeman. That's just the way it is in Lost Maidens Loch,' Tilda said, picking up Charybdis and holding her to her ear.

'What's that, catty? I know. He's being very grumpy, isn't he? We should call him Constable Grumpy, shouldn't we?'

'Tils! Don't be so rude!' Temerity could see that Angus didn't know how to take Tilda's teasing; Temerity knew that her sister's sense of humour was unpredictable, but you had to get used to it, or be pretty sarcastic or odd yourself in the first place. 'The Inspector said you were researching Molly Bayliss's family? She was adopted, right?'

'That's right. I was in Edinburgh looking at the records, but they had to send out for them. They're coming in about a week or so.'

'What relevance does that have, though?'

'Not much, probably. Just procedure.'

'Ah.' Temerity nodded.

'Hm. Well, I'd better be going.' Angus stood up and put his notepad in his pocket. Temerity could tell he was still disgruntled. 'Thanks for the information.'

'Angus, don't be like that.' Temerity held out her hand and caught his arm, but Hebrides chose that moment to fly to her and she had to back away and hold her arm out for the bird so that he didn't land on Angus. 'Hebrides! Off!' she ordered, but the bird squawked at her as if to say, *I'm doing you a favour here. Why do you want to be friends with him when you've got me?*

'See you around, Temerity.' Angus nodded curtly at her and shut the shop door behind him.

'Tilda! Did you have to be so rude?' Temerity sighed.

'I was only joking. Big policeman can't take a joke. What do you care, anyway? You don't like him... or do you?'

'Of course I don't like him.' Temerity made a dismissive gesture with her hands.

'Now you just look uncomfortable!' Tilda crowed. 'You do like him, you do! Temerity Love, as I live and breathe! A crush on Monotone Man.'

'I do not!' she snapped at her sister. Hebrides spread out his wings to their full span and flapped them regally. 'And you. You're a naughty fellow. What are you?'

'Clever Hebrides,' the parrot disagreed.

Chapter 21

'Dr Theakstone will see you now.' The receptionist, a boy barely out of his teens, called over the counter at Temerity, who was sitting in the doctor's reception lounge. There wasn't anything wrong with her, but she'd decided to *beard the lion in his den*, or whatever that ridiculous phrase was that Tilda kept using. Lions didn't even have beards.

Temerity's plan was to imply to the locum doctor that she wanted to pay him illegally to buy prescription drugs – not atropine, as that might look suspicious – but painkillers that she didn't need. She didn't have the Inspector's permission to do this, but if Dr Theakstone agreed to sell her the drugs, it would be pretty incriminating.

She'd dressed in an outfit she hoped screamed, *I'm addicted to prescription drugs!* although as Tilda pointed out as they'd surveyed her wardrobe, a) being addicted to something didn't mean you had to dress in any particular way and b) everything Temerity owned was fifties and Rockabilly style, so the chances of her pulling off any impression other than being in the cast of *Grease* was a stretch. In the end, they'd settled on some scruffy flat brown leather boots, the one pair of baggy jeans that Temerity owned and one of Tilda's more shapeless brown sweaters. Temerity hadn't applied any make-up either in an effort to look paler than usual. Her long black hair was in the same plait she'd slept in.

She shuffled into the surgery. Theakstone was putting something away in a cabinet as she walked in, with his back to her.

'Take a seat,' he called out. Temerity watched as he unsuccessfully tried to shut the cabinet door, but it kept springing open. After a few attempts, he swore at it under his breath and turned to her, leaving it to swing open slowly.

'Miss Love?'

Temerity resisted the sudden urge to purr, *Love by name, Love by nature*. It seemed like something an undercover detective in the 1950s would say, but she stopped herself. Talk about inappropriate.

'That's me,' she replied, instead.

'And what can I do for you today?' Dr Theakstone asked. He was a bit older than Temerity, perhaps in his mid to late thirties, unshaven and generally rumpled in appearance. Temerity noticed that one of the buttons on his shirt wasn't done up and the shirt itself looked as though it belonged the laundry basket. He didn't look as though he'd slept.

'Ah. Well, I've got a bad back,' she lied.

'Oh. How long have you had the pain?' he asked.

'Weeks. I can hardly walk some days,' she added.

'I see. And do you know what prompted it?' Theakstone yawned. Temerity thought his bedside manner could definitely do with some work.

'I fell off a ladder. In my shop,' she said, thinking suddenly that it was a little too close to reality and she shouldn't tempt fate.

'Right. Well, let's have a look at it.' He pointed to the treatment table at the side of the surgery and Temerity walked over to it and jumped up onto the surface.

'You don't seem to be in much pain with it just now,' Theakstone observed.

'Ah, well. It comes and goes, Doctor.' Temerity raised an eyebrow.

She pulled up her sweater as Theakstone examined her back. Every now and again she said *ouch* in as artificial a way as she could, making it obvious that she was faking.

'Hmmm. Rather inconclusive.' Theakstone listened to her heart and her lungs. 'I'd say that rest and maybe some over the counter anti-inflammatory tablets will help you manage it.' He returned to his chair and sat down heavily. His eyes were bloodshot and he blinked them exaggeratedly as if they felt very uncomfortable.

'Ah, well, you see, Doctor, I've been taking those. And they don't work when the pain comes.' Temerity tried to look as suspicious as possible. 'The thing is, I heard that you might... you know.' She lowered her voice. 'If people need something stronger. I've got money,' she whispered.

Theakstone sighed and rubbed his eyes.

'Miss Love, I don't know what you're suggesting, but ibuprofen should work well enough. If the problem continues, I can refer you to a physiotherapist.' He yawned.

Temerity sat forward in her seat.

'Are you sure you can't... you know? Find something in the storeroom for me? I can pay,' she hissed.

He frowned at her.

'I can prescribe you ibuprofen if you like, but it's much cheaper if you buy it from the chemist,' he repeated.

'Oh. I heard...' Temerity tried once more and gave Theakstone a significant look. 'You know? I heard that you help people like me.'

The doctor stared across the table at her for a long moment.

'Are you suggesting that I sell drugs illegally?' He leaned forward, his elbows on the desk. Temerity tried to read his face, but she couldn't get a sense of whether she should agree or pretend that wasn't what she was saying at all.

'Do you?' she asked.

Theakstone met her eyes.

'No,' he answered. 'That would be illegal.' He sat back in his chair and frowned at her again. 'Why are you really here, Miss Love? Because I know you don't have a bad back. I've seen you walking around the village quite happily this week.'

Busted, Temerity thought. *Time to come clean. Or, clean-ish.*

'Okay, You're right. I don't have a bad back. But I wondered if you can tell me if you've seen Ben McKinley recently.' She tried another tack; she wasn't going to tell Theakstone there definitely was a rumour that he sold drugs under the counter, but she could try to find out something new about the missing atropine.

'Ben McKinley?'

'Yes. He's a teacher at the school.'

'I'm aware of who Mr McKinley is. Yes, I've seen him recently.'

'As a patient?'

Theakstone smiled thinly.

'You must be aware of patient confidentiality, Miss Love. You know I can't tell you anything about what I've treated Mr McKinley for.'

So he has been here recently, Temerity thought. She tried a different question.

'Have you heard about the murder at the school?'

'Miss Love, if you're not here for a medical reason, then I will have to ask you to leave.' Theakstone stood up. 'I am not here to gossip.'

Then you'll be the only one in Lost Maidens Loch, Temerity thought. She got up.

'Look. I'm sorry I pretended I had a bad back. But I did hear a rumour that you might be… making certain drugs available to those who had the money,' she whispered. 'If that's not true, then tell me. Because it's not a rumour you really want to go around otherwise.'

'I've already told you it's not true.' The doctor sighed. 'Look, Miss Love. I know that when newcomers come to places like Lost Maidens Loch, the locals can get very suspicious. But I can assure you that the only thing I'm guilty of is not getting enough sleep. My daughter's three months old and she's got a cold. I've been up all night syringing her nose for the last three nights, if you must know.' He yawned.

That would account for the rumpled shirt and the red eyes. So, maybe not a drug addict himself, Temerity mused.

'I see,' she said. 'I'm sorry. I've been helping the Inspector out with the murder case and—'

'Atropine. I know. He's asked me about it. I've already told him that I didn't give it to anyone. We had a break-in and that and some other things were taken. The Inspector's looking into it for me.' He fixed her with a level gaze. 'So, if that's all?'

'That's all. Thanks for seeing me.' Temerity walked out of the surgery, feeling embarrassed.

Brenda had thought the locum had a drink problem because he seemed hungover every morning, but that could certainly be explained away by sleepless nights. If the Inspector already knew about a possible break-in, then that meant all that was left was rumour and Theakstone was right. Lost Maidens Loch was a rumour mill and usually none of it was true.

So the real question is, if there was a break-in, who did it? And did that person murder Molly Bayliss? she thought as she walked up the street to the shop. It was still possible that it was Theakstone, but it seemed less likely. She sighed. Her plan had worked, though not in the way she expected: it had reminded her not to believe in gossip. She never had, often being the subject of gossip herself, but this time she'd let it get to her.

Maybe Tilda was right. Maybe she needed to get away from Lost Maidens Loch for a while.

Chapter 22

A crowd was milling in the middle of Kirkaldy Street when Temerity walked around the corner the next day, on her way to the library to return some of Tilda's romance novels. She saw Ken MacDonald in the crowd, who ran the glass-blowing studio in the village. Ken was probably in his seventies with a white Santa beard and perennially warm smile. Today he was wearing a blue bobble hat, with his glass-blowing apron over corduroy trousers and an old sweatshirt.

'Hi, Ken. What's going on?' Temerity asked. The crowd was at least three people deep and there didn't seem to be much happening other than a hubbub of chatter. 'Tourists coming up by the library now?'

Ken nodded to the house opposite, a plain stone terrace with a white door.

'Naw. That's Ben McKinley's hoose. Inspector and the Constable's just gone in tae search it,' he said.

'How come everyone's here?' Temerity spotted various familiar faces in the crowd. 'How did they know?'

'Muriel caught wind o' it.' Ken raised his eyebrow. 'From Dora, probably.'

'Ah. They must be searching for atropine. That was what poisoned Molly.'

'I heard that the new doc might hae done it,' Ken said.

'Don't believe everything you hear.' Temerity sighed. 'I mean, he might have. But you know what rumour's like in Lost Maidens Loch.'

'I do,' Ken agreed.

'So, how long are we going to stand here?' Temerity stamped her feet against the cold.

'They've been in there a wee while. Reckon if they find anything, it'll be soon,' Ken said. 'See, Ben's standing there. Looks guilty as sin.'

Temerity was amazed to see that Ken was right; Ben McKinley stood outside his house in a dressing gown and slippers, while the villagers stared at him and whispered.

'I think anyone would look pretty uncomfortable standing in their bathrobe in the street while the whole village stares at them, to be fair,' Temerity said. 'I guess he didn't know when they were coming.'

'Element of surprise.' Ken touched the side of his nose. 'That's what I'd do.'

'But surely if he had anything incriminating in the house, he'd have got rid of it immediately after the murder?' Temerity frowned.

'Aye. But they're lookin' for trace elements. Bits of this and that. Chemicals. Things show up under that blue light, don't they? I've seen it on TV,' Ken said.

'I suppose so.' Temerity thought she should take the books back to the library; she wasn't that comfortable hanging around Ben's house. The villagers were suspiciously like a small mob that she could imagine turning nasty. She had made up her mind to go when the front door to Ben McKinley's house opened and Inspector Hyland strode out, carrying a small plastic bag.

'Ben McKinley. I am arresting you for the murder of Molly Bayliss on the twenty-first of February. Do you understand?' he addressed McKinley, who seemed to crumple into the Inspector.

There was a loud gasp from the watching crowd.

'No!' McKinley started crying. 'I didn't do it! I swear! I loved her!' he shouted. The Inspector nodded grimly and led him to the patrol car that was parked slightly up the street.

'All right, fella.' Temerity was close enough to hear the kindness in the Inspector's voice as he guided McKinley away from the crowd.

Someone started shouting. *Murderer! Murderer!* The words rang against the stone walls. Angus came out of the house, carrying various pieces of investigation equipment, followed by Alf Hersey. Alf acted as coroner and forensic crime scene investigator in the village as well as doctor; Temerity knew from Tilda that he planned to be back in post as the village doctor in a couple of weeks.

Temerity realised, when he stepped out of the house, how much a part of everyone's life Alf was: he'd been everyone's doctor for as long as she could remember. Maybe his description of Dr Theakstone as drug-addled and irresponsible came more from jealousy that someone else was fulfilling that role for the villagers, even if just for a while? Temerity thought that if she was as important to the people of Lost Maidens Loch as Alf was, she probably wouldn't like the feeling she'd been replaced, either.

'What did ye find, Alf?' someone shouted, but Alf shook his head. He wasn't so unprofessional to stand there and give the crowd a blow-by-blow account of the search, but Temerity guessed that if Tilda called around later with a bottle of whisky, he'd be happy enough to talk.

'Go home!' Angus strode towards the crowd and they stepped back. The chanting stopped and Temerity watched as the patrol car drove off. She guessed that Ben would be held in the one police cell overnight and then taken to a larger facility until... what? A trial? Was that it? It seemed a sudden end to the case.

'There's nothing to see. Go home!' Angus shouted again. Temerity turned away, towards the library. The crowd started to disperse, mostly walking back down towards the loch. Temerity thought that Muriel would be doing a fine bit of business pretty soon, as everyone would gather in The Singing Kettle for a good gossip.

'Temerity. Wait!'

She looked back and saw Angus run after her. She waited up the street for him.

'Hi, Angus. I wasn't involved in that awful chanting – I didn't even know anything was going on until I walked up here. I was taking books back to the library.' She proffered the books in her hand as proof, realising too late that she didn't want Angus to think that Tilda's romance novels were hers. Tilda, despite her caustic shell, always chose books with titles like *His Savage Secret* and *Love Me, Letitia*, which made it all the sadder that Tilda had never had a romance of her own. People who read *Love Me, Letitia* believed in earth-shattering, tumultuous love that changed your life completely: Temerity knew Tilda secretly yearned for that kind of storybook love, but also knew that she was too afraid to look for it herself. When asked, Tilda would say that Lost Maidens Loch was tiny, full of all the same people she'd known her whole life and no one here would ever understand her, so it wasn't even worth trying.

However, Angus barely glanced at them.

'I know you weren't.' He looked uncomfortable.

'So... what did you want to say?'

Angus looked at his feet.

'Ummm... it's... I, errr...'

Temerity frowned.

'What's up? Do you need me to look at something in McKinley's house?' she asked.

'No. Nothing like that.' He shuffled his feet. 'It's just that, now that the case is pretty much over, I was wondering whether you might... err, maybe, come out with me one evening?' he asked, looking away.

'What?' It was so unexpected that Temerity couldn't think of anything else to say. 'Oh! I see.' *But I didn't think you liked me at all*, she thought and then realised that she had forgotten to answer properly. 'Well, that's very kind of you to ask.' She was flummoxed. 'The thing is, I don't usually... I mean, I don't really date.' She knew it was an awful answer, but she hadn't really thought of Angus Harley in that way and she was generally unprepared for any indication that anyone might want to ask her out.

'Oh. Right.' He actually stepped away from her and nodded. 'Sure, of course.'

'Please don't be offended. It's not you. It's...' She caught herself before she could say *It's not you, it's me*, although that really was the truth. 'I'll see you around, though. Okay?'

'Sure.' He gave her a little wave. 'See you around.'

Oh gods, Temerity berated herself as Angus Harley's tall frame walked away from her. *Why am I such an idiot? Why couldn't I just say yes?*

She knew why: whenever a man had asked her out, it had always felt like she was betraying Patrick. For the first time, she wondered if it was time to move on. Patrick was gone and she was alive. Wasn't she allowed to have love in her life? Or at least some kind of fun?

She shook her head as she turned away and walked up the hill to the library. This time, she imagined what Tilda would say if she'd witnessed that car crash of a conversation:

Tilda: *Angus Harley just asked you out.*
Temerity: *I know.*
Tilda: *Is your brain actually connected to your mouth, or are there some loose sinews just flapping around in there?*

Temerity: *I was surprised. He surprised me.*
Tilda: *Gods help you if a child pops a balloon anywhere nearby. You might be rendered completely mute forever.*
Temerity: *[howls sadly]*

In the library, she pushed the pile of novels towards Kerry Cohen, the librarian.

'Any good?' Kerry asked, turning the cover of the first novel towards Temerity with a raised eyebrow. The cover featured a painting of a steamy clinch between a woman in a low-necked dress and a man in a ripped shirt.

'I wouldn't know.' Temerity sighed. 'They're Tilda's.'

Kerry rolled her eyes.

'Surprised your sister reads books like this. Isn't she too busy boiling frogs or something?'

Temerity, still distracted, had temporarily forgotten that when she and Tilda were at school, Kerry had been on Tilda's hockey team. They'd been friends until their late teens when Tilda started taking more of an interest in their parents' books and began teaching herself herbalism and witchcraft. Kerry and the other girls had pulled away from Tilda then; they didn't have the sports field to exhaust their energies on any more and they didn't understand that Tilda was still Tilda, only she'd swapped a hockey stick for a broomstick. They had been cruel to Tilda, for a time, until Tilda hid away in the shop.

'Don't be ridiculous, Kerry. That's the kind of comment I'd expect from one of the old ladies in the café,' Temerity snapped. 'Don't you think it's time you gave it a rest? You and Tilda used to be friends.'

'That was a long time ago. She went… weird,' Kerry retorted.

'Oh, for heaven's sake.' Temerity rolled her eyes. 'You're a librarian and you still live in Lost Maidens Loch. Don't act like you're too good to go out for a drink with my sister. Who, by the way, is a rare books dealer, so you'd actually have quite a lot in common.'

Temerity swept out of the library as regally as she could, given that she was wearing her one pair of jeans, sourced from the charity shop tucked into green wellington boots, the leather deerstalker Tilda had given her (with her hair in one long black plait over her shoulder) and a bright yellow wool coat belted over the top of everything. If she'd have known that she was going to have two uncomfortable interactions this morning, she might have paid more attention to her outfit.

Chapter 23

Temerity settled herself into one of the wide leather booths that ran along the side wall of The Singing Kettle and opened her magazine. It was a week later and Tilda was away on one of her occasional book-buying trips and Temerity hated cooking, so she'd decided to treat herself to dinner at the café. She'd ordered as soon as she'd come in: haggis, neeps and tatties – a classic Scottish meal of sausage, turnips and mashed potatoes – and some of Muriel's famous apple pie and cream for dessert.

She had the most recent Sotheby's auction catalogue to flick through, which she considered light reading: she liked to keep up to date with the world of normal antiques, like lamps and china and paintings, even though she specialised in what Tilda called *Strange Items Belonging to the Ancient Dead, Probably Cursed*.

The Alaskan university had also got back in touch, asking how they could persuade her to do the keynote speech at the conference and it was playing on her mind. Maybe she *should* go. She'd only the week before been thinking that maybe it was time to have a break from the village.

'Good evening.'

Temerity looked up to find Angus Harley standing awkwardly next to the table. He wasn't dressed in uniform for once and looked really quite nice in jeans, hiking boots, a plain sweater and a rainproof jacket.

'Oh. Hello.' Temerity immediately regretted not having put any make-up on; she had her hair in two plaits, pinned around her head, and she wore wellingtons over her red capri pants.

She had, at least, thought to put a clean baby pink long-sleeved cardigan on before she left the shop.

'Lovely evening…' he continued awkwardly. Temerity looked out of the café window where rain was battering the street outside.

'Very fresh,' she agreed. This was awkward.

'Here for dinner?' he asked as Muriel placed a steaming plate of haggis in front of Temerity along with a tall glass of cherry cola.

'Remarkably, yes.' Temerity looked at her dinner and back again at Harley. She hadn't meant it to come out so sarcastically.

'Ah.' He nodded and looked out of the window. 'I come a couple of nights a week. I'm not much of a cook.'

'Tilda usually cooks dinner, but she's out,' Temerity replied.

There was an uncomfortable silence. Temerity wondered if he'd already eaten and was on his way out, or whether she should ask him to sit down. She hoped he was just going. She hadn't seen him since his awkward asking her out a few days ago and she didn't know whether to bring it up or not. *Remember when you asked me out for a drink and I flatly refused? Fun times.*

'Mind if I join you?' he asked. 'I'm not the greatest fan of eating alone. I mean, if you'd rather read your magazine, that's fine, of course…' he trailed off.

Temerity felt herself blushing and was immediately mortified. It was just Angus Harley, the most socially awkward man in Lost Maidens Loch, after all, possibly the child of an unusual family of redheaded, pale-complexioned Romany pedlars who had lost their child one lonely Transylvanian night. Yes, he was good-looking and yes, they had recently had an unfortunate and deeply embarrassing encounter that would haunt her forever, but they could be grown-ups.

Muriel reappeared and gave Angus a menu.

'Specials are trout, cod or haggis, pet,' she said, assuming he was sitting at Temerity's table and surreptitiously nudging him so that he sat down.

Thanks, Muriel, you nosy old harridan, Temerity thought, trying to transmit the thought to Muriel through the ether.

'Ah – I'll have the same as Temerity. Thanks.' Angus gave Muriel the menu back; Muriel beamed at them both and sauntered back behind the counter, singing something under her breath. 'Sorry... I think Muriel decided that for us.' He grinned ruefully. Angus smiled so little that Temerity was surprised at what a difference it made. He was like another person.

'I don't mind,' she found herself saying. *What? I do mind, actually. What am I saying?*

'Okay.' He was still awkward. 'What're you reading?'

'Auction catalogue. Like to keep up with the industry,' she explained.

'Ah.'

There was another silence. *Great decision. Loving this so far*, she thought, cynically.

'Also, I was just... oh, you don't want to hear about it,' she mumbled. *Gods, why am I acting like such an idiot?* She was annoyed at herself.

'Hear about what?'

'Oh, it's just that university. The keynote speech. I'm still umming and ahhing over it.'

'You should do it. Share that expertise of yours far and wide.'

'Hmmm.' She folded one page of the auction catalogue in half and then straightened it out again. 'Maybe. I don't know.'

'What's stopping you?' he asked. 'It's just a conference.'

'I know.'

She remembered what she had wanted to ask him and snapped her fingers.

'That was it. What did you find at Ben McKinley's house? The other day?' *You know, before you asked me out and I said no, remember?*

Angus frowned.

'I'm not sure I should tell you. You're not a police officer.'

'Oh, come on. I know everything else. I was just curious.' Temerity smiled her most charming smile; usually she thought smiling made her look horsey.

Angus sighed.

'Fine, fine. It was a powder in a small bag. We've sent it off for analysis, but we think it's the poison. Powdered form to add to drinks easily.'

'I see,' Temerity mused.

'Here ye are, darlin'.' Muriel came back with a plate identical to Temerity's and set it in front of Angus. 'Enjoy, young lovers!'

'Muriel! We are *not* lovers!' Temerity protested. 'We hardly know each other!'

'Ach, now, come on, I'm only messin' with ye. Fine couple ye'd make, though,' she mused. 'Maybe I'll get some ae that lovers' potion from the big hoose and slip it in ye food next time.' She smiled benevolently at them as if she were a mother duck. 'Might speed things up, ye never know.'

'Sorry?' Temerity chewed her haggis and frowned. 'Love potions?'

'Ach, aye. Many years, she's been makin' them for the villagers. Many a weddin' and a bairn has come of those wee sachets, I can tell ye.' Muriel looked sharply at Temerity. 'No' getting any younger, ma darlin'. That's all I'm sayin'.'

'No, I mean, who's making love potions?' Temerity repeated. The only herbalist she knew was Tilda and she was pretty sure that wasn't who Muriel was talking about.

Angus frowned and leaned forward.

'Sachets?' he repeated.

'Ach, dear, I assumed ye knew. Lady Dalcairney, of course. Mind ye, nowadays she's that frail, she doesnae make many. Time was she's be over every week, droppin' wee sachets and bottles of this and that off with me to pass on to all and sundry.' Muriel wiped the table with a cloth as she spoke.

Temerity exchanged a look with Angus. She'd told the Inspector all about her and Tilda's visit to the Manor house: the strange meeting with the elderly Lady Dalcairney, about Liz and the Laird's story about a curse. She assumed the Inspector had passed it on to Angus.

'Lady Dalcairney... makes love potions?'

'Aye, yes. Skilled herbalist in her day. Lots of other ones, too, she used to make. Healing, protection, that type of thing.'

Temerity frowned.

'And you distribute them?'

'If she asks me to, aye.' Muriel looked suddenly defensive. 'What? It isnae wrong. I havenae done anything' wrong. It's all herbs, all natural, no harm done.'

'Has anyone collected a... potion from you recently?' Angus put his knife down on his plate. Temerity could see what he was thinking: the small bag of powder recovered from McKinley's house could have been such a thing.

'Ah, well, I don't really like to say.' Muriel looked uncomfortable, clearly regretting saying anything.

'Muriel, I'm off duty, but I can come down tomorrow morning when I'm on duty and you can tell me then,' Angus warned. 'Who came and got a potion from here recently?'

'Ach, hell mend ye, Angus Harley,' the cook muttered. Harley took out his police notebook from his overcoat jacket and looked at her enquiringly.

'Last chance, Muriel. Or I can come back with my badge.'

'Ach, fine. But I didnae want tae tell ye, okay? He's in enough trouble.'

'Who was it, Muriel?' Temerity prompted her.

'Ben McKinley. All right? Are ye happy now? She left him a love potion. No doubt tae get that Molly tae love him. Stuck on her, he was.' Muriel shook her head. 'Such a shame he never had the chance tae use it. Think what might have been.'

Angus exchanged a glance with Temerity.

'We'll see. Thanks, Muriel,' he said. 'You don't happen to know what was in these potions, do you?'

'Ach, no. I'm just the pick-up point,' the woman replied. 'I shouldnae have said anything.'

'No, you absolutely should have.' Temerity reached out and touched her arm. 'If it's innocent, then Ben hasn't got anything to worry about from you telling us. As you say, a love potion isn't illegal in itself.'

The door opened and a group of tourists looking for their dinner after a day out on the loch came in; Muriel moved away reluctantly to serve them.

'Well, what d'you think of that?' Temerity asked.

'I think we need to go up to the Manor and ask Lady Dalcairney exactly what she put in that love potion.' Angus raised his eyebrow as he ate. It irritated Temerity that he was even good-looking shovelling mashed potato into his mouth.

'But why would she put poison in it?' Temerity had a small word with herself and made herself look at her own food. 'It doesn't make sense that she would. I mean, did she know Molly? How could she? She never leaves the house.'

'Hmmm.' Angus heaped the mashed turnips on his fork. 'McKinley poisoned it, then.'

'But... if he wanted to poison Molly, why did he need to put something into a love potion? Either he wanted her to love him, or he wanted her dead. Not both,' Temerity pointed out. 'And Muriel says *she* passed Ben the love potion. So that rather throws doubt on the idea of him being the murderer, don't you think?' She sipped her cola.

'I don't know. All I can think is that we've got a witness who says she gave McKinley some kind of herbal concoction and then his... not girlfriend... love interest – in his eyes anyway – Molly Bayliss is found dead. Doesn't look too good, does it?'

'No, it doesn't,' Temerity mused and looked at her watch. 'Have you got the patrol car?'

'It's in for a service.' He gave her an enquiring look. 'Why?'

'Maybe we should go now,' Temerity suggested. 'We could still walk over.'

'Where? To the Manor? I'm off duty and you haven't eaten your pie.' Angus pointed to the pottery bowl Temerity had put to one side which held a generous slice of pie and a stainless-steel jug of cream Muriel had placed next to it. He gave her that warm smile again and despite her initial assessment of him, Temerity felt herself melting a little. *Maybe you do have a personality, under the ridiculously uncomfortable formality*, she thought. *It's within the realms of possibility.* 'Why don't we finish our dinner first?' he looked at his watch. 'It's still early.'

'You'll go with me after that, though? The surprise approach, as it were.'

'It is a little irregular.' He swallowed his food. 'But maybe you're right. And I could do with a walk to digest all of this.'

'I am right and a walk would do us both good, I'm sure,' Temerity replied archly, grinning at him. For a moment, their eyes met and for the first time Temerity saw something more than duty and formality in Angus's gaze. A smile played around his lips. 'Aren't you curious to find out what all this is about?'

'Curious. Yes, I suppose you could say I am,' he replied. *Gods, was that flirting?* Temerity thought. It was hard to tell, but she thought maybe that it was.

Damn. He did look good when he smiled.

Chapter 24

It was a clear night and the stars were starting to come out over Lost Maidens Loch by the time Angus and Temerity had finished their dinner.

'It's beautiful,' she sighed as they made their way down the narrow cobbled path from The Singing Kettle and turned right along the wide pathway that led walkers alongside the loch. To their right, the village was already quiet; they passed the boat shed which was closed for the night, then Ken MacDonald's glass-blowing studio, where he made colourful paperweights, vases and other trinkets for tourists. Next there was the bakery, where Mrs Black stringently resisted any modern innovations in baking and churned out the same selection of unsliced farmhouse, cob and bloomer, crusty white rolls, sandwiches and teacakes she had for forty years. Temerity didn't care that she never varied; she loved Mrs Black's bread. Tilda, being Tilda, complained that, in the twenty-first century, Mrs Black's choice of sandwich cheese being either sliced or grated cheddar was unacceptably basic.

Next to the bakery was a line of modern wood-panelled townhouses which looked over the loch; the wood was painted blue and the houses featured white picket fences and white windowsills, maybe to give them a kind of fisherman look. Unlike the older stone cottages, these modern properties had attracted a few new inhabitants to the village.

'Have you heard? The old guard want those taken down. Say they're not in keeping with the village and should never have been built.' Temerity nodded to the houses, two of which still had FOR SALE signs on them.

'Taken down? What do they think's going to happen, they just fold up into a shoe box or something?' Angus shook his head. 'This place. It takes a lot of getting used to.'

'It certainly does.' Temerity nodded. 'They're just grumbling. They don't like change.'

'No, I noticed that.' He jammed his hands in his pockets as they walked along.

'How long have you been here now?' she asked him. Neither of them had mentioned the incident outside the library. *Also, who in their right mind gets in the mood to ask someone out by doing a house search?* Temerity pondered. *It's weird. One minute you're dusting for fingerprints, the next, you're proposing romantic drinks. Maybe it's a policeman thing.*

'A month. I was posted here from Glasgow.'

'Pretty different, huh?' Once they were past the village and started alongside the loch path, it was so quiet that Temerity could hear the occasional plop of a fish breaking the water to catch a fly on the water. The last time they'd walked this path together, they'd been part of the search party for the missing boat with the helicopter circling overhead. Tonight's ambience was kind of nicer.

'You could say that. I think I told you I was in the fire service originally. Joined the police about two years ago. After…' His face clouded over and Temerity recalled the scars she'd seen on his back.

'You can tell me what happened,' she said, gently. He smiled wanly and stared at his feet on the path in the gathering dark.

'We were called to a fire. I went in with some of the others. We were trained, we'd done it hundreds of times before. There was a kid trapped in her bedroom. She was crying out for us, so she hadn't succumbed to smoke inhalation yet.' He took in a deep breath, but continued plodding along. 'We broke the door down. Got her out, passed her along the line, back outside. I was the last to leave. The ceiling fell in on me. I was knocked out. Next thing I know, I woke up in hospital.'

'It must have taken a long time to heal,' Temerity said, quietly. The scarring had spread right down one side of Angus's torso. Even though he was awkward, she was at fault, too. She knew she had been purposefully cold with him, if only in her own mind. To some degree it was her and Tilda's caustic sense of humour, but it was also a self-defence kind of thing. Temerity purposefully kept people at arm's length, using humour as a defence mechanism. It was kind of difficult to stop, sometimes.

'Months. After that, I dunno… I couldn't face it. Going back into a fire. Long story short, I got accepted for police training instead. And here I am. Lost Maidens Loch.'

'Here you are,' Temerity agreed. She sensed he didn't want to talk about the fire in great detail, so she changed the subject. 'Has anyone told you about the legends about the town?'

Angus laughed. 'I read that damn brochure, whatever it was. It's all haunted, or something.'

Temerity laughed. 'I don't know about that. I've never detected any hauntings in the places it described. Elsewhere, occasionally. But the real legend of Lost Maidens Loch is that once, nobody knows when, a beautiful young woman—'

'It's always a beautiful young woman.' Angus rolled his eyes. 'Why can't it be an average, middle-aged woman in this type of legend? Or an old man?'

'You won't get any argument from me.' *Registering modern views about women: check*, Temerity thought. 'It'd be nice if the victims in these old tales were middle-aged men. But, nonetheless, the legend holds that a beautiful young woman drowned in the loch. No one knows why; some say she was swimming out to her lover who waited for her on the other side. Some say that she was abducted by a dragon and taken to live under the loch as its Queen.' She rolled her eyes. 'Silly, right?'

'Not exactly believable,' Angus agreed. 'But there have been other deaths, too, right? Other drownings. Not always women. I did my research before I came here. And… I mean, you told me about your loss, too. It can't be easy walking past here every day, remembering what happened.'

Temerity gave a half smile.

'The legend goes that, now, the loch requires a new victim every few years. I think it's kind of sick that people think like that, but there you are.'

There was an uncomfortable silence; Temerity felt the grief she normally suppressed rising up in her.

'Why do you stay?' Angus reached for her hand; she stopped walking, surprised at the contact. 'I'd have left years ago. I don't think I could stand it.'

'I don't know,' she said, taken aback at the sudden contact. 'I suppose… I feel I can't leave. I'd be leaving Patrick.'

'Is that why you don't want to go to that conference?' he asked softly. Temerity looked away, not wanting to talk about it. 'But he's gone,' Angus said, softly. The warmth from his hand seemed to transmit itself to her, along with a sadness that she was surprised by, but recognised.

Temerity closed her eyes; touching Angus gave her access to him in a totally different way and she realised how similar he was to her. They were both hiding something, an old sadness. She couldn't tell, for him, whether it was the fire or something else, but there was something there, hidden. *Come on, now. Don't make me empathise with the Wolfman*, she thought, but she couldn't help it. There was something there. Something familiar.

'I know,' she sighed. 'I know it's stupid, but I can't help it.'

'It's not stupid. I suppose… I just don't think someone like you belongs here.'

'Someone like me?' Temerity wondered what he meant. 'A witch? You think I'm too much of a weirdo to live with all these normal people?'

He dropped her hand; the last flash of emotion she got from him before her skin lost contact with his was guilt and embarrassment. She wasn't angry, but grateful for an excuse to divert attention away from her grief by pretending to be irritated.

'You might think what I do is weird, Angus, but I can assure you that there are lots of people – even in boring little Lost Maidens Loch – who appreciate my talents. And, I think you'll find, when you've been here a little longer, that the Loch isn't as normal as you think it is.' She wagged her finger at him, and instantly remonstrated with herself: *Oh dear lord, did I just wag my finger at him? What am I, eighty?*

'That's not what I…' he sighed. 'It doesn't matter,' he said gruffly.

Temerity was glad that Angus didn't have a psychic bone in his body, because if he could have heard her thoughts, she felt sure that he would have thought she was a crazy witch for sure.

They walked on in silence.

Chapter 25

It was the Laird who opened Dalcairney Manor's heavy oak front door; Temerity had expected Liz or Sally. He looked surprised.

'Constable. Miss Love. I wasn't expecting you. Oh, excuse me, where are my manners? Come in!' He ushered them into the long, carpeted hallway. 'Did we make an appointment? I'm so sorry, but I'm on my way out just now.' He shrugged on a black dinner jacket over a dress shirt and black trousers. 'Fundraising dinner. I expect I'll see the Inspector there.' He smiled. 'It's all a bit of a fuss, really, but one must do one's duty. Liz'll be back in a minute, if you want to wait? She popped out into the garden, I think.' He waved his hand distractedly in the general direction of the side of the house where Temerity had discovered the overgrown herb garden.

'No problem. We just popped in to talk to Liz,' Temerity lied; they actually wanted to speak to Lady Dalcairney, but it seemed safer to pretend that they were paying a call on a friend. 'Just to say hi, really. We were walking up this way and thought she might take pity on us and make us a cup of tea.'

Temerity could sense Angus's slight incredulity at the ease of Temerity's lie, but she ignored it and reached for his hand instead. He tensed immediately. *Some detective you are*, she thought, still cross in a not-very-cross way at him. She had invented the argument to have a reason not to have to talk about Patrick, but for the rest of the walk she had engineered an argument with Angus Harley in her mind, soundly debating him on issues of faith, life after death and the healing power of crystals. Therefore, by the time they came to the beach at the edge of the Laird's land, Temerity felt argued out.

Also, the more that David Dalcairney believed they were here as a couple, out for the evening on a romantic walk and not as an off-duty policeman and his psychic, unofficial colleague coming to ask difficult questions, the better.

'Ah, right you are. Well, I'd better be off, but do wait in the lounge. As I say, she won't be long, I'm sure.'

'Thanks.' Temerity stood a little closer to Angus as the Laird busied himself with a scarf and his shoes and waved them goodbye; Angus was as stiff as a board. Touching his hand, she knew instantly that he was uncomfortable, but when she realised the reason for his lack of comfort, she was mortified. He was quite deeply attracted to her and he was uncomfortable about the little show she was doing for the Laird's benefit.

Temerity felt immediately embarrassed and as soon as the door closed, she stepped away from Angus and let go of his hand.

'That was a close one,' she said, brightly. 'Hope you didn't mind me holding your hand then. I just thought if it looked like we were on a date, then he'd be less suspicious.' *Mortified, mortified, OH MY GODS*, she thought, madly. *He really likes me. What am I doing?*

'Oh. Right, yes, of course.'

'I mean, we're not on a date,' she added, making it worse.

'Clearly,' he answered.

'I mean… it's not really the time to talk about it. The date thing. You asking me out.' She blundered on, wondering when she'd stop. *Not showing any signs yet*, she thought. *Rambling on really quite badly at this point. Yep.* 'Is it? I mean, we could talk about it. Maybe we should.'

'Maybe not right now.' Angus gave her a look that implied he thought she was at best batty and at worst, unhinged.

'Right.' Temerity tried to regain some of her usual composure. 'Okay. We should find Lady Dalcairney. While Liz is outside. I don't know where Sally is.' Temerity pushed her own feelings to one side. She didn't know if she did have feelings for Angus – sure, he was attractive, if you liked that kind of tall, healthy, Scottish warrior kind of look – *Temerity, focus* – and anyway, her feelings about Patrick always got in the way when she thought she might be interested in someone. This was the good thing about antiques. They were little mysteries Temerity could solve. People, on the other hand, not so much.

Also, they were alone in Dalcairney Manor, but it wouldn't be long before they weren't.

'I don't know if I've met Sally,' Angus commented.

'Oh, you'd remember.' Temerity lowered her voice in case the maid appeared suddenly. 'She's… kind of creepy. Wears black. Doesn't talk. Glares a lot.'

'Well, I can't imagine being a maid is that much fun,' Angus shrugged. 'Let's focus on Lady Dalcairney, anyway. Where is she likely to be?'

'Upstairs. If Liz comes in while we're up there, we can say… I don't know. We heard a cry and we went up to check she was all right.'

Angus shook his head.

'You're quite devious, aren't you?' he said as he followed Temerity up the imposing staircase.

'I suppose it comes of being a witch,' Temerity replied archly, glad for a change of subject.

The whole interior of the house was panelled in dark varnished oak and the staircase had an elaborately carved siding and wide banister. The image of a stag's head, engraved into the wood, flashed into Temerity's mind; she turned to Angus, halfway up the stairs, whispering.

'I saw a stag when I first picked up the hand mirror found on Molly Bayliss's body. We know that it had belonged to Lady Dalcairney. Liz told me that it disappeared on the same day Ben McKinley visited.'

'We can assume he came to request some kind of potion from Lady Dalcairney and stole it when he was here. Why, though?' Angus whispered back. 'Maybe he's into witchcraft.'

Temerity rolled her eyes and continued walking as quietly as she could up the stairs. 'Why do you always say that straightaway? Oh, she's got a broom, she must be a witch. He's got a cat, he must be a witch. There's a bit more to it.'

'He might be, though.'

'I highly doubt he is.'

'Why? You don't know.'

'I'd know, okay?' Temerity hissed. 'I know my own kind. I've got radar.'

'Well then, why would Ben McKinley steal the mirror? Doesn't make any sense. Unless he knew it could be used for some kind of purpose.'

'What purpose?' Temerity whispered back. 'If he wanted to kill her, then the poison did the job. What difference does putting a mirror near the body make?' She frowned and stopped on the stairs.

'What?'

'No, it's just...' Temerity broke off as a new thought came to her. Opposite her, on the wall, a full-length mirror in an elaborate gold frame reflected herself back to her.

'What?'

She turned to him.

'What do mirrors do?'

Angus gave her another meaningful look.

'Show us our reflections,' he said, as if he was talking to an idiot.

'Yes. They reflect. But they also *de*flect. If I shone a torch onto a hand mirror and angled it, the light would go elsewhere. I can't believe it's taken me this long to realise it,' she mused.

'So?' Angus was frowning.

'So, a magic mirror – with the glass painted black, like the one found on Molly's body. One way it could be used is for scrying. Seeing the future and suchlike.'

'She didn't have much of a future. Minutes, at best, after she ingested the poison,' Angus said.

'Right. But witches *also* use mirrors to deflect curses. It's like psychic self-defence,' Temerity continued. 'What if the murderer placed the mirror near the body to put us off the scent? What if that mirror was enchanted to deflect attention away from the killer? Put there to make us think that Molly was caught up in some kind of witchcraft, herself – but instead, what it was actually doing was diverting our gaze from the truth?'

'That would mean that the murderer was a witch. Or knew enough about witchcraft for it not to make much difference,' Angus replied. 'That doesn't leave us with a very wide pool. In fact, it incriminates you and Tilda more than anyone.'

Temerity walked up the last few steps. At the top of the stairs, a wide, wine-coloured carpeted hallway stretched out, with various doors leading from it. *This feels ominous*, she thought. *Not in a good witchy way, either.*

'Maybe. But it also points to one other person. Someone who makes herbal potions for the villagers. Someone whose son thinks he's been cursed.' Temerity looked wide-eyed at Angus. 'Someone who made some kind of herbal concoction for the number one suspect in a murder investigation. And if the mirror was… enchanted somehow to divert our attention away from the real murderer, if it worked, then Ben isn't the one responsible—'

Angus finished her sentence. 'We have to find her.'

Chapter 26

Angus opened the first door on the left and switched on the light; it was a bathroom. 'Try the others.' He nodded, opening the next door on the left which appeared to be a guest bedroom.

Temerity tried the first door, but it was locked. The second was a utility cupboard containing all the usual things: vacuum, mop, cleaning products. She very nearly managed to knock everything over, but caught the mop at the last minute and righted it. *Come on, Temerity. Just try not to be clumsy for once in your life*, she willed herself. *This really isn't the time.*

She expected another spare room when she opened the third door, but when she turned on the light, there was a weak cry and she saw that she had woken Lady Dalcairney, who looked tiny in a wide four-poster bed, propped up by pillows. Temerity looked at her watch; it was only a little past seven p.m. Surely the Lady couldn't be asleep already, even if she was a little fragile these days?

'Oh! Lady Dalcairney! I didn't mean to…' Temerity began, but the old woman screamed a feeble, thin warble and clutched the sheet under her chin.

'Leave me alone! Liz! Liz!' The old woman was genuinely terrified at Temerity's sudden appearance and Temerity felt awful. She approached the bed with her hands up, as if she was being arrested herself. *Oh gods, this escalated fast. Where's a man raised by wolves when you need one?* It wasn't the time to make jokes, but her nerves were on edge.

'It's okay! It's all right, Lady Dalcairney. I'm Temerity Love, I visited last week with my sister,' Temerity explained in as soothing a tone as she could manage. Lady Dalcairney twisted the thick, blood-red duvet in her thin hands.

'Witches! Be gone! I'm a good Christian woman!' Her shaking hand reached around her neck and she pulled out the same gold crucifix as before, holding it up in the light as if it was a shield. Temerity stood nervously by the side of the bed.

'Please, Lady Dalcairney. I'm not here to hurt you. I just want to ask you some questions,' she repeated, trying not to sound as panicked as she felt. This was straight out of a bad horror movie but about two thousand per cent less entertaining.

Angus appeared in the doorway.

'David? David, is that you?' the old woman's voice quavered and Temerity wondered if hers and Angus's theory was right. How could Lady Dalcairney be Molly's murderer? It didn't make any sense.

'No, Lady Dalcairney. I'm Constable Harley, Lost Maidens Loch Police,' Angus said, coming in and sitting at the end of the bed on the opposite side. 'I'm so sorry for the late hour, but we wanted to ask you something about the herbal... potion you made for Ben McKinley.'

The grey–haired woman sat up a little on her pillows and reached out for him.

'Oh, thank goodness. Constable, this woman is trying to put a curse on me. I knew she would show herself, eventually. She's tortured me all these years.' The Lady was on the edge of tears; kindly, Angus reached for her bony, birdlike hand with his wide, reassuring palm.

'Maybe you're confused. Miss Love runs the antique shop in the village,' he said.

'I know who she is! Witches, all of them. Cursed me! Cursed us all!' Lady Dalcairney screamed. Temerity took a deep breath.

'I'd never met you before last week. How could I have cursed you?' Temerity asked, appalled that anyone could think she really had done such a thing, but also saddened by what was clearly a reasonably advanced stage of dementia. She knew Lady Dalcairney was a confused old woman, but it was still hurtful to be accused of something so horrible.

Angus nodded at the door, indicating Temerity should stand way from the bed. As soon as she did, the elderly woman seemed to calm down a little.

'I'm a godly woman. This is a godly house,' she repeated to Angus, who nodded.

'Of course, Lady Dalcairney. I can see that. When you say that someone has cursed you for years, what do you mean?'

She shuddered.

'They think they can get in here, but I'm protected by my faith,' she said, still gripping the crucifix. 'Years, it's been. When Emma drowned – and her going to have a child, too, I knew it then. There was a curse on us. Then Claire left us. Anthony was always a difficult boy, of course. We had to work hard to discipline him. And then, David was consorting with them.'

'Them?' Angus enquired evenly.

'The ones in the shop. Evil. Demons in that place. David used to come home stinking of that smell, that smoke they used to call their familiars. I told him, *They've cursed us. Don't go there any more*. But he didn't understand. He thought they were helping get rid of it.'

So far, Lady Dalcairney wasn't telling them anything new, although Temerity doubted that David Dalcairney would have shared his beliefs about the curse with his mother. But if he hadn't told her, it was strange that they had somehow come to the same conclusion.

'Tell me about the things you make for the villagers.' Angus changed the subject. 'My grandmother used to give me peppermint leaves in hot water when I had a stomach-ache. That kind of thing. She seemed to know all the old cures.'

Temerity was surprised that Angus had even the most basic knowledge of herbal medicine, but more than that, she was impressed at how he had managed to calm the old lady down. She'd never seen him like this before.

'Oh, yes. My mother taught me, her mother taught her. The old ways. When I was just a teenager, I was friends with the baker's daughter in the village. I'd go over in the boat and pick up the bread order for our housekeeper; I liked to do it. I could steer that boat as well as any boy.' For a moment, a light appeared in Lady Dalcairney's eyes.

'One day, I was there, playing with Jill in her back garden before I took the bread back in the boat and the baker, Mr Eadie, came out coughing from the bakery. He was trying to stop himself coughing all over the bread, I suppose, but he looked fit to die. Anyway, Mother had told me, for coughs, you should mix thyme and mallow root in milk if you have it. In those days, of course, we knew how to recognise plants. So I made it up for Jill's father and his cough went away.'

'I see. So, after that, people asked you to help them?'

'Yes. Mother told me other things, too, when I got a little older. Little love powders, old ways to protect your house, simple things to do. But they seemed to work.' Lady Dalcairney closed her eyes. 'I'm so dreadfully tired all the time, dear. I don't know why.' Her voice grew slower.

'Lady Dalcairney? Please, if I can just ask you one more question. What was in the love potion you made for Ben McKinley?' Angus asked. Her eyes fluttered open.

'McKinley? I'm sorry, dear. I don't know names.'

'He's a tall fellow. Teacher at the local school. Dark hair,' Angus said. 'He came here and you talked in the garden.'

Lady Dalcairney closed her eyes again.

'I don't remember, Constable,' she said. 'But my memory has been very bad lately.'

'Can you tell me what you put in the love potion?' Angus tried again. Lady Dalcairney sighed.

'Rose petals; dried, ground rosehip; cardamom seeds; dried hibiscus petals – grind them up and drink them in water like a draught,' she murmured as she closed her eyes. 'Simple things.'

Angus stood up; Lady Dalcairney was asleep.

The bedroom door swung open and Liz stood silhouetted in the light from the hallway. Behind her stood Sally, like an ominous shadow.

'May I ask what you're doing up here, Temerity Love?' Liz asked and her voice had none of its former friendliness.

Chapter 27

'Liz! Hello.' Temerity tried to make her voice pleasant and neutral, but she knew she sounded guilty. They had no good reason to be interrogating a frail old woman in her bedroom, even if they did think she might be a murderer. However, now that Temerity had met Lady Dalcairney, it seemed unlikely that she was.

'What're ye doin' here?' Liz repeated. 'Ye cannae be up here. Get out.'

Temerity felt immense gratitude that Angus was with her: at least, as a policeman, he could have a reason for being in most places. He stood up and Liz shrank back slightly; Temerity realised that she hadn't seen him, maybe because the light was behind her.

'We came to see you, Liz. The Laird let us in. We thought we heard the Lady in distress, so we came up. She was shouting for you; in the Laird's absence, surely, as the Lady's main carer, you should be in the house and not be leaving her alone?' Angus had his sternest expression on and Temerity marvelled at the effect it had on the housekeeper, whose tone changed immediately.

'Ah, I see. You're right, of course, Constable. I had popped outside very briefly to pull up some vegetables for tomorrow's meals and it took a wee bit longer than I thought. I did think David would let me know when he left, so I could come back in,' she explained. Temerity detected a sudden deference in her voice that absolutely hadn't been there when she had thought it had just been Temerity up here. 'Sally came and found me just now; she heard noises up here but was too afraid to come on her own.' Liz stood aside and indicated a frightened-looking Sally.

'I see,' Angus continued and led Temerity past Liz into the hall. 'Maybe we can talk to you now?'

'Oh, certainly, Constable. Sally will escort ye to the lounge. I'll follow ye. I've just got tae see to something.' Liz watched them go down before she entered Lady Dalcairney's room; Temerity could feel her stare on her back as they followed Sally down the stairs.

'She's acting strangely,' Temerity whispered to Angus, once they were downstairs. Sally showed them to the same room Temerity had eaten cake and drunk tea and whisky in the night of the rescue. As before, she stood silently in the corner, not saying anything, her arms by her sides. Temerity wondered if she was, in fact, able to speak at all.

'Yes. Maybe,' he whispered back. 'I don't think Lady Dalcairney can be the murderer. She can hardly sit up.'

'But she did confess to making herbal remedies – she could have poisoned Molly. And there's the stag, too. The Dalcairney motif on their coat of arms.' She pointed at the stone mantelpiece, where the stag's outline, chasing pheasants, was carved above the wide fireplace. 'I saw a stag in visions, twice. Once when I touched the mirror and when I touched the mug Molly drank out of. I'm sure it means that there's some connection between Molly's murder and the Dalcairneys, but if the murderer isn't Lady Dalcairney, who is it? David?'

'It might be,' Angus answered in a low voice.

Liz appeared in the doorway before they could carry on the conversation.

'Now then. Can I get you both something? Tea? Something stronger?' she asked. Her manner was wholly unlike earlier; now, she was as warm and welcoming as she had always been.

'Oh no, we're fine, thank you. We were just passing – walking – and we thought we'd drop in,' Temerity explained, seriously hoping that Angus could continue to finesse his way out of this situation and come up with a good reason for them dropping by.

'Ah, I see.' Liz looked curiously at them both. 'And what can I do for you? I'd normally be heading home by now, but of course, David has an evening appointment, so I'm here for the night.'

'Aren't you usually here at night?' Temerity asked.

'No. Sally is in night residence, as a rule,' Liz nodded at the silent young woman. 'You can go, dear. Make sure Lady Dalcairney has settled down, would you?' Sally nodded and left the room. Liz sighed. 'What a night.'

'Well, Liz,' Angus began. 'We were wondering if—'

A scream cut through the house, stopping Angus.

'What the...?' Temerity stood up, but Liz was ahead of them. She ran through into the hall and headed upstairs.

'It's Lady Dalcairney. I was afraid of this. It sounds like she's having one of her bad turns. Stay here, I'll go to her,' she panted, running up the stairs as the screaming got louder.

'Can we do anything?' Angus called up after her, but Liz shook her head. 'It's all right. This is fairly common, especially when she's had some kind of excitement or disturbance,' she replied. 'Probably best if we catch up another time, though. Do you mind? I just know I'll be up here a while calming her down.'

Temerity and Angus exchanged a glance; Temerity could see that Angus was as suspicious as she was. Somehow, the scream had come at exactly the right time to stop Liz having to answer any difficult questions – and just a few minutes after Sally had been told to check on Lady Dalcairney.

'Of course.' Angus nodded and handed Temerity her coat. 'If you're sure. Do you want me to telephone for an ambulance?'

'No, no. I'm sure. Thank you.' The screams intensified. 'If you don't mind, I have to leave you to let yourselves out!' she called from the top of the stairs. Temerity waved and opened the door; Angus shut it behind them.

'I don't like that one bit,' he said as soon as the door was closed. 'If that happens regularly, that woman should be in professional care.'

'Hmmm.' Temerity frowned. 'What d'you think Liz was doing up there? Before she came down, just now?'

'I don't know. Here, come on. I want to see what she was doing when we got here. Pulling up vegetables in the dark? I don't think so.' Angus took her hand and led her around the side of the house, avoiding the lounge that looked out over the loch. The garden was dark, but Angus produced a small torch from his pocket. 'Always be prepared.' He grinned at her and clicked it on; despite being small, the torch was bright.

'You're quite the boy scout,' Temerity quipped.

'On my evenings off.'

'Do you always have that with you?' Temerity asked as they followed a mud path between overgrown bushes; she thought some of them were brambles.

'You never know when you're going to find yourself blundering around in the dark. Admittedly, blundering with a witch gives it an added dimension.' He chuckled and Temerity was relieved that they seemed to have moved past their earlier uncomfortable moment.

'Fifth-dimension crime solving.' Temerity saw his confused expression. 'Don't worry. Witch joke.'

'Okay…' Angus moved the torchlight beam to the right. 'What's that?'

'What?' An owl hooted and Temerity suddenly started to feel spooked. Even though she was here with Angus Harley, a prickle of dread had just gone up her spine.

'That. Over there. Some kind of out-house.'

The torchlight picked out a shadowy, huddled wooden shed, partially hidden by a tree that grew next to it. They picked their way through more bramble bushes; as Temerity got closer she could see that ivy covered half of the planks.

'Spooky,' Angus said. 'But it looks like it's in reasonably regular use. Look, that padlock's pretty new.'

Temerity stopped at the door to the shed and examined the silvery padlock, which held the door closed. Angus rubbed at the window with his sleeve and peered inside.

'Too dark to see anything.' He shone his torch in and shook his head. 'Is it definitely locked?'

'Yep.' Temerity was disappointed; she really wanted to see what was inside.

'Hmmm. Why lock it, a random falling-down shed in a private garden? Think she was out here?'

'Who? Liz?' Temerity looked back at the house. 'I don't know. Maybe.'

Angus followed Temerity's gaze thoughtfully.

'I think we need to see inside,' he said.

'But it's padlocked,' she said. *We're still in a horror movie and now I've somehow turned into the girl who wails 'but what shall we doooo?' at the strong man*, Temerity thought. *How did this happen?*

Angus smiled and reached into his pocket.

'Boy scout,' he repeated and slid something into the lock and turned. It popped open.

Chapter 28

The shed was the size of a large bedroom. It may have appeared to be a shambling shack from the outside, but inside, it was almost cosy. On the bare wood floor, someone had placed a faded blue rug. The bare wood insides of the shed had been draped with a mixture of velvet and silk fabrics, stapled to hold them in place.

A side table sat against the back wall and on it were a number of objects that Temerity instantly recognised as witchcraft-related: half-burned white candles in cast iron candlesticks; puddles of wax that had pooled on the small table. There was a chalice and a small heatproof casserole dish that contained the remnants of incense resin burned on charcoal, but that was where the similarity to any altar of Temerity's ended.

Instead of fresh flowers, garlands and pictures of the gods, this table was littered with bird claws, bird heads and sigils – ritual markings – in what Temerity thought might be blood – animal or human – marked on white cotton. *Grisly. We're still in horror movie territory.*

Temerity wondered if all this belonged to Sally, and then dismissed the thought. As a witch herself she ought to be immune to being suspicious of people because they wore black and were somewhat forbidding in their manner.

On the table was a ragged poppet doll; on its head was sewn grey wool to represent hair and the Dalcairney crest was drawn on its chest. It was pinned by its hands and feet to a piece of cardboard covered in white cotton and a strip of the white material was tied around where its eyes should be, as if to blind it.

Angus went to pick up the doll, but Temerity batted his hand away.

'Don't touch it,' she warned. 'It's a poppet doll. And unless I'm very much mistaken, it's one representing Lady Dalcairney.' Temerity could feel the intent that had been infused into the doll and it wasn't pleasant. Just being near it made her feel choked and confused. She stepped away, looking around her.

'What's a poppet doll? Like a voodoo doll?' Angus made a repulsed face. 'I didn't know anyone actually did stuff like that outside the movies.'

'People do stuff like this,' she answered grimly. 'You can use poppets for good magic, healing, love spells, that sort of thing, too. But I don't think this is good. Look, she's being pinned to a bed. Blindfolded. Whoever made this wants Lady Dalcairney out of the way for some reason. Not dead, but incapacitated. Which she is.'

Angus raised his eyebrows.

'We've just seen that she can't get out of bed. But surely that's because of some kind of illness.'

Temerity gave him a look.

'Really? Even when you've seen this, you think she's just poorly? She's not. Someone's controlling her. They could be drugging her, too.' *Aaaand we're back to reality*, Temerity thought. *Magic versus logic. Only, I'm being completely logical here. No more B-movie heroines.*

Angus nodded.

'It definitely doesn't look good, I'll agree with you there,' he conceded. 'What's that?' he knelt down, pointing the torch at a box under the small table. 'Here, hold the torch.' He passed it to Temerity and opened it.

'Well, these look familiar.' He held up two Russian matryoshka dolls: one featuring a blue patterned dress and black hair and one with a yellow and pink colour scheme.

*

'Wow. That seems a pretty unlikely coincidence.' Temerity held out her hand for one of the dolls; she knew that Angus was, like her, thinking of the red matryoshka doll that had sat on the windowsill of Molly Bayliss's room.

'Agreed.' Angus shook out the box but there was nothing else in it apart from dust. 'We should see if there are the same kind of markings in these. Even without that, it's incriminating. Especially found under this.' He indicated the altar. 'We could probably get a handwriting expert to look at the markings on Molly's doll and compare them to those –' he nodded at the blood sigils, soaked into the white cotton – 'plus there's DNA testing. If that blood's human.'

Temerity could hear Angus, but she had closed her eyes instinctively on touching the wooden doll. She took a deep breath and saw a tunnel spooling in front of her; his voice was suddenly a distant echo.

What are you, where have you been, matryoshka? she asked the toy, inside her mind. The tunnel continued on: grey, without feature. No pictures or words came to her. However, Temerity was suddenly aware that though she wasn't receiving anything visual apart from the tunnel, she was getting a feeling and it was sadness. No, something a little different, loneliness even. And something else. A fierce sense of protection which was almost motherly.

She opened her eyes.

'I lost you there.' Angus looked concerned. 'You all right?'

'I'm fine.' Temerity remembered the last time she had performed her talent in front of Angus; he'd admitted there was something in it, but she knew he remained unconvinced. She thought, for now, she would keep her feelings to herself. 'What were you saying?'

'Blood. On the… napkin thing. Whatever it is.'

'It might be animal blood,' Temerity said, pulling herself together. 'But you should probably confiscate this entire shed. I mean, whoever this all belongs to is doing some shady stuff,' she added. The emotions were still with her. She placed the doll on the altar table, not wanting it in her hands; as soon as she put it down, the feelings evaporated. A terrible kind of gnawing sadness and fear. And that maternal sense of having to protect someone or something. What did that mean?

'Well, it can only really belong to the Laird or Liz,' Angus replied. 'Or Sally. Or it could be someone else.'

'Probably not Ben McKinley, though, right?' Temerity met his gaze.

'Probably not,' Angus agreed. 'But just because we've found a suspicious lair in the grounds of Dalcairney Manor doesn't mean Ben isn't Molly's murderer.'

'That's true.'

Temerity didn't want to be there any more; the energy of the whole place was hateful. As someone who was used to raising power, she could feel all the magic that had occurred there, but she could also feel how different it was to what she was used to. She could recognise power, but this was like the discordant hum of a child in a horror movie instead of an angelic song. It was all wrong; the shed was wrong, the altar was wrong, the Russian doll was wrong. *Tilda would have a big word for this, but it's… yucky,* she thought. *Top marks for vocabulary, Temerity.*

'What is it… Occam's Razor? The thing that people like you tend to quote?' she said, wrapping her arms around herself.

'People like me?' He glanced at her, but she couldn't make out his expression in the dark.

'You know. Self-professed logicians.'

'Ah.' Angus was searching the shed, but there didn't seem to be anything else particularly obvious. 'You mean, the likeliest person is the killer? If it looks like doggie doo and smells like doggie doo, then it *is* doggie doo?'

'If you want to put it that way, yes.' Temerity really wanted to leave, but she couldn't help smirking at Angus' obvious attempt to avoid swearing.

'Well, that *is* often true. But not always. McKinley might have been here. He'd been up at the house, after all. Or he could be in league with someone else. This isn't a crime scene, but it's suspicious enough to be relevant to our enquiries. And if it provides evidence that McKinley isn't the murderer, then we need to know that, too. On the other hand, this could relate to a separate crime. If we can in some way prove Lady Dalcairney's being drugged, that's another investigation.'

'Can we go now? This place is giving me the heebie-jeebies.' Temerity stamped her feet both to drive out the cold and the sense of foreboding and sadness about the place.

'I'm going to need to come back and dust this whole place for fingerprints and take proper pictures. I'll have to see if Alf's up for coming up and doing some DNA analysis, too. I'm guessing as it's not an official crime scene, we won't get the paperwork sorted to allow forensics up here until tomorrow now.' Angus sighed and looked at his watch. 'The Inspector's not going to be happy and I'm going to be up late.' He took out his phone and snapped pictures of the whole shed, close-ups of the altar, the poppet doll, the Russian dolls.

'Come on. Let's go.' He took Temerity's arm and manoeuvred her out of the shed, snapping the padlock shut behind them.

'Whoever owns all that will know we've been in there,' Temerity said in a low voice, as they made for the edge of the loch.

'How? We didn't disturb anything. I closed that box back up.'

'They'll just know. Energetically.'

'Well, maybe that will force their hand in some way,' he said as he took her hand; the muddy edge of the loch was uneven as it had been before. 'That's when criminals get sloppy; when things happen they weren't expecting and they have to react fast.'

It was a relief to have Angus Harley's strong, broad hand gripping hers. Warmth started to spread back into Temerity's fingers and toes.

She told herself that it was walking that was making her warm again; the benefit of movement and the relief at being out of that spooky wooden shack. But as they walked and the track levelled out onto an even pathway, Angus kept a hold of her hand and Temerity didn't do anything to stop him.

Chapter 29

The next morning, Temerity found Angus with the Inspector sitting at their usual table in The Singing Kettle. Temerity made her order with Muriel at the counter for a bowl of porridge with honey and a large mug of tea; she'd come straight from home without even having breakfast, curious about what the Inspector would say when Angus recounted the events of the night before at Dalcairney Manor.

She'd lain awake for most of the night, thinking about it and she couldn't get the Russian doll out of her head. There was no doubt in Temerity's mind that whoever had given Molly Bayliss a Russian doll as a child was the same person as the inhabitant, or user, of the wooden shack, but that meant someone at that house had known Molly when young. How had they known her and why had they given her gifts? Had this been a close relationship or an occasional one? It made no sense, except that it did, somewhere along the line and Temerity was irritated that she couldn't work out *where* yet.

On the counter, next to the cutlery, which was arranged in pottery jars, and the sauces – plastic bottles of ketchup, mayonnaise, mustard and brown sauce – was a pile of smallish pamphlets. Temerity picked one up, recognising the home-made appearance. She frowned at it and dropped it on the table before taking off her coat and hanging it on the nearby coat–stand.

'I see T.L. Hawtry has been at it again,' she said, dryly. 'New volume. This time it's *A History of Lost Maidens Loch*. Less immediately sensational, I suppose.' She smiled as she sat down. 'There might even be some facts in this one, you never know. Did you ever find out who was producing these things? Morning. Sorry.' Temerity remembered her social graces a little late.

Kim Hyland was halfway through a full Scottish breakfast and mopped up his baked beans with his potato pancake with a contented sigh. 'Never mind that, ye couple o' hoons. More like ye tell me what ye thought ye were doin' up at Dalcairney Manor without a warrant last night.'

Angus had nodded to Temerity as she sat down; she felt herself blushing, thinking about her hand in his on the entire walk home last night. He'd walked her to her door and for a moment she'd wondered if he was going to kiss her, but he had merely squeezed her hand and thanked her for her help. *If last night was a date, it was the weirdest date in the history of romance*, she thought.

'It was my fault. I suggested going there. Angus and I happened to meet in here for dinner last night and—' Temerity started, but the Inspector shushed her.

'I didnae need tae know aboot that. What I need ye to tell me is, this witchcraft stuff that Angus is tellin' me. It's not, I, how shall I say it? I'm not goin' tae go up there an' embarrass the Laird's religion or his, errr, kinky predilections, like? Because that could be quite awkward.'

Temerity remembered the Laird leaving the house for his fundraising dinner, saying that the Inspector would be there. They probably knew each other quite well; they were roughly the same age and they were both, in different ways, powerful figures in Lost Maidens Loch.

'I don't think so. I think it's real witchcraft and, in this case, malignant. I think someone in that house has put some kind of a curse on Lady Dalcairney. And we think the whole place needs to be fingerprinted and tested for DNA. Has Angus mentioned the blood?'

The Inspector sighed.

'Aye, he has. I just wanted tae check with ye that ye thought it was connected tae the case. Thing is, I'm very friendly with the Laird, so… I want tae have good reason to have tae fingerprint the man.'

'I understand. But we don't think you can ignore this.' Temerity nodded at Angus. He showed the Inspector the photos he'd taken and the Inspector's expression changed from his usual easy calm to a deep frown. *Yep. Pretty gruesome*, Temerity thought. 'The biggest link from the shed is the Russian doll at this stage. If we can prove it's the same make as the one Molly owned, it would suggest a link from someone at Dalcairney Manor to her.' Temerity frowned. 'Though, admittedly, a weak link. It's all connected somehow, though; the witch mirror, the altar in the shed, the love potion. I think whoever put that mirror on the body is the same person that uses the shed. And that means they've put some kind of curse on Lady Dalcairney,'

The Inspector raised his eyebrows.

'Good Lord,' he muttered.

'There's something else,' she said. 'It doesn't mean anything in particular, but I've been… seeing signs,' she said, trying to work out how to explain the feathers.

'Signs?' Hyland asked.

'Yes. Like… portents. Not road signs.'

'Portents of what, lassie?'

'Umm… well, Tilda and I did a, err… ritual a few weeks ago. Like a kind of meditation,' she added hastily, seeing both Hyland and Harley's expressions cloud over. 'I was told in that… *meditation* that I would start seeing feathers on people whose judgement was coming.'

'And you've seen them?

Temerity nodded.

'On three people so far. Beth, Ben McKinley and Liz up at Dalcairney Manor. Well… Liz's skirt had a feather pattern on it, I took it as the same thing.'

'And you think this means they're guilty? Of the murder?' Angus asked.

'No. But it's guilt of some sort. Involvement somehow. Beth Bennett was charged with shoplifting. We know McKinley's involved in Molly's death somehow. Liz, I don't know.'

'Right. Well. Lots of guilty people in the world, lassie. But we're investigating one murder, aye. Still, it's good tae know.' Hyland smiled at her. 'We'll drive up tae the Manor in a wee while an' I'll talk tae Liz and David aboot all this. Might as well eat first.'

Muriel brought Temerity's porridge and tea to the table and placed it in front of her.

'More propaganda, Muriel?' Temerity held up the pamphlet with one hand and sipped her tea with the other.

'Aye, well, in a place like Lost Maidens Loch, there's a lot of history.' Muriel bridled. 'It's not like ah wrote it. Just doin' a public service, stockin' them. Fer tourists and the like.'

Temerity opened it towards the middle of the brochure to a double page of black-and-white photos that looked as though they weren't taken very recently; it was entitled *Lost Maidens Memories*. Her eyes skimmed the captions which had been typed on what looked like a manual typewriter, cut out and stuck under the pictures with glue before photocopying.

Misty Loch, 1991. Sutherland's Boat Hire, 1968. Dalcairney Manor staff, 1979.

The first picture, of the loch, was identical to how it looked now on a misty day. The picture of Sutherland's Boat Hire featured what must have been the previous Mr Sutherland with, Temerity estimated, a four- or five-year-old Henry Sutherland, the current owner, standing next to his father and squinting up into the camera. Temerity ate a spoon of porridge and revelled in its sweet creaminess.

The last picture was of a group of men and women. The women wore maids' uniforms. Even though the picture was dated the late 1970s, they wore black dresses with white pinnies and the little white caps Temerity would have guessed belonged to the 1940s or before. Next to the four women, who looked to range in age from teens to middle age, there were two men in smart suits standing next to a couple of expensive-looking cars. The chauffeurs, maybe, or a butler and a driver.

As Temerity peered at the faces of the women in their ridiculous caps and aprons, she could swear that one of the younger ones – maybe she was twenty? – was Liz. Temerity spooned up more of the porridge.

Temerity passed the open pamphlet to Angus across the table and tapped the picture. Muriel had returned somewhat huffily behind the counter.

'Look familiar?' she asked. He stared at the picture and frowned.

'Liz?'

'That's what I thought.'

'It does look like her. But I didn't know she'd been at the house that long.'

'She told me she'd been employed as housekeeper a few years ago.' Temerity looked up at the Inspector, who was finishing a sausage. 'How long has the Laird's housekeeper worked for him? Liz?' she asked.

'Aye, Liz has been there forever,' Kim replied. 'Knew her a bit when she started as a maid. I was just the Constable then. She used to be friendly with Mrs Hyland. That's how we met, in fact. Time was that the young Laird would go tae discos and parties with some of the girls on the staff. Not very seemly, I suppose, but they were of an age. I think Liz was keen on him, but o' course nothin' was ever goin' tae happen. A wee while later he met Emma, his first wife.'

'Liz had feelings for the Laird. All that time ago,' Temerity said slowly, piecing it together in her mind. She remembered the terrible feeling of sadness she'd felt in touching the Russian doll. If it was Liz that used that shack and everything in it, maybe she had a grudge against her employers. Maybe the Laird had broken her heart, once, when they were young. But what was the link to Molly? And why stay in a job that makes you wait on a man that spurned you?

Angus looked at the pamphlet again.

'It does look like her,' he admitted. 'So why lie about it?'

'I don't know,' Temerity mused. 'It seems odd.'

The Inspector pushed away his empty plate.

'Come on, then. I take it yer comin' with us, Temerity Love? I can't see ye stayin' away, not with that inquisitive look on yer face.'

'Yes, please,' she said and followed the Inspector outside where the patrol car was parked. Yet, as soon as they left the café, Temerity knew something was wrong.

The normally clean, cold air of Lost Maidens Loch smelled of Tilda's occasional log fires when she burned wood that was too green. It was the smell of smoke and instinctively Temerity looked over, across the loch.

On the opposite side of the loch, a huge cloud of grey smoke was billowing up into the morning air. Beneath the smoke, they could see fire flickering up against the walls of the tall stone house.

Dalcairney Manor was on fire.

Chapter 30

When the patrol car screeched to a halt halfway up the long drive to Dalcairney Manor, smoke was billowing from the upstairs windows, but the house seemed eerily deserted.

'Oh, no,' Temerity gasped as she got out of the car and held her sleeve over her nose and mouth to avoid breathing in the acrid smoke. 'Is anyone still in there, do you think?'

The Inspector was on his radio, calling for assistance.

'Fire crew cannae get here for about another half hour at the best. I've called in an ambulance, they'll be here as soon as they can, but looks like it's just us for the moment.' He grimaced and went to the back of the patrol car, pulling out two oxygen masks. He handed one to Angus.

'We'll have tae go in, lad.' Hyland looked grim. 'Every minute counts. I need yer experience in this, okay?'

Angus had gone white, but he nodded and pulled on the mask. It was attached to an oxygen canister that could be strapped around the body. 'Follow me.' He nodded at the Inspector.

Oh, no. Temerity thought. *This is his worst nightmare.* The story of how Angus had got his scars was horrifying. Surely he couldn't go back into another burning building?

She caught at Angus's sleeve.

'You don't have to. I know you're scared,' she tried to reassure him, but he shook his head.

'I do have to. Someone could be trapped in there.' Angus shook her hand away and refused to meet her eyes. She could tell from touching him how terrified he was; Temerity had a sudden vision, when she touched his arm, of Angus running into another burning building; of the smoke in his lungs, coughing, coughing and then looking up to see the flaming timbers about to fall on his head. She knew he felt like a frightened child, dwarfed by the house, by the fire that they could all see blazing in the upstairs windows.

David Dalcairney came running around the side of the house. There was a black soot mark across his face in the shape of a feather.

Is that just me imagining it now, or is that a sign as well? Temerity wondered and filed the sight away for future analysis in her mind. She tried to catch Angus' eye, to see if he could see it too, but he was looking up at the Manor house.

'Oh, thank God. I couldn't find my phone... and the house line isn't working. Please, Kim, have you called an ambulance? Call whoever you can. Mother's trapped in there.' The Laird's eyes were wild and he was out of breath. He leaned on the outside of the Manor wall and coughed.

'Where is she?' Angus demanded.

'Upstairs. In her room. But the stairs are burning... I couldn't get to her...' The Laird coughed again, doubling over.

'What about the other maid? Sally?' Temerity demanded. The Laird shook his head.

'She's not here. She went home earlier this morning. Night shift.'

Convenient, Temerity thought.

'Temerity, look after David. There's whisky in a flask in the car and get the first aid kit out. Check him over, aye?' Hyland gripped the Laird's shoulders and looked him in the eyes. 'David. It's okay. I've called the fire service and the ambulance, but they're not goin' tae be here for a wee while, so me an' Angus are goin' tae see if we can get in. Apart from Lady Dalcairney, is there anyone else in the hoose?'

'Aye. I mean, I don't know. I haven't seen Liz; she should have been here, but I can't see her.'

'All right.' The Inspector nodded. 'C'mon, Harley. Let's go.'

Temerity watched, her heart in her throat, as both policemen stepped cautiously through the warped Manor house doors. Beyond, the hall was thick with black smoke. They disappeared into it like ghosts.

*

'How on earth did it start?' Temerity guided the Laird to the patrol car, made him sit in the passenger seat and handed him the flask, which she found in the glove compartment along with a map of Lost Maidens Loch, a fishing magazine and a half-eaten packet of peanuts. *Good to see the boys are concentrating on the important elements of police work,* she thought dryly. *At least there aren't any doughnuts.*

'No idea,' the Laird confessed. 'I'd gone for a sail and when I came back, this had happened. I walked into the hallway and it was full of smoke. I thought immediately of Mother – she was in her room… but I couldn't get to her. The whole upstairs is alight. I—' His voice broke.

'It's going to be okay,' Temerity reassured him, even though she was pretty sure they both knew it was a lie. 'Come on. We'll split up and search for Liz,' she suggested, watching as David Dalcairney drained the whisky flask, wiped his mouth and handed it back to her. *Fair enough,* she thought. If there was any time to drink an entire flask of whisky, she supposed that watching your house burn down was probably it.

'Do you think that's a good idea?' He looked up at the Manor. 'I don't think we should go into the house.'

Temerity tried not to think about what might be happening inside, right at this moment. Angus and Kim had oxygen. That was the main thing.

'I agree, but we can look outside and in the parts of the house that aren't burning. I'll go around to the back. I seem to remember you can get to the kitchen through the back door. I'll go that way and see how far I can get,' she suggested.

'All right. I'll check the conservatory and the boot room. I don't know how far the fire has spread,' he replied, wiping his hand over his face; the soot mark smudged into a random splodge of black on his skin.

'Okay,' she said, wrapping her scarf around her mouth to protect against the acrid smoke that filled the air. The house was devastated: the glass in the old-fashioned panelled windows was cracked, the stone was stained with soot. As they stood there, Temerity jumped as a whole window at the far end of the house from where they were standing fell out and smashed onto the drive.

'Maybe we shouldn't stand here. I know I'm a witch, but I've got no desire for any Wrath of God-type injuries,' she muttered. 'I'll meet you back here, okay? Be safe, David.' Temerity thought there was no point calling him Laird now; if you couldn't resort to first names whilst saving people from a burning building, then when could you?

She made her way to the side of the house and followed it around, taking care to stay as far as she could from the walls to avoid any other falling glass or something worse. The noise of the fire was intense; she would never have imagined that the sound of a house fire would be so chaotic, but she could hear regular crashes as, she supposed, furniture fell over; there was an ongoing creaking noise and other sounds she couldn't identify; a whistling, a kind of screaming noise.

Towards the back of the house, she came upon the untended vegetable garden again. She went to the back door of the kitchen, remembering when she had been here before and tried it, but the door wouldn't open. It was either locked from inside or the heat had warped the wood, making it difficult to open. Temerity tugged on the handle but to no avail. She peered through the glass. The kitchen didn't appear to be on fire, but it was filled with smoke. She concluded that the fire must be mainly upstairs, remembering what the Laird had said about there only being smoke in the hallway, too. Yet there was still a lot of smoke in the air, even at the back of the house which seemed less affected than the front.

There was no one in the kitchen as far as she could see, which was a relief. She joggled the handle again, but the door didn't open.

Stepping back, Temerity looked around her. Something wasn't right.

She walked away from the house and followed the path through the bushes and trees towards the shed she and Angus had investigated the night before.

Through the trees, there was light, but it shifted and leaped. Temerity's heart was in her mouth: she knew what she was going to see before she saw it.

The shed was on fire, too.

Chapter 31

She knew it was too late before it crumpled into a heap in front of her, the flames licking the old wood. She thought of the fabric wall hangings and the rugs; all it would take would be a candle flame flickering the wrong way and the whole thing would go up in a matter of minutes. But the Manor house and the shed at the same time? Too much of a coincidence.

The fire was too savage to get close to; Temerity could only stand by helplessly and watch it all burn. All the evidence they were going to trace; the fingerprints, the poppet doll pinned to the bed. The box of Russian dolls. She was glad she'd taken that one home; at least there was something left. But it was obvious: whoever the murderer was had known that she and Angus had found their secret place and set fire to it to get rid of the evidence.

Yet, why burn the house down, too? Temerity pondered, dejected that their discovery had been denied them. If you were the murderer and you had to destroy a shed, you could probably burn it to the ground without anyone knowing. What was the sense in setting fire to the Manor house, which would draw much more attention than you needed? Unless you had to silence someone who was in the house. Who you had been controlling by drugging them and using a poppet-doll curse.

Temerity shivered and turned back to face Dalcairney Manor. *Angus, be careful*, she thought, her heart clenching in sudden anxiety. If the murderer knew that she and Angus had seen everything, then they both might be in danger. She didn't care about herself; she knew that her sixth sense would protect her.

But Angus didn't have the gift of precognition. He didn't have visions or an uncanny sense of whether to trust people or not.

She wondered briefly if the Laird had found Liz; there was no sign of her here. She looked up the path, back to the house, as the kitchen door banged open. The Laird appeared from the inside, his arm over his mouth. *Speak of the devil* she thought. *And I was just thinking about precognition.* She waited for Liz to follow him out, but he was alone.

Temerity ran back up the path.

'David! Are you all right? I tried to get into the kitchen but the door was locked, or jammed,' she called out.

The Laird nodded to her and coughed for a few moments as he regained his breath.

'It was locked, Miss Love. Are *you* all right?' he spluttered.

'I'm fine, don't worry about me,' she reassured him. 'You sound terrible.'

'It's the smoke. I got in through the boot room. I tried to get up the back stairs but I couldn't,' he panted. The soot was all over his skin and clothes now.

'Look, there's something else.' Temerity beckoned him down the path; the shed was still blazing. The roof had fallen in and the flames were eating the walls. Melted, twisted shapes lay among the ash that had fallen around the outside; whatever they had once been, they were unrecognisable now.

'Oh dear Lord!' the Laird exclaimed. 'How did the fire manage to spread out here?' He looked confusedly back at the house. 'I don't understand… how is this possible?' He took a few steps closer to the burning wood. 'The whole garden would have to be on fire for this to have caught.'

'I don't think this was an accident,' Temerity said quietly. 'And maybe the house isn't an accident either,' she continued. 'Last night, Constable Harley and I found this shed. It was being used as some kind of… ritual space, by someone. There was a poppet doll there. I think it was meant to represent your mother.'

The Laird's eyes widened.

'What? This is just an old shed. There's nothing but garden tools in there. Maybe some bags of compost, a bit of weedkiller, that sort of thing. We haven't had a gardener working up here for a few years, so it's gone to ruin a bit, as you can see.' He held his hand out to indicate the garden. 'What do you mean, a ritual room?'

'You know what I mean. You visited Mother and Father. You spent time in theirs.' Temerity frowned.

The Laird looked at her blankly.

'Who would… I mean, I don't know who would be… doing that kind of thing. I mean, Mother, maybe… but she's been more or less bedridden for the past year or so.'

'Your mother? It seems unlikely, not least that she'd make a poppet-doll spell confining herself to her own bed.' Temerity found herself irritated, suddenly. It was obvious to her that the shed hadn't been used by Lady Dalcairney; she had felt no trace of her there apart from her hair, fixed onto the poppet. She was sure that the Lady had never set foot in there.

'She makes these lotions and potions, you see. Or at least, she used to,' the Laird continued. 'Time was, she was very active in the garden. Growing unusual plants, making up herbal tinctures and whatnot. Maybe she kept some of her old stuff in there. She never said, but she's a secretive old bird. That's probably what it was. Somewhere to dry herbs.'

Temerity shook her head.

'That's not what it was, David. I know the difference between hanging herbs and a space someone's been using for magic. And it had been used recently, too. There was a pentagram drawn on the floor. Lots of sigils drawn on, candles that had been used. There was an altar set out. You don't set out an altar and then leave it for a couple of years. That's something that's meant to be used.'

He frowned and looked at the shed again.

'Then I don't know. It could have been a stranger, I suppose? Looking for some kind of secret place to do their... sorcery?'

Temerity stared at the Laird in disbelief.

'Do you really think that's likely? Someone comes onto your land, repeatedly, at night, uses one of your outbuildings and you don't notice?' she interrogated him.

'It's feasible,' he shrugged. 'Someone could come up from the loch.'

'Don't you think that it might have been Liz?' Temerity suggested gently. 'We can't find her. There might be a reason for that.'

David Dalcairney stared uncomprehendingly at Temerity for a moment. Behind them, Temerity could hear sirens approaching. *Thank goodness*, she thought.

'Liz? A... witch?' he repeated. He looked back at the house. 'She did this?'

'Maybe. I don't know. And I don't know if she's a witch. She could be.' Temerity sighed.

'No. I can't believe it,' the Laird said, his brow furrowed. 'I'd have known. All these years she's been here. Inside my home. She's like family.'

'It makes sense...' Temerity continued. 'For some reason, she wanted to hurt your mother. Keep her bedridden and confused. She might very well have been doctoring her medicine. Drugging her. Why would she do that?'

'I have no idea.' The Laird frowned. Temerity met his eyes, but he looked away. 'Look, Miss Love. This is all very strange. But I think we should go back and see if Liz has turned up and I need to know what's happening with Mother. I can't be away long. I just hope the Constable and the Inspector managed to get to her.'

'But…' Temerity started to argue, but she realised he was right. The shed wasn't going anywhere and whatever evidence had been in there was lost now. *Angus*, she thought.

They had started a fire and Angus Harley had run into it, despite his fear. Like a poppet doll being pushed by an unseen hand.

Temerity started running towards the front of the house again. She was dimly aware that the Laird was following her.

'Angus!' she shouted, turning the corner. 'Angus, be careful!' she shouted. He was in danger; he'd been in danger from the minute he entered the house, but it was more than just the fire that might want to hurt him.

There was no point in shouting as he couldn't possibly have heard her, but she shouted nonetheless. The noise of the fire was almost deafening, worse as she approached the driveway that led to the front of the house. She jumped over a row of ornamental bushes and narrowly avoided landing on a large terracotta plant pot. Temerity had the strange feeling that she was too late, but she didn't know what she was too late for.

Her first feeling was relief when she saw the ambulance and fire engine.

But when she saw Angus Harley being wheeled out of the house on a stretcher, the relief evaporated like smoke.

Behind Angus, two firemen wheeled another stretcher. On it was a small figure; her grey hair was spread out over the white sheet.

'Mother!' David Dalcairney cried and ran to her side.

Yet, behind Lady Dalcairney, there was another stretcher, holding a body which was completely covered by a white sheet.

There were two people who hadn't been accounted for; either of them could be lying burned under that cover. Liz and Kim Hyland.

Chapter 32

'She battled on for a few days, but she was too fragile to recover from the smoke inhalation.' Tilda shook her head as the sisters listened to the radio in the kitchen. *There will be a memorial service for Lady Jane Balfour Dalcairney and Elizabeth Maitland at 11 a.m. on 29 March at St Peter's Church. All welcome, with refreshments after at The Singing Kettle.*

'It's terribly sad. And to have lost Liz, too.' Tilda looked forlorn. 'Such a terrible way to go.'

'Terrible, terrible,' Hebrides repeated. He was sitting on the back of one of the kitchen chairs; Tilda put a bowl of seed on the table and he hopped down to peck at it. His plumage was as grand as ever: deep cerulean blues merged with midnight and teal, depending on how his feathers caught the light. Temerity stroked his head.

'She was in the shed, the firemen said. It collapsed on her.' She shivered. 'It must have caught fire and either she was trying to put it out, or she set it on fire and got caught in there somehow. No one knew she was in there for ages. When we were there we looked for her. The Laird and I watched the shed burn. We… we didn't know. It had already collapsed.' Temerity started crying. After the bodies had been wheeled out, she'd been relieved to see Kim Hyland stagger out of the Manor house, soot-blackened but very much alive. But then she'd realised who had been under the sheet of the last stretcher that was taken onto the ambulance. 'They said they found her first. We were standing there arguing, but we didn't realise in all the confusion.'

'Oh, love. You couldn't have known!' Tilda enveloped her sister in a bear hug. 'You were doing your best.'

'I know, but I feel terrible.' Temerity sniffed.

'Terrible, terrible. Murdered!' Hebrides squawked.

'Hebrides! Not now!' Tilda scolded the parrot, who made a clicking noise and returned to eating his seeds. 'Is the Constable all right? You said he came out on a stretcher.'

'He's all right, apparently. Just minor smoke inhalation, so he'll have a cough for a little while, but that's all. He did pass out just as he got outside the building, though.' Temerity didn't add that when she had seen Angus being wheeled out with an oxygen mask on his face, her heart had skipped a beat and a terrible sense of dread had filled her. She also didn't describe the relief she felt when the Inspector had called her earlier in the morning to let her know that the Constable was all right and to enquire after her own health.

'So, d'you think Liz was the murderer?' Tilda made Temerity sit down at the kitchen table and sat opposite her, holding both her hands.

'It's the only logical conclusion. She panicked when she saw that someone had been in the shed. She must have suspected it was Angus and me; we'd visited unannounced. Liz could easily have doctored the love potion Lady Dalcairney made for Ben McKinley and she could have lied about him stealing the mirror.'

'Good grief.' Tilda shook her head.

'She didn't want us to see what she was up to, so she enchanted the scrying mirror – probably one she'd stolen from Lady Dalcairney and blacked out herself to turn it into a witch's mirror – and gave it to Ben when he visited that day. Muriel was used to Liz being courier for Lady Dalcairney's powders and potions, now that the Lady was more or less bedridden,' Temerity continued.

'Liz! Murdered!' Hebrides repeated, flapping his wings.

'He's getting upset. Picking up on your emotions,' Tilda said, clicking at the parrot and holding out her wrist. 'Hebrides. Come to Tilda. Cuddles.'

Hebrides flew to Tilda, who stroked his wings gently and crooned a little tune until he settled.

'But I don't understand why Liz wanted to kill Molly Bayliss – or keep Lady Dalcairney under her control, either,' Tilda continued in a quiet voice, handing her sister a muffin with her spare hand. 'Go on, eat. You're too thin.'

'That's what we need to find out still, about Molly, anyway.' Temerity frowned. 'I got a feeling when I was in that shed. There was terrible loss, sadness. Jealousy, too. Maybe Liz was jealous of Lady Dalcairney. You know, the haves and have-nots. Liz was a maid there all her life. It must have made her bitter. Taking care of the rich all her life.'

'Hmmm. I don't know,' Tilda mused, drawing the bowl of seeds to her so that Hebrides could eat them again. 'She could have found another job. Something kept her there. I think she was in love with the Laird and he didn't love her. Remember? The Inspector told you Liz and the Laird went to parties together, even though she was in service at the time. Alf told me once that David Dalcairney broke a few hearts in the village when he was younger.'

'Maybe,' Temerity said. 'But that doesn't explain it. Why kill his mother and a teacher she had no connection to?'

'Maybe the Laird was having an affair with Molly,' Tilda suggested. 'Liz was jealous.'

'He was a bit old for her.' Temerity made a face. 'If I'm being honest, I don't see it.'

'But he's a powerful man. Rich, titled. Molly might have gone for him.'

Hebrides made a rude noise.

'There's been no suggestion they were seeing each other, but I suppose it's possible…' Temerity mused. 'I'll mention it to the Inspector. But now he's got Ben McKinley in lock up, he thinks the murder's been solved. The fire was an unfortunate accident.'

'Really? What about the shed, the Russian dolls?'

'Coincidence for the dolls and one person's spiritual proclivities. He says the shed obviously belonged to Liz; she might well have been up to no good, cursing the Lady, but they're both dead, so case closed. That information hasn't been released to the public. He doesn't want to add fuel to the gossip mill. No point bringing it all up now, he says.' Temerity shrugged.

'Protecting the Dalcairney name.' Tilda shook her head.

'Well, not necessarily.' Temerity had thought of that, but she didn't think that was what was going on. 'There is no point going over all that if you genuinely believe that what happened at the house wasn't connected to Molly Bayliss's murder.'

'But you don't believe that, do you, Tem?' Tilda peered into her sister's eyes. They both had brown eyes, but Temerity's were deep brown and Tilda's were more of a hazel. Temerity shook her head.

'No. They're connected, but I don't know how. And it's suspicious that Sally wasn't there when the fire happened.'

'The one who hates you,' Tilda observed. 'But she wasn't supposed to be there, you said. Night shift.'

'I know, but it's suspicious that the fire starts at about the same time she would have left to go home, isn't it?' Temerity brooded.

'I'm sure the Inspector will check it out,' Tilda said.

'Liz. Murdered,' Hebrides said, followed by one of his little songs; part of a jingle he'd picked up from the radio. *You've tried the rest now try the best: Abercrommmm-beeees!*

'Hebrides, shhh.' Tilda shushed the parrot. 'I'm going to let him out for a fly. I think he needs it. Go and do some work.'

'Hmmm.' Temerity played with the paper muffin case. 'If I take my mind off things, a connection might appear.' She thought of her multiplying inbox as clients from all over the world emailed her with their provenance requests.

'Probably a good idea,' Tilda agreed as she went to the back door and opened it, letting in a burst of wind. Hebrides flew out. 'There. That should help him settle down. I'm going for a bath.'

Temerity hardly noticed her sister as she padded back through the kitchen and up the stairs. She had opened her laptop and was looking at her emails. The first one was from Angus Harley.

Chapter 33

Dear Temerity,

I'm in Edinburgh at General Register House, where they've been helping me continue researching Molly Bayliss's family. I thought you would want to know what I found out and the Inspector says it's okay for you to know, as long as it's kept confidential.

It seems likely that Molly Bayliss was David and Emma Dalcairney's daughter. As you'll see from the attached certificate, Emma Dalcairney gave her maiden name of Ross on the birth certificate. Your visions of the stag were correct – there was a connection between Molly and the Dalcairneys.

We can surmise that the then-pregnant Emma obviously didn't drown in the loch, but left David Dalcairney. Either they had a row and she left and maybe he started the rumour that she had drowned, or she left and he believed the rumour started by someone else.

'Well, I didn't see that coming.' Temerity muttered to herself as she read the scanned birth certificate attached to Angus' email. She went back to the email.

Emma gave Molly up for adoption as soon as she was born and Molly grew up with the Bayliss family in Ayr. She was adopted as a baby.

They were very upset when I spoke to them on the phone earlier. The family hadn't spoken to her for a few months; she'd

fallen out with them when she left Ayr for Lost Maidens Loch.
They didn't say what the argument was about and it was difficult
to ask – I'd just told them their daughter was dead, after all.

However, Mrs Bayliss did say something I thought you'd
find interesting. When Molly was quite young, this middle-
aged woman had turned up on the doorstep saying she was
Molly's natural aunt. She had some kind of paperwork with
her that made them believe she was genuine (I don't know
what this was and Molly's mum couldn't remember, only that it
seemed official). She visited Molly a few times and brought her
presents. Said she was a nice woman, Scottish, conservatively
dressed and wore a thistle pin on her cardigan.

'Liz!' Temerity exclaimed and sat back, amazed. It certainly
sounded like her. Had Liz been the one that had given Molly the
Russian doll? Temerity had seen in her vision something of that
memory: it could have been her.

If Liz Maitland had visited Molly Bayliss as a child and given
her the Russian doll that had sigils drawn inside it, what was the
purpose of those visits? To monitor her development, maybe? To
keep an eye on her, maybe on the Laird's instruction? But why the
sigil? It had felt restrictive and dark to Temerity. Not something
protective and good.

We have no way to prove that Liz was the visitor, of course,
especially now that she has passed away, although I will
visit the Bayliss house in person and see if Mrs Bayliss can
identify Liz from a photograph.

It seems likely that the shed was Liz's, given the doll
connection. And, now that we have a renewed connection
between Liz and Molly Bayliss – and the new knowledge
of Molly's parentage – the Inspector is reopening the case.

We will keep McKinley in custody for now, as he certainly had some involvement in the murder.

However, as you can appreciate, there are now complexities that should be explored.

I'll see you soon but the Inspector (and I!) wanted to get this news to you as soon as possible, in the event that you had any other insights.

I will be attending the funeral, as I think you and Tilda will, so I will look forward to seeing you there or before,

My regards,
Angus

If nothing else, this is proof that I should read my emails daily, Temerity thought, as the details from Angus's email embedded themselves in her mind.

If Molly Bayliss was Molly Dalcairney, then she was the heir to the Dalcairney estate after the Laird's death, as the child from the first marriage. There was a son, Anthony, in London. The son of the second Lady Dalcairney, Claire.

The Laird had been ill. Temerity didn't know exactly how ill, but she guessed that if his condition was reasonably bad, then inheritance started to become a potential reason for murder.

Temerity chewed the end of a pencil thoughtfully, then pressed Reply.

Dear Angus,

Thanks for the email. Most illuminating. Questions:

Can we find Emma Ross? If we can talk to her about why she left Dalcairney, I feel that it might shed a lot of light on the investigation.

Ditto Claire, the second Lady Dalcairney. Liz told me once that Claire lived in Italy.

What do we know about Anthony? Could he have found out that Molly existed and threatened his inheritance?

What do you know about the Laird's health? If he has something serious, I'm sure, like me, you will have realised that this whole case could be about inheritance.

More of a comment than a question: I believe it's considered bad form to arrange a date at a funeral. I'm a witch, not a ghoul.

Best regards,
Temerity

She stared at her laptop for a few moments, then pottered upstairs to Tilda's library.

She had some research to do.

Chapter 34

It took a while to find the right ones, but eventually Temerity found the Laird's name in her mother's *Book of Shadows*.

There was a row of notebooks in varying sizes that ranged along one of Tilda's shelves. Some were plain black or green or blue, held closed with a rubber band; some were more ornate, with patterned covers. However, all of them contained her mother's slanted handwriting, diagrams and drawings.

The cats, Scylla and Charybdis, snaked around her ankles as if they were deliberately trying to trip her up.

'Carrie-cat! Scylla!' Temerity chastised them, but they ignored her. It was unusual for them to be so active; on the whole, they resented having to get out of their fluffy cat beds to eat, never mind be playful. Temerity looked out of the sash window – there wasn't a storm coming in, either. 'What are you so interested in?' she mused. 'Do you want to see Mum's books?'

She sat down on the floor and opened up the notebook in her hand. The cats purred and pushed their heads against the books, scent-marking them. Scylla reached out a paw and seemed to stroke the pages, but Charybdis butted the book with her head suddenly so that it fell on the floor.

'Naughty!' Temerity tutted and picked up the notebook.

A *Book of Shadows* was the name popular since the resurgence of modern witchcraft in the 1960s of a magical record: a journal of sorts that tracked a practitioner's dreams, vision work, ritual, seasonal celebrations and other related information.

The book had fallen open on a page which read like a diary entry and Temerity raised her eyebrow in disbelief when she scanned the page and found David Dalcairney's name. She frowned at the cats, who purred and nestled against her.

'Thanks.' She stroked their heads and read the page.

May 5

We received David Dalcairney again today. He is a seeker of wisdom, he says and is a broken man. He has lost his wife in mysterious circumstances. Rumours say that she's dead, but I scryed for her presence in the spirit world and Rory and I enacted a calling to her spirit, but there was no answer. I have the strong feeling that she is alive and have told Dalcairney this, but he is too deep in despair to believe me. (Note: Hebrides squawked, Alive, alive! when I asked him. He is becoming a knowledgeable and trusted familiar.)

He says he thinks there is a curse on him, though I could not detect one with an initial scrying. I offered to undo it. I asked David who would have set this curse on him? He said he didn't know, but I detected something hidden about him. He is a very charming man, even in his grief, but there is something underneath it.

I have suggested to him that he comes to us regularly to be trained. He has a natural gift for magic: a strong imagination, a strong league of spirit around him (his ancestry, for the most part), a strength of character. If he gains in craft and power, he is all the more likely to be able to lift this curse himself. He has agreed.

Temerity flicked further through the book, looking for David Dalcairney to be mentioned again. Her gaze was caught by her regular acronyms recorded in her mother's slanted handwriting; she surmised that DD meant David Dalcairney.

June 1

DD came for what we have jokingly started calling a coven meeting. We are also working with Elen, who had already come to us for training and taken her witch name. We started on some of the basics, setting space and the elemental powers. The energy was good between us all. DD seemed withdrawn at first and then lost his inhibitions. Elen has few inhibitions to begin with.

Temerity wondered who the person described as Elen was and whether she still lived in the village. She read on.

June 21, *Midsummer*

DD and Elen joined us for a solstice celebration. As the weather was good, we went out onto the moors and enjoyed what turned out to be a very spirited affair. DD and Elen have a definite chemistry and Rory and I both felt that they enjoy being able to express it within the confines of our little group. We have talked to them about attraction and magical power and how magical partnering differs greatly from friendship and romantic relationships. They seemed to understand, though DD is more reluctant than Elen to put aside his hang-ups about the social niceties.

We stayed up to see the sunrise over the moors and were blessed to see the sun catch the old menhirs at Kirkgraig Ring.

Temerity flicked through the pages leading to the end of that notebook; the cats had by now spread out, dozing, on the carpet. She wished the diary entries were more detailed, but it sounded as though the Laird had certainly been more involved with magic than she thought. He hadn't mentioned anything about the regular meetings her mother was describing.

The last entry in that notebook was written in Temerity's father's upright handwriting.

August 18

Dalcairney has given us our notice and will not be attending our meetings henceforth. He has not given us a reason why, but we suspect it is something concerning Elen, who is continuing the training. Maria is disappointed he will not be continuing on the path, but I am somewhat relieved. I do not know if Maria and I should be teaching magic to these village folk, Laird or otherwise.

Rory Love had always been the more conservative and cautious of her parents, Temerity thought as she closed the notebook thoughtfully. What had happened to put David Dalcairney off his magical training? How far had he got? And who was Elen, who, she assumed, had continued with whatever her parents had taught?

Chapter 35

The bells of St Peter's Church echoed across the flat surface of Lost Maidens Loch, which was shrouded in heavy mist.

Temerity stood next to Tilda inside the small stone church where, it seemed, the whole village had gathered to pay their respects to Liz Maitland and Lady Dalcairney. Next to them in the long wooden pew, Alf Hersey and Harry Donaldson rubbed shoulders with Muriel from The Singing Kettle and Ms Hardcastle, the school Headmistress. Temerity caught Angus's eye across the aisle; he stood next to the Inspector and Mrs Hyland, a rather glamorous woman in her early sixties with softly curled blonde hair, red lipstick and a smart black skirt suit.

There were the usual stares as they walked in; dressing in black, even though it was customary for a funeral, just made Tilda and Temerity look that much witchier. Temerity caught Kerry Cohen's eye, who looked away without smiling. She hadn't mentioned that day at the library to Tilda; what would have been the point? She didn't want to hurt her sister's feelings.

'Did Liz have much family?' Temerity whispered as the pews continued to fill up; soon there was only standing room at the back.

'Don't know. Don't think much,' Alf replied. 'But there are quite a few unfamiliar faces, so I can't be sure.' He nodded over at the front couple of rows to their left. 'That's Anthony Dalcairney in the front row, next to David. I don't know who the man next to him is. Then I think…' He squinted and peered closer; Harry nudged him with his elbow.

'Don't be nosy,' he muttered.

'If I can't be nosy at a funeral, when can I?' Alf whispered peevishly. 'Now. Ah! That's John, he used to be the chauffeur over at the Dalcairney house. I treated him for shingles once. Nasty case. And that's Elsie Maitland, Liz's sister. She was in service with Liz there, back in the day. They must be her children with her.'

Temerity recognised all the village usuals: Ken MacDonald, the glass-blower, looking unusually smart in a dark blue suit and tie; Mrs Black from the bakery wearing a calf-length black dress and pearls. Henry Sutherland from the boat shed stood in the pew in front of Temerity with his family, including his two eleven-year-old twins who were watching something on their phones with earphones in.

Temerity wondered about all the connections between these people, Liz Maitland and Lady Dalcairney. The friendships, passing acquaintances or rivalries they'd held; the times they'd said hello as they passed each other, or remarked on the weather. Temerity thought ruefully that probably only Muriel knew even half of it.

'So the second Lady Dalcairney hasn't come.' Tilda nodded at the back of Anthony's head. 'She's the one that lives overseas? Obviously no love lost between her and the old Lady Dalcairney.'

'No, I suppose not,' Temerity mused. She wondered whether Claire and David Dalcairney really had divorced because he couldn't get over his grief for his first wife, or whether it was something more than that.

The Minister cleared his throat and she listened as he began the ceremony.

Yet, suddenly, in her mind, Temerity was remembering another funeral service, long ago and tears sprang to her eyes, even though she fought them back.

*

Temerity was sipping a glass of ginger wine at the wake and listening politely to the Minister talk about the evils of social media when her phone rang. She frowned at the name on the screen. The Inspector and Angus Harley had left as soon as the service was over. Why was Angus calling her?

'Angus Harley, I *told* you. Funerals really aren't the time or place for sexy chitchat,' she turned away from the group and answered it, smiling.

'Hi, Temerity. You at the wake?'

'Yes. I thought you were going to be here,' she replied, wondering if yet again she'd misjudged the flirtation. She honestly wondered if she would ever get it right.

'Something came up. Police business.' It was difficult to hear Angus's voice against the hubbub inside the town hall, so she walked out onto the small cobbled street outside. Obviously, because of the fire, the wake couldn't be held at Dalcairney Manor.

'Gods, it's freezing,' Temerity muttered, folding her arms over her chest, wishing she had brought her coat outside with her. She was dressed in a black, full-skirted 1950s Rockabilly-style dress with a black tulle underskirt, a black cardigan over the top, black tights and yellow kitten heels. Her hair was tied up in a yellow scarf. Tilda had told her she looked like a bumble bee, which she had ignored.

'What?'

'Nothing. Why are you calling me?'

'We had some important last-minute information that had to be followed up. I wanted to check if you were still at the wake.'

'I just told you I am.'

'Okay, good. Is everyone else there? The Dalcairneys?'

'Yes…' She frowned. 'Look, by the way. I searched my mother's journals and I found a few entries in one of them, about the time when Emma Dalcairney was supposed to have drowned. It's nothing incriminating *per se*, but it suggests that David Dalcairney knows more about magic than he's letting on. It's possible that the stuff in the shed could have been his.'

'Right, okay. Interesting. We've spoken to Emma Ross, his first wife, and Claire Dalcairney in Italy. They had some interesting things to say.'

'You tracked Emma Ross down? Did you tell her about Molly?' Temerity sheltered the phone against the wind with her hand as best she could.

'She was understandably upset. She said she left because David was very controlling. From what she told the Inspector, it's what would now be described as coercive control. Mind games. Incremental physical and mental torture. Emma said when she found out she was pregnant, she knew she had to leave him. She couldn't stand the thought of him around a child.'

'Gods. How awful.' Temerity looked through the window of the Town Hall and watched as David Dalcairney laughed at something Muriel had said. He seemed so pleasant. He'd taken his own boat out with Angus to find the missing tourists; had always seemed every inch the benevolent landowner. But you never knew what people really were, beneath the surface. And Temerity had heard about men like David Dalcairney, who were experts at deceiving people into thinking they were kind and decent.

'There's a lot more, but we need your help with one more thing. Keep them there until we get there, okay? David and Anthony.'

'Of course.' Temerity shivered and listened to the rest of what Angus said carefully. 'Okay. I'll see you soon.'

She ended the phone call and went back inside. She really needed another glass of ginger wine.

Chapter 36

The main room in Lost Maidens Loch Town Hall had seen many village pantomimes, birthday parties, wedding receptions, wakes, Town Council meetings, dancercise, karate and yoga classes, but the smaller room which connected to it through double doors was musty and dank.

On one wall, a heavy cabinet with glass partitions held a series of leather-bound notebooks which held the minutes of every town council meeting since 1947; the previous records had been lost in World War Two. Lost Maidens Loch had escaped being bombed, but an overzealous member of the local Home Guard had hidden them away from potential invaders and then had died without telling anyone where they were hidden.

Temerity sat opposite Angus Harley at a green baize-topped oval card table with the Inspector and David Dalcairney to her right and Anthony Dalcairney, Tilda and Alf Hersey to her left.

Above them, apparently cascading from the ceiling, were hundreds of black spirit feathers that pooled on the table. Temerity stared up at them in wonder, knowing that only she could see them and wishing that the others could, too: it was such a strange and beautiful sight. All of them were for one person, but who?

She'd never met Anthony Dalcairney before; she remembered Liz telling her that he lived in London and didn't visit much. He was well dressed in an expensive-looking black suit with black tie; his shoes shone and his straight black hair was combed neatly. While Angus was shuffling some paperwork, conferring with the

Inspector, they made small talk. When Temerity asked what he did, he told her that he was a stockbroker.

'It wasn't what I wanted to do, but Dad pulled strings in the City after university and… London seemed like a good change of scene,' he explained. 'Don't get me wrong. I know not everyone has someone to pull strings for them.' He trailed off, meeting his father's stare.

'Anyone would think you weren't grateful, son.' David Dalcairney's tone was jolly, but Temerity detected an edge in his words. 'Perhaps I shouldn't have bothered with that expensive education.'

Anthony looked down and said nothing.

The Inspector stood up.

'Thanks tae ye all fer hangin' aboot. I didnae want tae make this long and I know yer all wantin' tae get home and put yer feet up, so I won't keep ye.'

'What's all this about, Hyland?' David Dalcairney asked; he looked tired.

'Aye. Well, the thing is, some information's come our way and we wanted tae talk it over with ye,' the Inspector continued.

'About the fire?' the Laird asked. The Inspector nodded.

'Now, Anthony, lad. I wanted tae ask ye aboot the insurance policy ye took out recently for the Manor.'

Anthony Dalcairney sat up straighter than before; his expression was defensive.

'What of it? Dad asked me to look into it for him. We'd been talking about it and I realised that the policy he had wasn't fit for purpose, so we updated it to something much more comprehensive,' he explained.

'Ah, I see. Protected against fire, I take it?'

'Of course.'

'Aye. So you'll earn a pretty penny from the payout when it comes through, I'm guessin'?'

Anthony Dalcairney shrugged. 'When you consider everything that has to be repaired and replaced due to fire damage, it's not as though we'll be making anything on the policy. I don't see what this has to do with my grandmother's death.'

'Hmmm. Well, of course, the wake isn't just for your grandmother's death, is it? It's for Liz, too. You were close tae Liz, weren't you, Anthony? Like the mother you never had?' Angus took over the questions; Temerity watched Anthony's face.

'Liz was like part of the family,' Anthony replied, but there was a catch in his voice.

'More than that, wasn't she? You told her in this email you considered her your mother and that, quote, *the sooner that crazy old bitch and my abusive father are out of the picture, the sooner we can be family again.*' Angus handed a printout of an email to Anthony, who read it and passed it back.

'I didn't mean anything by it. It was a turn of phrase.' Anthony took in a deep breath, avoiding his father's gaze.

'Rather a strange turn of phrase. You called your father an abuser. Would you like to elaborate on that?' Angus continued.

'No.' Anthony met Angus's stare.

'Fine. We'll tell you what your father's first wife has to say about him, then.' Angus took out his notebook and caught a few confused expressions. 'Yes, Emma Dalcairney – or, Emma Ross, as she's now known, is alive. Liz Maitland started that rumour to hide the truth; to protect Emma and her baby. She told you, David, that Emma was suicidal; that she'd seen her wading into the loch in just her nightdress, one night when you were out. But of course, the body was never found.' Angus nodded. 'Emma was terrified of you, David. What had started as a whirlwind romance turned into a controlling and violent relationship. When Emma found out she was pregnant, she knew she had to leave. She didn't want any child of hers growing up under your roof. She feared for her own life and the child's.' Angus passed a picture of a young Molly to David over the table. 'Did you know that Molly Bayliss was your daughter, David?'

Tilda gasped; Temerity was expecting the news, after Angus's email, but the reveal was still shocking.

The Laird took the photo and stared at it for a moment, then pushed it back over the table at Angus.

'Yes, I knew. She came to see me a few weeks after she'd moved to Lost Maidens Loch. She'd found out about me somehow. It was… it was wonderful. It was a second chance.'

'But then you found out, didn't you, David? That Liz had known about Molly for all those years. That she'd kept her from you,' Temerity interjected. 'I found my Mum's magical journal from the year that you came to her for magical training. You didn't stay with it for very long, but your fellow student did. And she got really good, didn't she? She got so good that she was able to enchant a present she gave little Molly one time she visited – a Russian doll – to protect Molly from you. It deflected your attention away from her, should you have ever gotten suspicious that Emma's body had never turned up.'

'Oh. *Liz* was Elen. Elen must have been her witch name.' Tilda shook her head. 'Elen. She's a British deer goddess. Deer. Stags. It all makes sense with your vision, now.'

'Yes. She trained with Mum and Dad for quite some time and I think she used witchcraft to protect herself and others from David. Presumably it was only ever Mum and Dad that called her Elen; no one else would have known that name. You thought she stayed because she loved you, didn't you?' Temerity turned to the Laird. 'The Inspector told Angus and I that Liz had been in service at the house for years and that you had a habit of dating the staff when you were young. She was probably stuck on you for a while, maybe some years, until she saw who you really were. When Emma told her about the mind games, the abuse.'

Temerity didn't want to be near David Dalcairney anymore; her psychic senses were too sensitive. Now that the truth had come out, she could feel his slipperiness, his lies and obsession around her like a cloud. 'She didn't love you. She loved Anthony and she drove away anyone else that got close to you for their own good. And then, Molly arrived.'

'Aye. Anthony's mother, Claire Dalcairney – we spoke to her in Italy. She told us about what your father did tae you. Why she left.' The Inspector's tone was kind. 'It's nothing a child should ever experience.'

Anthony Dalcairney sat with his head bowed. When he spoke, his voice had lost its earlier composure.

'My grandmother and my father made my life hell after Mother left. They refused to let her take me with her. And then when Liz told me that my half-sister had come to the village and come and met Dad up at the house, I wanted to warn her about him. So I came up to the village and I met up with her.' He started crying. 'But what I could have never predicted was that she was exactly like him.'

'How was Molly like your father?' Tilda asked. 'How could you tell?'

'I didn't at first. She was quite charming. She said was so happy to have found her family again. She invited me around to her house for dinner. Her housemate came home and there was a bit of an atmosphere between them, but I just put that down to the normal stresses of cohabiting.' Anthony kept looking at his hands, folded on the table in front of him. 'The housemate, Beth, I think her name was? She went up to her room and left us alone, anyway. We talked. She asked me a lot about Dad's health, the estate. What it was worth. I told her – I thought she had a right to know.'

'David. I've told the police the extent of your health problems.' Alf Hersey spoke up. 'I had to.'

The Laird shrugged and stared into the corner of the room.

'Doesn't matter now,' he said, tonelessly.

'Go on, Anthony,' Tilda encouraged him gently.

'Molly was… she was so charismatic. That should have put me on the alert, but it didn't. Dad was like that too; that was why no one ever suspected him of being anything other than a genial Laird. But he was controlling. His temper was terrible. He'd punish me for the smallest thing; I was locked in a cupboard for forgetting to say please or thank you, for not finishing my dinner, forgetting to say my prayers at night. Grandmother was the same, only with her, there was a kind of unhinged sprinkling of religion in there, too. She had her own strange version of God, a revenging angel.

'She lived in fear of everything; I think she was afraid of my father. She knew that after Emma was supposed to have died, Dad went for help to Tilda and Temerity's parents. After that, she was convinced that he'd brought a curse onto the house. She used to make me take boiling hot salt baths to get the curse off me. I know she took them too. She'd make up these bundles of foul-smelling stuff and smoke the house out with them, trying to cleanse the house in her own peculiar way, I suppose. She got more and more paranoid the frailer she got. By the time I was old enough to leave home, she was convinced the devil had cursed her.'

'Isn't it true that Liz was drugging your mother, David?' Alf asked. 'I think she must have been doing it for some time. Did you find that out?'

'No comment,' the Laird muttered. 'I'm allowed to say that, aren't I? I don't have a lawyer here.'

'Aye, ye can say that,' the Inspector agreed. 'But it's nae goin' tae help your case.'

'She did it because I asked her to,' Anthony interjected. 'Grandmother was insane. People thought she was this slightly eccentric aristocratic old lady who made herbal remedies for the people in the village now and again. She wasn't. Before Liz and I agreed that we should take control of the situation, Grandmother had tried to burn the house down on more than one occasion. She thought it was cursed and the only solution was to burn it all. Ironic, really. That's why I took out the insurance policy. Liz took care of things her end. We thought if we could keep Grandmother more or less bedridden, we could just wait until they both passed away, then I could come home. Take over the estate.'

'I think someone planted the idea of a curse in her head, though,' Temerity said, looking at David. 'You told us when we were at the house that you went to our parents because you believed you were under a curse and you needed their help lifting it. In fact, Mother's diary is quite clear that you were a part of their training coven for some time. You went there for power, nothing else.'

'No comment,' the Laird said, a smile playing around his lips.

'You planted the idea of a curse in a vulnerable woman's mind and let it fester there.' Temerity shook her head. 'How could you?'

'No comment,' the Laird repeated.

Kim Hyland put his hand on Temerity's and gave it a gentle squeeze as if to say, *enough for now*. He turned to Anthony.

'You knew that your father was ill,' he said. 'You were waiting for him to die, too.'

'From what Liz said, I knew it wouldn't be long,' Anthony said. 'I was stupid enough to tell Molly all of this. I even told her that we could share the estate; I was happy to do that. She had just as much right to it as I did, after all. But then, things got a bit… strange. She'd come to visit me at my flat in London, so that we could get to know each other better. Away from Lost

Maidens Loch. She said she had a boyfriend who was beginning to be a pain, he was stalking her and she wanted to get away. We talked, she told me about her childhood.'

'What was Molly like?' Temerity asked.

'She was… it's hard to describe. Two-faced, I suppose. She had this way of suggesting something and then if you said no, laughing it off like it was a joke, but she hadn't meant it as one. That first day, we were having dinner at a restaurant near where I live and when the bill came, she said, *Aren't you going to pay, Anthony? You're the rich one, I'm just a humble teacher* and the thing was, I was going to pay anyway, I wouldn't have thought of asking her to go halves, but it was the way she said it. And then, when I said, of course I would pay, it was my treat, she was all smiles and *Oh you're so kind, Anthony, I can pay if you want me to, I was only joking.*' He shook his head. 'That probably sounds like nothing, it's hard to describe.'

'Nae at all, Anthony. Carry on. What else happened that weekend?' Hyland prompted the young man gently.

'Later that night we'd had a few glasses of wine and the conversation got around to Liz; I think I mentioned she'd been the only one who ever really cared about me, the only one who ever did anything nice for me. Liz kept me out of harm's way more times than I could count. Molly said it sounded like Liz was interfering with family business. I hadn't told her about what we'd agreed about Grandmother, of course. I tried to explain that Liz was good – that she was the only good person in my life, really – but she refused to understand.

'Anyway, we got into a huge argument about it. She said, didn't I think that Liz was just trying to get half the estate off me? And, I don't know… up to that point I had every intention of getting my solicitor onto the paperwork, to recognise Molly as my co-heir to the estate. But after she left, the next day, I decided to wait a while until I knew her better. Turns out I was right.' Anthony sighed and wiped another tear from his eye. 'I know that she must have had scars, being adopted, growing up knowing her parents didn't want her. But there was something else in her. Something that was off.'

'Meanwhile, Ben McKinley had visited Lady Dalcairney after hearing that she made love potions. We have to assume that Liz was telling the truth about that day – that he did visit. Liz would have been the one to let him in; maybe he called in advance and she realised who he wanted the love potion for. Or, she found out when he turned up unannounced. Either way, she saw an opportunity. Anthony had telephoned and told her what Molly was like and that he had concerns about her and the implications for the inheritance,' Hyland said.

Temerity turned to address Anthony. 'Both you and Liz were so scarred by years of mistreatment from the Dalcairneys, that the thought that Molly might have been just like your father must have been intolerable. You had your plan in place and it seemed as though your long suffering was almost at an end. You could come home, finally, once they had both died, of more or less natural causes. And I think Liz's protective urge kicked in. Maybe it was panic. She put something in that powder, somehow, before Muriel came and got it. She would have had ample opportunity.'

'I don't know what she did. But when I heard about Molly's death, I knew it was Liz. I hadn't asked her to do that. I called her on the phone; I couldn't believe what she'd done. Yes, Molly was… I don't know. She was damaged, I think. But she didn't deserve to die. We argued. Liz tried to explain, but I didn't listen to her. It was the last time we spoke.' Anthony fought to get his emotions under control. 'I was planning to come back. I was going to come back and see her. We could have found a way out of all this…' He trailed off.

Angus cleared his throat.

'We can confirm that what we think is crushed, dried belladonna leaf was added to the love potion Lady Dalcairney gave to Ben McKinley. We found the bag on the premises at his house – amazingly, he'd hidden it in his bathroom cabinet and not got rid of it after Molly's death. As he had no idea the powder was poisoned, he panicked after being arrested.'

'So what happened on the night of the fire?' Tilda asked.

David Dalcairney gave Tilda a level stare.

'It had been brewing all those years, between us. I don't know why Liz stayed. God knows she was miserable being at the Manor, but she wouldn't go. So we all co-existed there for years in a kind of mutual contempt. I knew she loved Anthony and she'd convinced herself she was staying for him, God knows why. But I knew the truth. She was in love with me. You're wrong to say that she wasn't,' Dalcairney said to Temerity.

Temerity said nothing, but exchanged a glance with Angus.

'She was obsessed with me, it would be truer to say. She always had been. And when we spent that small amount of time training with your parents – learning magic together – ahhh, yes. We did have a connection. A magnetism. She was drawn to me and I to her. In that time, I won't deny that we had a rather… physical relationship. But she… she grew too demanding. I had to end it. I expected her to leave the house after that, but she didn't. For many years I didn't realise that she continued her training with your parents.'

Angus cleared his throat.

'The night before the fire, Temerity and I found the shed. We found blood there on the altar, mixed up in whatever Liz was making. I took a sample of it when I was there. It was Liz's blood type, so I think we can assume she had used her own blood to intensify the power of whatever curse or magic she made, or thought she'd made.' Angus met Temerity's eyes. 'Just in case you were wondering.'

Anthony looked repulsed, but didn't say anything.

'That just proves she was crazy!' Dalcairney cried.

'Not necessarily,' Tilda interjected coolly. 'Using one's own blood for spell work is an old folk practice. There's nothing evil about it, though it's not that common these days.'

The Laird waved his hand dismissively at her. 'Mad, all of you! Are you hearing this, Hyland?' he cried again, but the Inspector shook his head.

'Please, continue with your account. You were telling us about the shed?' he replied evenly. David Dalcairney held the Inspector's gaze for a long moment in which neither spoke: *a battle of wills*, Temerity thought. Finally, the Laird looked away and began to speak again.

'Fine. On the night of the fire, I found her there. In the shed, amongst all her magical ephemera. I'd worked it out, you see. Molly had met Liz when she came up to the house and told me about Liz visiting her as a child. Liz had lied to me all that time; about Molly's existence, about Emma drowning in the loch. I was furious with her, as you can imagine.' Dalcairney appealed to the Inspector across the table. 'Kim. You're a father. You must know how I felt.'

The Inspector nodded.

'Go on, David,' he said neutrally.

'Well. The argument got a bit out of hand, I'll admit that. I slapped her face, reasonably hard, I suppose. She fell over but I didn't help her up, I was too angry. I told her that she could pack her bags, I didn't want her in my house any more. I walked out. I didn't look back. I went down to the loch and took the boat out for a row. I needed to get my head together. When I came back, the house was on fire. I couldn't find her.'

'We estimate that she took a fall, knocked herself out on the edge of a table or on the floor. She must have knocked over a candle or two and the whole thing set alight. It was full of fabrics. They would have caught fire very quickly,' Angus said, quietly.

'Murderer!' Anthony lunged at his father, but Alf jumped in between them before he could make contact.

'Hey! Settle down,' he said, pulling Anthony back. David Dalcairney remained where he was, in his seat. He laughed at his son.

'Look at the knight in shining armour I raised,' he commented to no one in particular.

'You left her there to die!' Anthony screamed at his father. 'She burned alive!'

'How was I supposed to know that?' the Laird replied calmly. 'However, it doesn't explain the house fire. The shed was nowhere near the main house. There was a whole garden full of damp soil in between. Got any answers for that?'

'What about the maid, Sally? She was the only one who wasn't there. She could have set the fire before she left that morning,' Tilda said suddenly. 'She's been pretty suspicious from the start, always hanging around, watching, never saying anything,'

The Inspector shook his head.

'We questioned Miss Shearing after the fire. Her ma and pa confirmed that she'd come home at her normal time with nothin' amiss. They also explained tae us that Miss Shearing was aboot tae leave Dalcairney Manor; she were unhappy workin' there because of the –' he consulted his notebook – 'difficult atmosphere between the Laird and Miss Maitland and was serving oot her month's notice. Terrible thing, actually – her faither told me that the wee gurl had a stroke when she were eighteen, at nursing college. Now, she suffers with somethin' called Apraxia, so she mixes up the syllables in her words. She's havin' speech therapy but it's takin' a while for her speech tae come back. Which is why, ah'm guessin', she didnae talk tae ye when ye were at the hoose.'

'It doesn't mean she didn't start the fire,' the Laird muttered.

'Well, in fact, it does, sir,' the Inspector continued. 'Miss Shearing was so unhappy tae come tae work that she'd asked her faither tae accompany her tae the Manor on the night before the fire, tae keep her company on the night shift. So her pa was with her, and he swears she didnae set anything' on fire.'

'Poor thing.' Tilda blushed. 'I'm so sorry we thought so badly of her now.'

'Not yer fault, Tilda,' the Inspector reassured her.

'What did the fire crew say?' Temerity asked.

'They weren't able tae find anything particularly incriminatin'. They suggested it might've been an electrical fault. All they could really say was that the fire started in Lady Dalcairney's bedroom.' The Inspector closed his notebook.

All Temerity could think of was the poppet doll, burning in the flames. It had worked well enough for years, keeping Lady Dalcairney under control. Had she managed to finally achieve her goal and somehow set the fire herself? Or had something else been at work? Something more magical?

The poppet doll had burned in the shed along with Liz. Didn't it then make some kind of sense, if only from a magical point of view, that Lady Dalcairney had ultimately died from being inside that burning building? She had died of smoke inhalation, but it had been the fire that did for her, just the same. Temerity knew that theory would never make it past the Inspector, never mind a trial, but she rather suspected she was right.

'Then *she* started it, the mad old bitch,' Anthony said angrily. 'She burned down my home. My future.'

'We may never know,' the Inspector said, sadly. 'However, I am arresting you, David Dalcairney, for the manslaughter of Elizabeth Maitland.'

The Inspector stood up and walked around to the Laird. He held out his hand and helped Dalcairney up from his seat.

'Thank ye all for bein' here. I suggest ye all go home and have a stiff drink,' he said, nodding to them all. He guided the Laird out of the room, followed by Angus. 'We'll take it from here.'

'Well, that was dramatic,' Tilda said, getting up and shaking out her shoulders. 'I need a dry sherry or a ginger wine at the very least. Maybe both.'

Anthony slumped in his seat, holding his head in his hands. Temerity could see he was crying. She sat down again next to him and motioned to Tilda, whose face crumpled with sympathy. Completely uncharacteristically – she usually eschewed physical contact with most people except Temerity and the cats – Tilda rubbed Anthony's back in wide circles.

'Ah, you poor thing. We're here for you, okay?' Tilda crooned and Temerity held out her hand for Anthony's.

'Come home with us. You don't want to be alone tonight,' she said, kindly. 'We've got room as long as you don't mind cats. And a parrot.'

'I need a drink,' Anthony mumbled, rubbing his hands over his face. Temerity squeezed his hand. She could feel his grief for Liz. She expected to feel his hatred for his father, but a wave of deep sadness washed over her instead. Her heart wrenched for him. Anthony Dalcairney was alone in the world now, except for a distant mother in another country.

Tilda seemed to read her mind.

'Come on, everyone. Back to ours. I've got loads of food in. I'm going to make us all a feast and we can raid the drinks cabinet,' she said bossily; Temerity knew that she wouldn't accept no for an answer.

'I'll be in that,' Alf said and put his arm around Anthony's shoulders. 'Anthony, lad. It's good to see you again after all these years.'

Anthony stood up, wiping his eyes. He handed the hankie back to Temerity.

'Sorry, it's all rumpled,' he said. His eyes were as large and sad as a puppy's.

'Keep it,' she smiled.

'How's that old football injury?' Alf guided Anthony out of the room; Temerity watched as all the black feathers that had been falling from the ceiling disappeared. She heaved a sigh of relief. It was over.

'It's fine now,' Anthony replied. 'All healed a long time ago.'

'Ah, well. Time heals all wounds,' Alf agreed as they walked out into the night. The mist had cleared and the stars twinkled in the darkness. The moon shone on the water, making it gleam.

'I'd forgotten how beautiful Lost Maidens Loch is,' Anthony Dalcairney said, as they headed back towards Love's Curiosities, Inc.

'Aye, it's beautiful all right,' Alf said. 'It's a strange place, but it knows who belongs here and who doesn't. You belong here, lad. It was always your home.'

'And it always will be.' Temerity said, linking her arm in Anthony's.

Chapter 37

A week later, Temerity Love sat at her desk in Love's Curiosities, Inc, holding an ornate dagger with both hands and her eyes closed. The dagger was an antique *sgian-dubh*, or *skien-dhu*, a small, single-edged knife worn as part of traditional Scottish Highland dress, most often tucked into the top of a sock. Originally used for eating and preparing fruit, meat and cutting bread and cheese, cutting material or even being pulled out in a fight, they were reasonably common. The contact who had got in touch with Temerity had been asked to identify the dagger, but was having difficulty finding its true provenance. Though it seemed to date from the seventeenth century, he couldn't be sure which clan had owned it: there were no conventional markings.

Temerity was starting to go into a trance, getting ready to feel her way through the layers of history and back to something: a place, a date, a name, when the door opened and Angus Harley walked in. She put the dagger down on the desk, irritated. *No one comes in for days and the moment I'm trying to concentrate...* she thought.

'Angus,' she greeted him. 'Do come in.'

'Hullo, Temerity. Sorry to disturb you. Did the Inspector not say I was going to pop by?' he asked, going back a few paces to the doormat and wiping his feet.

'No. I was just in the middle of something, actually. How can I help?' She smiled brightly. There was a slight artificiality in her expression that she hoped he noticed. *Don't mind me, I'm just trying to see into the past*, she thought. *No biggie.*

'Oh. Well, he said to bring this by. He thought you might want to look at it before we gave it back to Anthony.' Angus walked over to the desk and laid Lady Dalcairney's hand mirror on the desk. Temerity frowned and picked it up.

'Why?' she asked, immediately getting that same feeling touching it as she had before: it was unpleasant, but now she knew what lay behind its enchantment. Liz had, in her own mind, been protecting the son she had never had.

'He just thought it was your type of thing. If you wanted to, you know, do your thing with it one last time.'

Temerity turned the mirror over in her hands.

'No,' she said, slowly. 'I think I know enough. But there is something that should be done with this.'

She picked it up, took it into the kitchen and ran some water into the sink basin. She opened a cabinet and took out a box of sea salt and threw a handful into the water, swishing it around with her fingers until it was dissolved.

Carefully, she lowered the hand mirror into the white ceramic basin of water and washed it with her hands, stroking the surfaces carefully with her fingers. As she did so, she repeated something her mother had taught Tilda and Temerity when they were girls:

Rest in the Lord and wait patiently for him: fret not thyself because of him who prospereth in his way, because of the man who bringeth wicked devices to pass.

Cease from anger and forsake wrath: fret not thyself in any wise to do evil.

For evildoers shall be cut off: but those that wait upon the Lord, they shall inherit the Earth.

For yet a little while and the wicked shall not be: yea, thou shalt diligently consider his place and it shall not be.

But the meek shall inherit the earth; and shall delight themselves in the abundance of peace.

'What was that you were saying?' Angus came up behind her and watched as she took the mirror out of the water.

'An old psalm, or part of one,' Temerity said, wiping the mirror carefully on her skirt. 'It's a traditional way of breaking curses. The salt will do most of it, but it never hurts to add something else in.'

'Right. So this is no longer… magicked?'

Temerity smiled.

'No longer magicked,' she agreed and handed it back to him. 'So. Trial date set yet?'

'It will be soon. The Inspector's waiting to hear. McKinley and the Laird are being kept in custody in Edinburgh. It's bound to be a few months at least.'

Temerity shook her head.

'What is it about Lost Maidens Loch, eh?'

'There's definitely something in the air, I'll admit that,' Angus said. 'I think it's possibly the strangest place I've ever been to.'

Temerity thought Angus was probably right about that.

'It's got some redeeming features, though, wouldn't you say?' she asked. Angus blushed and looked away.

'It's very… scenic,' he said.

'Hmmm.' Temerity decided not to push Angus any further for a compliment of any kind; clearly, that wasn't his thing. 'One thing I've been wondering. Ben McKinley was the one that put what he thought was a love potion into Molly's mug at school, right?'

'Yes. He's admitted that. I think when it goes to trial he'll get a reduced sentence, but he still stalked the girl. And he had no way of knowing that whatever was in that paper sachet wasn't harmful. He may not have intended to kill Molly, but he still spiked her drink.' Angus was always much happier talking shop; he visibly relaxed as he talked about the case.

'Agreed. The thing is, how did he get it in there? And what about the mirror? It was next to Molly's body when I got there that day.'

'Well, McKinley says that he made Molly's tea for her most days. That day, he made it as usual before he went outside for playground duty and added the contents of the sachet into the cup. The other teachers assumed she'd made it herself because McKinley had popped in quickly just before break and done it and so by the time they all came in, she was probably already drinking her tea.'

'Okay... so, the mirror?'

'As to the mirror, he says that Liz gave it to him. She told him that it was an extra part of the spell and that if he could get Molly to look into it, it would complete an enchantment on her. He'd brought it into school that day, intending to show her at break time, then forgotten he was on playground duty. He says he left it on the side of the chair in his rush to make the tea and have it waiting for her. He intended to put the mirror away in his locker and show her later.'

'If he'd remembered to do that, the case would have been much harder to solve,' Temerity mused. 'So the series of events must have been that he went up to the house to ask for the potion. While he was there, Liz overheard, realised there was a way to poison Molly and made her plan. She put some kind of masking spell on the mirror and gave it to Ben before he left Dalcairney Manor that day. In fact, she'd enchanted it to deflect attention from herself as murderer and towards Ben. Muriel gave Ben the potion when it was ready, a few days later: Lady Dalcairney likely needed a few days to make it. Then she got a message to Muriel that she had a package that needed delivering.'

Angus nodded. There was a silence in which one of the cats snored.

'Well, that's everything, I suppose,' Temerity said, after a pause.

'Um. Right. Yes.' Angus smiled uncertainly. 'Oh. While we're on the subject of drugs – the surgery break-in. We couldn't really find anything, but Theakstone has confessed that he thinks he might have left the surgery unlocked one night; he knows he's not been that alert these past few weeks, being sleep deprived with the new baby and all that. Anyone could have got in.' Angus shrugged, open-handed. 'Probably a tourist found the door open and tried their luck; looking at what went missing, it was a random selection of stuff that just happened to include the atropine. A quick grab of what was closest, what they could carry, probably. Thing is, with it being a doctor's surgery, if we fingerprinted the place, we'd find more or less everyone in the village in there, plus a lot of unknowns. We're just going to write it off as a mishap.'

'He hadn't slept much when I saw him last,' Temerity admitted, though she thought it prudent not to mention the circumstances of her visit.

Angus stood awkwardly, shifting his weight from foot to foot. 'What?'

'Oh. Errr. It's a nice day outside. I was just wondering… Do you fancy a walk or something?' He looked at his shoes. 'I'll be on my lunch break in a few minutes, so…'

Maybe he wasn't so much raised by wolves as just painfully shy, Temerity thought.

'All right,' she said. 'I could do with some fresh air, I guess.' She picked up her baby blue cardigan and slung it over her shoulders.

'Frrreshhhh!' Hebrides called out in a shrill voice from his perch, making Angus jump.

'Damn. I didn't see him there,' he muttered.

'You're still afraid of Hebrides, aren't you?' Temerity grinned.

'Of course I am. He's a killer,' Angus said, seriously.

'Hebrides is *not* a killer! He's a sweetie. You just have to let him get to know you.'

'Hmmm. I might not, if it's all the same to you.' Angus grinned as Temerity locked the shop door.

*

It was certainly a bright Spring day and Temerity was grateful to feel the sun on her face. Happening to look at the other side of the road, she noticed Beth Bennett going into the bakery. She nudged Angus with her elbow.

'Look,' she hissed, aware she was acting like town gossips Muriel and Brenda. 'Beth Bennett. Your biggest fan.'

'Could you not?' Angus rolled his eyes at her.

'Avoiding her, are you?' Temerity teased.

'No, I am not. Mind you, I did find something out about Miss Bennett.' Angus raised his eyebrow. 'It's not particularly relevant to the investigation, but Muriel told me – heaven knows how she knows, of course – that her boyfriend, the guy that Molly apparently stole from her? Molly didn't – he left Beth. She lost her job after they found out about her little shoplifting adventure, too.'

'Oh.' Temerity was surprised that she felt sorry for Beth. They weren't exactly ever going to be best friends, but Temerity could still sympathise with the girl. Everyone made mistakes. 'I mean, we've only got Beth's word that Molly and he were ever involved. She denied it to Ben McKinley, but then, she would,' Temerity mused. 'It might have just been sour grapes on Beth's part, if Molly flirted with him a little. She wouldn't be the first person to try and make it sound like someone had tempted away their lover when in fact they'd just been dumped.'

'Possibly. We shouldn't really gossip,' Angus chided her.

'You started it!' Temerity elbowed him again. 'So, the Laird's in custody now?' she asked as they walked along the main street of Lost Maidens Loch. As if she had conjured them be saying their names, Temerity could see Muriel and Brenda, the primary school cook, on opposite sides of the counter inside The Singing Kettle. Their heads were together and Temerity had no doubt that they were chewing over the details of the case just like she and Angus were.

'Yes, but the Inspector doubts he's going to make it to trial. Alf says his cancer's progressed pretty quickly. He'll likely be in hospital before long, maybe a hospice.'

Temerity blew out her cheeks.

'That's tough. I mean, I know he's not exactly a great person, as it turns out. But that's no fate for anyone,' she said. 'Do you think the Inspector knew that the Laird once trained as a witch, with Liz? They seemed to know each other quite well.'

Angus shook his head.

'I don't think so. Dalcairney kept that pretty secret and so did Liz. They'd known each other a long time, but only socially. You know, local council, dinner dances, that kind of thing. And it turns out that David Dalcairney didn't have any close friends for a good reason.'

'Hmmm.' Temerity nodded. 'What's Anthony going to do now? He hasn't got much of a house to come home to.'

'I spoke to him this morning. Nice lad. The good thing is that he did invest in that insurance policy when he found out Lady Dalcairney had taken to arson, so he's intending to rebuild. It'll take some time, though.'

'He was pretty withdrawn after the funeral. Understandably, of course.' Temerity shaded her eyes from the sun which glinted off the flat, black water of the loch. 'He was mourning Liz.'

'It's such a sad story. Liz didn't have anyone except Anthony. And he loved her like a mother.' Angus sighed.

'He survived. Not everyone does,' Temerity said, looking at the still water of the loch and thinking about Patrick, Liz, Lady Dalcairney and Molly Bayliss, who had come home only to join the ranks of the disappeared in Lost Maidens Loch. The loch itself might not have taken Molly, but her heritage had. She looked at Angus and touched his shoulder gently.

'You survived, too. You faced your fear.'

He gave her a questioning look.

'You went into the fire and you survived,' she continued. 'Don't you think you've conquered your fear, just a little?'

'Maybe. Maybe we're both survivors.' Angus took Temerity's hand. 'You know what you should do? Now this is over?'

'What?' Temerity smiled, glad to be outside on a sunny day, holding the hand of someone she liked. Maybe life could be simple sometimes, if she just let it.

'Go to that conference. The one in Alaska. There's still time, isn't there?' Angus asked, looking at her, seriously.

Temerity frowned. In fact, the conference organiser had emailed again this morning: the programme was about to be finalised and she wanted to try one last time to persuade Temerity.

'Yes… I mean, it's very last minute… I wasn't intending to go.' She looked away, embarrassed. 'I thought you understood.'

'I do understand, Temerity. I understand you're scared. But sometimes we have to do things that scare us. As survivors.' He stopped walking and gave her a meaningful look. 'You can do this, Temerity Love. I believe in you. And I'll be here when you get back. Believe me, nothing in Lost Maidens Loch will change when you're away.'

Angus squeezed her hand, leaned forward and kissed Temerity on the cheek.

'I'll be here,' he repeated. 'I'm not going anywhere. You've got this, okay? You're a world-renowned psychic provenance expert, remember.' A grin twisted his mouth at one side. 'I believe in you.'

'I didn't think you believed in anything that wasn't logical.' Temerity grinned.

'I didn't… and then I met you,' he replied and Temerity felt herself blush.

Nervousness danced in her belly, but there was excitement, too. Everything was changing.

'Okay.' She took a deep breath. 'I'll go.' She realised she'd made the decision this morning, reading the email in the shop; she'd started thinking, *would it be so terrible to go*? But, somehow, it took Angus asking her to make it real. 'I'm going to Alaska.'

Angus whooped.

'Good on you, Temerity Love!' he cried, picked her up by the waist and swung her around. Laughter bubbled up from inside her. She felt freer than she had for a long time.

She wasn't betraying Patrick by leaving; all of this had made her remember how much Patrick loved an adventure. *If he was here, he'd have decided he was coming with me the first moment I was invited*, she realised. *Patrick would be appalled if he knew that his memory was keeping me here. And I'll be back, anyway.* She could leave Lost Maidens Loch; it was her home, but not her prison.

And when she got home, Angus would be waiting.

A Letter from Kennedy

Hi! I hope you enjoyed *A Spell of Murder*. If you did enjoy it and want to keep up-to-date with all my latest releases, just sign up at the following link. Your email address will never be shared and you can unsubscribe at any time.

www.bookouture.com/kennedy-kerr

Scotland is such a beautiful country, imbued with thousands of years of magic and mystery among its purple mountains, green valleys and mysterious, silent lochs. It also has its own tradition of witchcraft. My family, though not witches like Temerity and Tilda, are originally from Ayrshire, a place of great rural beauty.

I adore curling up with a mystery book and a hot chocolate on a rainy afternoon and I began to want to write my own book about a little Scottish village alongside one of those strange, sometimes ominous lochs. A gossipy, cosy village where, sometimes, strange things happen and two local and very modern witches are on hand to investigate…

I hope you enjoyed reading all about Tilda and Temerity's adventures in Lost Maidens Loch as much as I enjoyed writing them.

With all my good thoughts,
Kennedy

9 781838 880965